LEARN TO LIVE

LEARN TO LIVE

CRYPTID ASSASSIN™ BOOK SEVEN

MICHAEL ANDERLE

DISRUPTIVE IMAGINATION®

Copyright © 2020 Michael Anderle
Cover Art by Jake @ J Caleb Design
http://jcalebdesign.com / jcalebdesign@gmail.com
Cover copyright © LMBPN Publishing
A Michael Anderle Production

LMBPN Publishing
PMB 196, 2540 South Maryland Pkwy
Las Vegas, NV 89109

First US edition, June, 2020
eBook ISBN: 978-1-64202-983-3
Print ISBN: 978-1-64202-984-0

THE LEARN TO LIVE TEAM

Thanks to our Beta Readers

Jeff Eaton, John Ashmore, and Kelly O'Donnell

Thanks to the JIT Readers

Dorothy Lloyd
Deb Mader
Jeff Goode
John Ashmore
Diane L. Smith
Peter Manis
Jeff Eaton

If we've missed anyone, please let us know!

Editor
Skyhunter Editing Team

CHAPTER ONE

Niki took a deep breath and leaned back in her seat to watch Maxwell demolish a prodigious amount of pizza all on his own. He'd mowed through almost a full pie while he was distracted, reading through one of the case files that had been dropped in their laps. She had no idea why Speare couldn't simply send them the case files electronically. It would have meant far less material they had to physically destroy once they were finished.

But no, she reminded herself belligerently, the man was old-fashioned and mistrusted anything to do with the computer age. Given the skills that lay in her family, she had no desire to challenge his beliefs on that. Both Vickie and Jennie were the kind of people who would make her eat her words if she insisted that anything sent to them was safe if it was sent electronically.

A little bored by the wait, she turned her attention to Jansen. He nibbled on his third piece and sipped a glass of coke intermittently while he occasionally took notes on a nearby pad. The man shared their boss' mistrust for all things electronic. He had his origins in intelligence so she could understand that he might have his reasons as well—although he didn't make his issues known to his partner, who took notes on a tablet.

She didn't need to take notes herself. That was what she had her team for, after all. So, while they waded through the information, she only had to focus on the food part of the working lunch for now. And honestly, if there was anything in the world better than pizza, she had failed to find it.

The wide variety available across the country and even across the world did mean there was a possibility of a few misses here and there. She wasn't as against pineapple on pizza as much as others might be and anyway, there were bigger transgressors. For one thing, people added mayo. The only thing worse than that was peas and corn. She'd even heard of places in Sweden where bananas were used.

In the end, while she didn't feel it was right to judge individual personal preference, no one on earth would ever convince her that bananas belonged on a fucking pizza.

But still, there were more hits than misses, she reminded herself thankfully. A personal favorite was one that could be found in the great city of Chicago. While there were New Yorkers out there who would have shouted at the tops of their lungs that deep dish pizza was not pizza but a casserole or something similar, Niki told them they could stick their opinions where the sun had difficulty reaching.

Chicago deep-dish was pizza. End of discussion. And it was damn good pizza too.

"Do you guys think we'll need to order more?" she asked as she took her third slice. They had ordered two, which had seemed like enough for the three of them until she saw how quickly the large agent attacked the food.

For the moment, they still had about a third left.

Maxwell looked up and shrugged as he swallowed his mouthful. "I wouldn't complain. We can keep anything we don't eat and take it home, right?"

Home. That was a concept she hadn't thought about for a while. She technically had a place of her own that she rented out since she didn't spend much time in any particular location, and that wasn't likely to change. It was a nice extra source of revenue and was handled by a friend who owned a real estate agency. The woman made most of the money from the rent, but that felt fair since she did most of the work to keep the property livable.

Still, it was a nice little nest egg for her to fall back on if she ever needed it. For the moment, though, she mostly relied on the short-term living situations she could afford or could bill her bosses for.

Finally, when Maxwell looked expectantly at her, she shook her head and raised a hand to call the attention of a nearby waitress. The woman moved quickly to the booth they had taken control of for the past hour.

"Can we get another pie—meatball and sausage, extra cheese, and some refills, please?" she asked and the server nodded and hurried to the kitchen.

Jansen raised an eyebrow. "We'll have to leave her one hell of a tip. That girl has waited for us to leave for a while now."

"We're working here and ordering regularly," Maxwell

pointed out as he picked another piece up and put it on his plate. "I know they need the turnover, but it's not like we're here during the rush hour. We're giving them a steady stream of business when they would usually not have much to do."

Niki nodded. The eatery was mostly abandoned since the dinner rush hour was a few hours away. This left only a handful of booths still occupied, mostly by people like them who preferred the peace and quiet of the venue, as well as the free Wi-Fi, while they enjoyed the food and got some work done. One group wore suits and could have been working on a project for one of the nearby law firms. There were a couple of student groups too and finally, the three of them. She wondered what theories the bored wait staff had made up about them.

It was how her brain worked when she was in a similar position.

"Well, we'll leave a good tip anyway," Niki asserted and picked up the next file from her stack. "I'm still not a fan of the whole tipping system, though. The assumption should be that people will receive a fair wage for their work, and tipping should only be required if they did an exceptional job. Like, above and beyond. In this case, we require these people to go above and beyond in order to earn enough money to survive."

"I'll go ahead and guess you were a waitress once?" Jansen asked, his focus still fixed on his file.

"Yes, but you don't need to have the experience to know it's a fucked-up system."

Maxwell smirked around another mouthful but didn't add anything to the conversation. She had a feeling he was mocking her somehow but decided not to engage. That would come later.

Jansen's phone buzzed on the table and vibrated energetically enough to dance across the surface for a few seconds before he picked it up. He narrowed his eyes at the sight of the caller ID and finally pressed the button to answer.

"Yeah?" He didn't sound happy to speak to whoever was on the line, but the more he listened, the more interested he seemed and even jotted notes on his pad. "Okay, thanks. I'll wire you the usual amount." He hung up quickly and looked Niki firmly in the eye. "I have an informant who says he might have something that's in our realm of expertise, although it's not certain yet. Either way, it looks like something weird is happening in Louisiana—New Orleans, to be precise. Since we're mostly waiting for shit to happen, do you think we should…"

His voice trailed off. He didn't want to seem like he was ordering the team around, but she stared curiously at him. It wasn't like him to take information like that and act on it immediately. His style relied far more on collating data in files for her and Speare to look at first.

"I don't see why we shouldn't investigate," she said finally, and Maxwell nodded in agreement. "It's been a while since I've visited New Orleans. And if there was ever a bad place for something Zoo-based to go wrong, it would be in the area of the largest wetlands in the country."

"So, the plane?" Jansen asked and looked from one to the other. "It shouldn't be a long flight to New Orleans, and we can be wheels up in an hour…maybe an hour and a half."

Niki nodded. "Get on the phone with the hangar staff to prepare it for immediate takeoff. Filing a flight plan and everything shouldn't take that long, right?"

He had already begun to dial, while Maxwell stared at her, then the waitress, who returned with the pizza that they had ordered.

"Is there any way for you guys to put the leftovers in a doggy bag for us?" Niki asked and tried to keep her voice as polite as possible when the woman moved within earshot. "We've been called away and we can't bear the thought of letting any of this amazing food go to waste. And we'll need the bill too, please."

"Of course," the woman replied with a smile and beat a hasty retreat to pack their food for travel before she returned with the bill and a bright smile.

Niki signed off on a twenty-five percent tip, along with the rest of the bill, and handed her the credit card Speare had issued her with to cover their work expenses. The man had to know the fact that they were on the road for their work at least ninety percent of the time meant most of their living expenses would be funneled back to them.

She hadn't bothered to take it up with him and there hadn't been any complaints about the amount of money he forked out to help them to be ready to work at a moment's notice. He had promised that no one would nitpick at every little detail of her budget and so far, the man had delivered in spades.

Niki could only assume that was because she had delivered in a similar fashion.

With the food packed and claimed quickly by Maxwell,

they stood and moved out of the restaurant to where their SUV was parked.

"So, will you tell me what weird something is happening in New Orleans?" she asked as they mounted up. "You know, aside from the Saints probably making a run at the playoffs this year?"

"I'll write a report for you on the plane," Jansen answered as the other man started the engine. "You know how Speare loves him some paperwork."

"I won't like it, will I?"

He paused and scratched his jawline idly for a few seconds before he shook his head emphatically. "No. No, you won't."

———

"So, you're telling me you put a pause on the whole operation because you wanted to have a burger?"

Taylor tilted his head and scowled when his jaw tapped lightly against the top of his armor. It wasn't painful but enough to feel uncomfortable. He would need to put the helmet on soon.

Vickie didn't sound happy about being dragged out of her comfortable location in Vegas to New Orleans, but it was unavoidable. He needed to do this and she would be his backup, which meant she had to be much closer than she had been during their last operation.

"First of all," he commented as he fidgeted with his helmet, "I have waited out here in this fucking heat—which remains long past sundown, mind you—for fucking hours waiting for the stars to appear. So yes, you're fucking right

I went to get myself something to eat. Secondly, you say that like I picked up something from the drive-through of a crappy brand fast food joint."

"Didn't you?"

"You have access to my location through GPS, so I'll give you one more chance to rectify that error."

She didn't reply immediately, which told him she probably had no idea where he had gone. "So, you went to this...Clover Grill. It doesn't look like anything special, honestly. Hell, their site looks like it was made in the nineties and no one has bothered to upgrade it since then."

"Be that as it may, you should know that the Clover Grill has operated since 1939."

"Clover Grill...it doesn't even sound interesting."

"You don't need to sound interesting when you've served the best burgers in the country twenty-four hours a day for over a century. Oh, and they serve beer with those burgers."

"Huh. And so does McDonald's—except for the beer part. Here in the US, at least. I've heard they're allowed to serve beer in a few European countries, so maybe it's not even that inventive to add an alcoholic beverage. Hell, New Orleans probably has fast food joints that serve beer just because."

"They don't serve burgers like this," Taylor asserted with a great deal of confidence he felt was more than warranted in this case. "Honestly, if I were to die during this operation, I'd be happy to have a Clover's burger as my last meal. Hell, the fact that they're still in operation today despite opening on the same year that World War Two started—and have kept their venue on Bourbon Street all that time—should tell you how many people keep coming back for more."

"That simply means they have a dedicated fan base, not that they're any good. Nostalgia is one hell of a thing. Seriously, Taylor, it's only a meat patty slapped between a couple of sesame buns and here you are, getting all melodramatic."

"Sure, but it's meat that makes you come to it. Over and over again."

"Jesus H Fucking Christ. You make it sound like you're describing a piece of ass. And I hate you for making me picture that shit."

"It's better than a piece of ass," he admitted as he began to check his weapons. The smaller suit had a different build to his usual one, which made carrying the larger assault rifles difficult and aiming almost impossible. He was, therefore, stuck with sidearms and a shotgun. In this kind of urban environment, though, it would be enough. "It's never turned me down and it's never made me sleep on the couch, which makes it better than roughly eighty percent of my trysts."

"You pulled that number out your ass, didn't you?"

"Sure, but the point remains."

"Well, quit thinking about the dirty things you would do to one of those Clover burgers. It looks like we have ourselves a green light—or as green a light as we'll ever get."

Taylor looked across the street from the small abandoned shop where he had set up. Lights had begun to go off in the target location, and people now left from the back entrance. The establishment was closing down for the night, a little later than he would have preferred but it wasn't like their delays would interfere with his operation.

"Okay, it's time to get your head in the game. You can keep telling me about how beautiful those burgers are later."

"Give me..." He pulled his helmet on and checked the time on his HUD. "About two minutes and we'll go live on my mark."

"You know, I've always wondered where this 'mark' term comes from. Do you think it was because of some dude named Mark who wanted to leave his 'mark' on history somehow or something—"

"Mark!"

"Oh, shit. Right, there we go."

He eased out from the shop where he hid for so many hours. As part of his preparation, he had plotted his course through the darkest parts of the street minutes before and now, it was only a matter of making sure everything was still the way he'd seen it and heading out.

Vickie tried to lean back in her seat and grunted softly when her head bumped into the side of the paneled van they had rented for the operation. They always made the vans look much roomier in the movies. Or maybe Taylor had skimped and stuck her in this tiny piece of shit because he was a cheap motherfucker.

Either way, it wasn't quite the space she was used to. Thus far, being the literal "woman in the van" had turned out to be much less glorious a job than she'd thought it would be.

Still, watching him try to sneak through the streets of New Orleans, even in the deepening shadows, in a suit that weighed close to half a ton was hilarious. And, she decided, it almost made it all worth it.

Her head snapped around at the sound of a second call coming in. It was adorable how Niki tried to mask her caller ID like she thought she wouldn't see right through it.

"I love you, cousin, but I'm a little busy right now. You have about forty-five seconds before I have to take care of business."

"What business? You don't take care of business." Niki sounded a little stressed and like she was in a car.

"Is that how you want to spend your forty-five seconds?"

"Whatever. It doesn't matter. I want you to tell McFadden to get his ass on the road now. I don't mean sometime tomorrow, mind you. I mean right now. I'll need him in Louisiana immediately, if not faster, and I won't wait around because he won't get on a fucking plane like a normal person."

"Deal," the hacker replied and stared morosely at the tight confines of the van. Night was falling and it still felt as hot as it had been at midday. At least Taylor had the presence of mind to park her in the shade and leave the air conditioning on. "We'll be there when you land."

"Wait, what?"

Her eyebrows raised when she realized her mistake. "Oh, would you look at the time? I have to go—bye!"

She pressed the button to end the call with a little more force than was necessary and shook her head.

"Yeah, you can keep world-class data miners from digging into your life, but the moment your mouth opens, you share all that information anyway," she muttered aloud.

"What was that?" Taylor asked and she realized her line with him was still open. "It sounded like you were talking to Niki—something about her landing somewhere?"

"Son of a bitch. Nothing…nothing, Taylor. You know what she's like and how she always calls at the worst moments to chat. Everything's fine here. How are you?"

He didn't answer, not that she expected him to. It was better to simply move past this whole fiasco and pretend it was all simply a bad dream.

CHAPTER TWO

The tension in the plane was palpable and she knew her irritation was the cause. Of course, it wasn't that she had never been hung up on. It was annoying and she always immediately had the instinct to call the person again so she could hang up on them.

Niki stared at her phone for longer than necessary and tried to focus on the facts rather than her reaction. Vickie had ended the call right after telling her that she and Taylor would be waiting for them when their plane landed. It could only mean one of two things—they were already in the area or Vickie was lying.

Either way, she needed more information.

Finally, she looked up and realized that both Jansen and Maxwell were watching her. They turned their attention to their work quickly, a little too late to avoid irritating her even further. She shook her head and pulled up her contact list. On some level, she wasn't sure how she felt about having Taylor's personal number and his business number.

The fact that this wasn't the first time she was forced to call both to get in touch with him also seemed unnecessary.

She pressed to dial the number and tried to relax in her seat.

"McFadden's Mechs, this is Elisa."

"Well, you're…cute," Niki muttered. The woman had a pleasant speaking voice, which was probably why she did so well in sales for the company. That was what Vickie said, at least. "Hey, this is Niki Banks and I need to have a quick word with Taylor. A business matter, you understand."

"Oh…hi, Niki," the woman mumbled. From her hesitant tone, she clearly recalled exactly who she spoke to. There were regrets about their first interaction, but it had been something of a volatile time. "Taylor isn't here at the moment. He was called out of town. Would you like me to take a message?"

"Oh, out of town, is he? Do you have any idea where he might be? Somewhere in the Southeast, perhaps? In a bayou?"

"I…I'm not sure—"

"Sure you're sure. You're a reporter, Elisa. Go ahead and report."

"Well, honestly, it sounds like you have more information than I do. I haven't been around long enough for them to entrust me with that kind of detail. I'm not in the chain of command and my boss is AWOL. I can transfer you to Bungees if you want."

"You go ahead and do that."

Niki took a deep breath and tried to remind herself that these people were her friends—or, at the very least, her contacts—and she needed to be nice to them or risk losing them forever.

No, she wouldn't lose Taylor or the rest of his team, but she still needed to put some effort into being a nice person. She shook her head gently.

"Niki?" Bungees asked as he answered. "Elisa says you're in a bad mood. How can I help you?"

"I'm not…whatever. It doesn't matter. Look, I know Taylor is in New Orleans and I only want to know what's happening."

"I can neither confirm nor deny your assertions," he stated quickly.

She sighed and rubbed her temples, which didn't seem to help.

"You were the one who said you wanted plausible deniability when it came to some of our less-than-legal dealings. I'm simply doing you a favor here."

"Fine. But you can tell me whether he is in New Orleans or not, right?"

The mechanic paused as he thought about it for a moment. Finally, he took a deep breath. "Fine. Yeah, he's in New Orleans. Why do you ask, though?"

"Because that's where I'm heading and I need a team there on the ground. And not only Taylor and Vickie. I'll need the whole McFadden team."

"We never agreed to be called that."

"Then work up an actual name for yourselves. Until then, I'll call you the McFadden Team. Or McFadden's Mercs. Yeah, mercs rolls off the tongue a little better."

"Yeah, it does."

"No matter, and don't worry. I won't ask why Taylor is

out there on his own with only Vickie for backup. Rack all the suits and pack them for a quick trip to Louisiana. I'll divert the flight to Vegas to pick you guys up. Make sure you and Tanya are ready for action and that my suit is too. Oh, and Bungees?"

"Yeah?"

Niki smiled. "You do him and your team proud. Oh, and know that when I find Taylor, I'll find out what he and my cousin are doing in New Orleans. If he's pulling another casino stunt, I will place the bullets in his body myself. You know, fair warning in case you didn't expect this shit to get graphic."

He laughed. "Yeah, it's nice to hear from you too, Niki. For what it's worth, even Taylor isn't stupid enough to run a casino heist solo, so whatever he's doing probably isn't that. Anyway, I'll see you soon."

He hung up and she stared at her phone for a few more seconds before she turned to Jansen.

"I'll change the flight plan," he grumbled and stood to go to the cockpit to talk to the pilot. It wasn't the first time they changed the plan mid-flight

She wanted to make a comment about how she wouldn't underestimate the depths of stupidity Taylor was willing to descend to, yet it felt a little unfair. The man was smart enough in his own right. Hell, he had pulled off robbing a casino in broad daylight and now reaped the benefits of it. As far as she knew, there were only a handful of successful casino robberies and very few had been performed without inside help.

Maybe he did have inside help. She wasn't sure about the details, and while that was intentional, she would have to hear the full story eventually. Maybe it would be a story he shared on their first date.

It was something to think about for the future.

Jansen returned from his errand and settled into his seat. Niki could already feel the gentle tilt as the plane began to turn.

"The new flight plan is filed," he confirmed. "We'll arrive a little later than expected, but I guess we'll make up for it by having our ground team in earlier than anticipated. You know that if Taylor isn't there, they could simply catch a flight and meet us in New Orleans too, right?"

"There is the small problem of transporting the suits. Not many commercial airliners will be happy about carrying weapons like that."

The man nodded. "I guess that's a good point and one I should remind myself of. Still, we might have to find a better way to go about this than having to either wait for them to drive to where we need them or go and pick them up."

"That's also a good point," she conceded. "But it'll work for now."

Bobby slid his phone into his pocket. He had hoped there would be a little more time between jobs, and Taylor's excursion in pursuit of vengeance had seemed to indicate some respite. The reality, though, was it was only a matter of time until Niki decided she needed their services again.

When it rained, it poured and all that bullshit.

He pushed from his seat and took a last swig of the

mostly lukewarm coffee before he wandered to where Elisa was still seated. The woman knew how to keep herself busy, and by the looks of it, she was working up profiles on the rest of the merc companies they could cold call later on in the quarter when they were ready to pick up more business.

It wasn't that they needed much more business these days, but Taylor had gone on at length about the controlled growth of the business. Bobby assumed this had to do with putting in the time and effort to make sure they didn't end up crushed by their business expansion.

Still, the guy was feeding his cash flows in other ways, which meant they could probably afford to push in a couple of new workers when he was ready. In addition to Elisa, of course.

"What kind of schedule are we looking at over the next couple of days?" he asked, leaned on the desk, and peered at the screen like he understood what was displayed.

"We have no new arrivals," Elisa stated. "Our next parts order will arrive next week, and the next suit deliveries are scheduled for three days after that, so we will have a ton of work to do then. For now, though, all we have on the docket is taking the suits we have apart and cleaning them in preparation for the parts we need to put in."

Bobby nodded slowly. At least, in this case, it meant there was nothing pressing they needed to attend to while they were off making their lives difficult with Niki.

"Tanya, we'll need to get ready for a trip out of here," he called to where the woman remained focused on taking one of their more recent deliveries apart.

"What kind of trip?" she asked without looking up from her work.

"The kind that requires us to bring our suits along," he replied and immediately tensed because he already knew how she would react to the statement.

Sure enough, she didn't disappoint. She pulled away from her task when she heard those words and tilted her head to fix him with a firm look. "Are you sure that's a good idea? Taylor was insistent when he said he didn't need any help out there for that little operation of his. In fact, I think his exact words were 'you need to sit the fuck down and recover from your last mission. Vickie and I can handle this on our own. Get better or I'll put you in a hospital bed myself.' I can't say I'll always agree with the guy's methods, but he does get some results that I'm a fan of."

The mechanic would never admit that being told to sit a mission out hurt his feelings, but that was what happened. He didn't like being sidelined, despite the fact that his entire right side still felt a little stiff and he needed the pain medications the doctors had prescribed him. No surgery had been required, fortunately, as nothing was broken. He'd been left with considerable bruising and the effects of twists and pulls that would inevitably need a few weeks to recover from.

Or so they said. It had been a few weeks, and the bruises had gone from purple to almost black and had now begun to fade a little. The pain and stiffness were easing, and while he wasn't raring to get back into the thick of it again, it wasn't a pleasant feeling to see a man he had come to think of as his brother head into action and order him to sit on his ass.

"Well, it looks like Niki will need our help now," he told her calmly. "She said she's heading into something and will need extra bodies on it. Also, she wants us to load all the suits, as well as hers, and get them to the airstrip. They'll meet us there."

Tanya frowned as he headed to where the suits were stored and stood quickly to move closer and stop him from loading his onto his truck. Taylor had taken Liz for his little operation, which coincidentally was in the same area to which Niki wanted them to go. That left Bobby's vehicle as the only large enough to transport the crates of suits if they needed to.

"What?" he asked.

"It's too soon and you know it. You're still recovering and if you pull or break something because you charged into the fray too early, it would piss me right the fuck off." She leaned in to press a light kiss to his lips and held his jaw between her hands as she pulled away to ensure that his attention was on her and nothing else. "I never thought I would fall in love with someone as crazy as I am, so I know a thing or two about what you're going through. With that said, now that I've found you, we need to make sure we don't get into crazy situations while still injured, okay?"

Bobby couldn't help a small smile as he placed a light kiss on her cheek. "Until I think we're no longer in agreement or the situation changes, we're good."

She scowled but patted him on the cheek and smiled. "I guess I'll have to settle for that, you obstinate man."

The suits had already been cleaned and readied for transport, which meant it wasn't long before they were on the road toward the tiny airstrip outside the city that Niki always used. The drive took a little while and they also had to wait before the plane landed and taxied to where they were parked.

The people who worked there responded quickly and efficiently to refuel as Niki exited. She left her entourage inside as she jogged to where they were parked.

"You're late," Bobby commented as the forklift drove to pick their cargo up to load it on the plane. "Do you know how long we had to wait here?"

"Yeah, my bad. We had to fly across the country to pick you guys up, no biggie," she commented and folded her arms as her keen eyes immediately noted the three suits that were being carried to the plane. "I told you guys to load all the suits, and unless I suddenly lost the ability to count, it looks like we're down one."

"You didn't lose the ability to count, but we're not down any," he replied quickly.

"What gives, Bungees?"

He shrugged. "I'm not Taylor, so I won't drop every-thing to help you out on a moment's notice."

She narrowed her eyes at him. "Okay, that's fair enough."

"I'm kidding, of course," Bobby cut in quickly with a laugh. "But in this case, there's a ton of work to be looked after around here. Honestly, I don't think I'm fully recov-ered from my last stint, so I'll watch this one from the side-lines. Tanya will take lead with you, one of your goons, and Taylor."

"And you still won't tell me what the hell he's doing in the Bayou?"

"You know, for someone who doesn't want to know about our illegal dealings, you sure sound like you want to know about them."

Niki smirked and patted him gently on the shoulder. "I thought it was worth at least one more try. Anyway, if I know McFadden at all, the chances are I'll find out on the news soon. But yeah, you should take it easy on yourself. I remember the condition of your suit after Taylor pulled you out of that facility."

"Yeah. Tanya insisted I stay behind for this trip, at least until something goes horrendously wrong and you guys need me to head in and bail you all out of whatever mess you've gotten into."

She smirked and extended her hand.

Bobby took it and shook firmly. "You take good care of Tanya out there."

"Of course."

Tanya snorted. "Like I can't look out for myself."

"Everyone needs someone to watch their back, especially in our line of work," the agent pointed out. "Okay, we should get loaded and take off as quickly as possible. Thanks for coming to my aid at the drop of a hat, guys."

"When you unpack it all, you might want to take a look at your suit," he advised. "Taylor and I repaired where it was dinged in the last mission and he put in a few additions based on your fighting style. I'm not sure how the man does it, but he does have an eye for making the suits work better for the person in them. We weren't sure which of your boys would head into combat with you, though, so he set the third suit into what could be called neutral, and he'll probably work it out when you guys land."

Niki uttered a low whistle. "I look forward to seeing what he put in there, but I guess I'll have to wait and see. For now, let's head out."

Bobby wasn't sure what he felt when he watched the two women walk toward the plane. He merely knew he wouldn't move from his position until he could see the aircraft taking off.

It wouldn't take long. The people working on the airstrip were professionals, and the plane was already loaded and refueled by the time the women boarded. It was clear that whatever they were heading out to deal with, it was an emergency and time was of the essence.

He watched as the plane turned, increased speed, and finally became airborne to vanish rapidly from view except for the blinking lights.

There was no telling how long he stood there. The workers had already left for the night, so he was mostly on his own except for the security personnel.

"They'd better take care of her," Bobby muttered under his breath before he finally spun on his heel and climbed into his truck again. It was lighter for the trip back but seemed to take twice as long. Elisa was locking up when he arrived at the shop, which meant the only thing for him to do was head home for the night. Maybe he could have a drink or two before that somewhere along the way.

It sounded like a good idea.

CHAPTER THREE

Having Vickie distracted during their mission was probably not the most auspicious of starts.

Still, the nature of the operation was essentially unfamiliar territory for Taylor and he needed to be focused. He had never been the kind of operative who worked in the shadows before. Most of what he'd done had been up-close and personal and not usually against humans.

There had been enough of that too, he reminded himself, but once he got to the Zoo, all that had been traded in for a brand-new set of skills that had been critical for his survival. It was the kind that would probably never be taught in any boot camp, although if anyone ever wanted to try, now was the time if they wanted to keep all their recruits alive and well in the jungle.

He wondered if the prospect of training specifically for Zoo-based operations would bring in more recruits or drive them away. Logically, the intelligent thing to do would be to run as far away as fast as possible. That said, he wouldn't credit the kids who joined the army barely out of their teens with an overabundance of brains.

No, that wasn't fair. He'd been one who'd acted stupidly, but many kids joined simply because they had no other decent choice in life. And that, he decided, was the saddest part when you considered how short many of those lives inevitably were.

"Are you still with me, Taylor?"

Fuck. He needed to stay focused.

"Yeah, I'm here," he rumbled as he inched toward the back entrance of the building he had studied for the past day and a half.

"It's been two minutes since your mark. Should I be worried?"

"You're the one who's supposed to be my eyes and ears in this. Isn't that what I pay you for?"

"True, but given that your eyes and ears are much closer and have a better idea of what they should be looking and listening for, I have to rely on them too. With that said, it appears our friends haven't put any security on the lower levels of the building. You should be clear to enter, assuming you don't make too much noise on your way in."

The suit he wore was the smallest available that qualified as a power armor suit, but it was still a heavy beast. It weighed in at almost half a ton and packed more punching power than a grizzly. Not that he knew how much punching power a grizzly had, he realized.

"Hey, Vickie, how hard would you say a grizzly bear could punch?" he asked while he moved as silently as he could through the narrow approach to the building.

"I don't know. I'm not sure if grizzlies can punch. Why

do you ask? Is it important to the mission? Are you facing a goop-enhanced grizzly?"

Taylor shook his head and immediately regretted the question. "No, nothing like that. Are you sure this is the right place?"

"Do you doubt my abilities, Taylor?"

"No, not at all, but when I picture a group that tries to steal my shipments by hiring mercenaries in Africa, I think more shady backdoor dealings and... Well, not a small warehouse in downtown New Orleans."

He picked the lock easily and slid through the doorway. The location looked like it had once been used to ship something in small quantities but with a high turnover. Electronics warehouses worked like that sometimes, with sufficient space for forklifts to move around in and shelves and pallets spread out to make as much use of as little space as possible. If they were involved in any way in the game of suit manufacturing, it was probably on the electronics side of things.

"I don't know what to tell you, Taylor. I've dug into these assholes for months now, and everything says they're based in this area. Have you considered the possibility that everything might not be what it seems? Like, against all logic, these people might possibly be trying to hide their illicit activities?"

Taylor could hear the sarcasm dripping from her voice and he didn't like it. Still, there was nothing wrong with what she said. Of course these people would put all the effort in the world to make themselves look like everyday businesspeople. If he was determined to unmask them, he would have to look past the veneer and get to the gooey, illegal center.

"Do you have any idea of where I'll find what we're looking for?" he asked and moved onto the floor of the warehouse. The structure looked far more solid than he'd thought. Concrete walls stopped at approximately the height of his chest and were likely in place to help support the weight of whatever they were stacking.

It seemed a logical deduction but he didn't know much about what a warehouse needed for operations.

"Do you expect me to do all the work for you, Taylor? I've literally pinpointed these guys to a single building on a planet full of buildings."

"Well, you are paid to gather intelligence for me, so yeah, I'd appreciate all the information you can find for me."

"Okay, find me a computer. When you do, you can plant those USB spikes I gave you and I can do what I'm paid for."

"Right. The spikes."

She had explained what they did three or four times and even gave him the name for the software he carried around, but it had mostly gone in one ear and out the other. He had a good mind for mechanics, but hacking was not his forte. He had a decent idea of the overall nature of it but it felt like speaking a second or third language. It simply didn't come naturally.

Not only that, but the kind of shit Vickie put onto the USB drives she gave him was also way beyond his limited knowledge. He defined it as somewhere along the lines of the most complex legal-speak in any given language and wouldn't even try to understand it.

He moved to one of the offices, thankful that the lighter suit enabled easy ingress through the doorway, and slipped behind one of the desks. Without so much as a pause, he retrieved the USB drive from one of the pockets on the outside of the suit and pushed it into the slot.

"What's…what's happening?" Taylor asked. "Nothing is happening."

"You have to turn the computer on, you moron."

"There's no need to be hurtful."

"I feel there is."

He sighed and leaned forward to turn the computer on. It booted quickly and he barely had to wait before Vickie took control of the operating system. He focused on the screen as she dug quickly through the office's servers for information.

It was interesting to watch her work, even if all he saw was the software she had worked up days or weeks before digging through firewalls and other defenses. He assumed she also rummaged around to make sure she could pull every piece of data available.

"Okay, for one thing, you are definitely in the right place," she asserted after only a few minutes of the device's activity. "I've already found the communications the manager here had with the mercs you ran into in Africa."

"How the hell did they know about our scheduling?"

"It's interesting, now that you mention it. Apparently, they have shipments moved by the same company, so whenever one was marked as stopping in Vegas before it headed to Africa, they made a mark on it. Eventually, they were able to extrapolate our schedule without any need to dig into our systems. It's kind of impressive, to be honest."

"Are you able to do something like that?"

Vickie didn't reply immediately and he felt like she was almost offended by whatever he had insinuated.

"Well, sure I could if I needed to. But I've never needed to apply that kind of low-tech solution, given that I'm more than capable of applying the more technological solutions that require much less effort."

"So what you're saying is that you're lazy?"

"Damn straight, and proud of it too— Fucking hell... shit, what's happening here?"

"What? Did I do something?"

"I don't know. I thought I'd disabled the alarm systems, but it looks like something was sneaking around and it only turned on at intervals. I assume it picked you up and triggered the alarm. I intercepted the signal sent to the police, but I wasn't able to catch a secondary alert signal in time."

Taylor looked up from the computer screen. "Well... where did that second one go?"

"I doubt it goes to the paramedics. The chances are these assholes are lined up with a couple of security companies—the kind with guns and guys with itchy trigger fingers attached."

That definitely sounded reasonable. He was surprised that any alert went to the police at all. Criminal types tended to prefer that law enforcement stayed as far away from their operations as they could, even if they were being robbed.

"Okay, so do you have any information on the teams I

can most likely expect?" he asked, hefted his shotgun, and checked his sidearm before he strode out of the office.

"Seriously, do you want to know anything else?" Vickie snapped. "What? How many men they have and how many of those men are married? Maybe how many kids between them? Or how many are having affairs with one of their comrades' wives?"

"Look, if you'd rather come here and fight off an unknown number of attackers while I sit in an air-conditioned van and type on a computer, be my fucking guest."

"Point taken. Okay, it looks like the response is on the way. There's no indication of ETA, but I'll go ahead and guess it's in the minutes range."

"Do you need me to stick around?"

"The spike is still digging through their data. If they remove it before I'm finished, we won't have everything."

"How long will it take?" When he received no response to his question, he took a few deep breaths. "Vickie?"

"Okay…gotcha."

"Gotcha what?"

"I found what I was looking for."

"You will force me to ask, won't you?"

"Come on. It's not as much fun if I have to talk to myself."

"Did you find any proof?"

"Of?"

"Illicit activity against us? Or any illicit activity?"

"Oh, I struck the mother lode of illicit activity. I found where they have been in talks with other companies to increase the marketing pressure to reduce the lower-priced mech servicing coming out of the United States.

That's the kind of insider trading shit the SEC loves to eliminate."

"Wait, this is a marketing company?"

"Well…no, not really. Not even kind of if their purchasing of ammunition and shit using their ordinance license is any indication. I thought marketing companies made their money by buying ads on Google and stuff like that."

"Okay, I guess that's all I needed to know."

"What the hell are you still doing there?" she asked. "You should be half the way back to me by now."

Taylor tensed. "You told me you needed me around to keep an eye on the spike until you were finished."

"Didn't you hear my 'gotcha?' That meant I'm finished."

"You have to tell me these things."

"Goddammit, I'm finished. Get the fuck out of there!"

Taylor chose to use the same route as he had on entry, but he froze when tires skidded to a halt outside the back door as well as the front.

"Okay, it's no longer an option. Are there any ways out that don't make me run through a gauntlet of armed security teams?"

Vickie tapped furiously on her keyboard. "I wish I had better news for you but…no, not really."

In response, his whole body relaxed and everything in him immediately felt calm. It wasn't like he'd expected to come through this without a scrap or two along the way.

"Are you still there, Taylor?"

"Yeah, I'm here. I'm getting ready for a fight."

He scanned his surroundings and chose a position that gave him a line of fire to both entrances to the warehouse but also provided some cover. The suit was set up to give him a degree of protection, but there was no point in testing it to the absolute limit.

"Good luck," she muttered.

Unable to reply, he nodded. The sound of the front door opening demanded his full attention.

Niki settled into her seat again as the seatbelt light turned off and left them free to wander about the cabin. In her case, it meant she could lean forward and get her work done with as little disruptions as possible.

Even so, there were still distractions. The small plane shuddered as it fought the elements and other people moved in the cabin, made the usual noises associated with activity, and talked quietly.

Not only that, but Tanya sat across from her and stared. She wasn't sure if the woman merely sat there and minded her own business. Maybe she didn't even realize she was staring and wouldn't unless someone pointed it out. Niki had done that on more than one occasion—her mind gone as she thought about something or nothing while her gaze wandered or fixed on nothing in particular that might become something in particular.

Eventually, she lost patience and looked at the woman, who didn't avert her gaze.

"So," the agent said briskly, determined to take control of the narrative, "how has work gone for you guys? I assume things are going smoothly if Taylor thinks it's a good idea to leave everything behind for a quick trip to

Louisiana, but it's still good to know about the details. And how is your new employee working out?"

She had hoped to slip the real question she wanted to ask in unnoticed, but the way Tanya's eyebrow raised the moment Elisa was mentioned, even without her name, said that her attempt to be subtle had failed miserably.

"Look, if you're interested in the woman's welfare, you can be direct and ask about it," her companion stated, brushed her black hair back, and tucked a few strands behind her ear. "Trying to beat around the bush, as it were, merely wastes everyone's time and honestly, directness would probably benefit you in other lines of questioning too."

Niki narrowed her eyes. "I'm not sure what you mean."

Tanya snorted derisively. "Yeah, of course you don't. Okay, I have a question for you. Why is it so difficult for you to admit that you dig the cut of the ginger giant's jib and that it annoys the hell out of you? Because if you want to hear it from someone who knows what she's talking about, listen to me when I say that the he and Elisa scenario isn't something either party is interested in. If you want to blame someone for the reporter being part of our crew, you can blame Vickie since her joining the company was the crafty little hacker's idea in the first place. Honestly, once you get that through your thick skull, we can move past all this high-school bullshit and get somewhere."

She hesitated, unsure whether she could disagree with anything the woman said. It did feel a little stupid, she decided when she thought about it, but it was like hearing the woman state it so bluntly was all she needed to hear. It was teenager bullshit, and she thought she had left that attitude behind her.

"When you say it aloud like that, I guess it does sound a little childish. And wouldn't you find it annoying that you're attracted to a guy who would stick almost anything with a pulse?"

"Hell, Taylor has some physical attraction to him, I won't lie. He's not my type, but many people still listen to that little lizard brain of theirs that tells them they should look for someone big, strong, and capable of defending their mate. There's nothing to be ashamed of in that. Also, I can't say this with much certainty since I don't spend much of my time with the guy after hours, but it would seem his little escapades have come to an end. Which is to say I haven't seen him wander in late in the morning, looking hungover and covered in scratches and hickeys, so I guess there is progress."

"Be that as it may, I already did my part. I told him I was interested in something a little more…intimate. Basically, I told him I was open to dating and left the ball in his court, and he still hasn't called and taken me up on the offer."

Tanya chuckled. "Hell, I don't know enough about the guy to guide you, but it does sound like he's trying to impress you. Kind of like his version of a mating dance, but he's not sure how it works. Put him in front of a cryptid and he'll find a way to kill that fucker in fifteen different ways. Tell him you want to go somewhere romantic and expensive for a nice dinner and conversation, and he cares enough to make the attempt? It seems like you broke his brain and he's trying to deal with it. You could either give him space and let him work that shit out or do like me and find a dark corner to push him into and shove your tongue so far down his throat that you can wrap it around his balls."

Niki's eyebrows raised. "I…that's a little…uh…"

The woman shrugged. "It's very crass, I know, but it's direct and that's my point. Testosterone has a way of giving guys like Taylor tunnel vision, so if you don't make your intentions obvious, he won't see past whatever he's working on at that given moment. It also makes him want to ensure that the woman he's interested in is safe, whether she asks for it or not."

The agent paused and leaned a little closer to the other woman. "So you think…"

She let her voice trail off until her companion finally smiled. "Come on. You two are so obviously interested in each other that it makes the rest of us want to puke. Well, except Elisa. That girl is blessedly ignorant, which is odd since she's supposed to be a top-notch reporter or some shit."

"So Vickie told you?"

Tanya chuckled in response. "Please. That girl is computer smart but is more than a little obtuse when it comes to the people around her. She's so naïve when it comes to reality, it's cute to the point of throwing up as well. I need the pink stuff around her." She leaned back in her seat and pressed the button to tilt it even further. "My two cents, which you haven't paid me for, is don't worry about Taylor. He knows the stakes. He won't do you wrong."

"He'd better not," Niki grumbled. "If he does, I'll shove a .45 up his ass—"

"And keep pulling the trigger until he coughs the bullets up. Yeah, I heard. The fact that Taylor knows that about you and is still interested in your crazy ass would be a warning sign to anyone else."

Niki scowled and leaned back as well. It was interesting to be able to see what he thought of her through another person's eyes, but also a little worrying. Exactly how did he see her, and what was it about her that made him interested in the first place?

CHAPTER FOUR

Fighting people was an altogether different animal than fighting cryptids. In both situations, he dealt with his opponents making poorly considered moves. Inevitably, they tried to attack him despite the fact that their survival instincts should have told them to run the hell away and not look back.

But that was where the similarities ended. Humans had the same ranged weapons he did, for the most part, and knew how to use them. Some had rudimentary tactics that evolved beyond what even the monsters could conceive. His current adversaries were smart enough to take cover and try to keep him from killing them.

Taylor merely needed a way to keep them out in the open, confused, and fighting something they didn't fully understand. He already had the advantage, given that the warehouse was in complete darkness and he was the only one who had anything resembling night vision.

The downside was that the group that advanced on his position was heavily armed. They mostly carried submachine guns, although he could distinguish a couple of assault rifles and even the odd shotgun thrown in. With that amount of firepower, even shooting in the dark meant they would hit him simply as a result of the sheer volume.

He couldn't tell if any of them wore body armor. It was best to assume they did and move forward based on that. He held his shotgun a little tighter and after a moment's thought, swung it to slide it into the holster on his back and drew his sidearm. He wasn't sure if he would regret the decision, but in the critical moment of closing the distance between himself and his attackers, he wanted a little more precision in his mid-distance shooting.

Once he was up close and personal, he had a feeling the shotgun would make a grand entrance into the fight—assuming he survived that long.

"Taylor, I'm trying to keep the police at bay and make sure the alerts go straight into the spam system they have to keep your average prankster at bay," Vickie explained. "That should work, but the moment there's any shooting in there, you can bet your ass there will be shots fired called in. Even if this is an older, less populated area of the city, it is still a city, so there are still people around."

"Roger that," he whispered and remained hunkered behind cover. "What kind of response time do you anticipate from the local law enforcement?"

"Not great. I'd say somewhere around ten minutes, assuming they don't have any cruisers in the area. In that case, you can expect them in fifteen minutes or so."

"Wait, how does that work?"

"Well, the cruiser is sent to investigate. The officer either doesn't hear the shooting and says nothing is going on. Or he hears it, proceeds to violently evacuate his bowels, and drives to a safe distance to call in the cavalry. It's a very efficient system."

Taylor scowled and wished she would take this a little more seriously. Then again, one of the reasons he'd brought her in was for her inability to be caught up by the pressure of the situations he was embroiled in. A side product of that, of course, was that she wouldn't take much of anything seriously. They'd need to try to find a balance.

"I've managed to keep everything off for the moment," she announced. "They'll have to find the electrical board and manually override what I'm doing. Everything will be dark in there. I assumed you wanted to keep the advantage of having night vision while they didn't. I was right, yeah?"

He nodded and grimaced when he remembered she wouldn't see him. "I was about to say something about that. Thanks."

"So, will you engage them or merely sit around and hope you have an opening to escape?"

"That was the idea, but they've left people to guard the entrances. I don't want to engage them and risk having people attack me from behind. So, yeah, if I want to get out, it won't be around. It'll be through."

"Did you practice that speech?" she asked. "Maybe mutter it to yourself to try to maximize the coolness factor?"

"Yeah. How did I do? I felt like I rushed it a little."

"No, it wasn't rushed at all. I liked it."

"Really? You're not simply saying that?"

"I'm not simply saying that. Seriously. I have chills, Taylor. Chills."

"Thanks," Taylor muttered and focused on the team that now advanced through the warehouse. The alarm had likely been in the large storage area of the building, which explained why they made sure to check the entire space. The size slowed their advance, though, and spread the group of twelve across the entire space.

There was, he realized, a way for him to take advantage of that too.

He eased from behind his cover but remained hunched. The suit was surprisingly silent, at least compared to the heavy boots clattering around the warehouse. They likely didn't think they needed to sneak anywhere.

Hell, they probably didn't, not with those numbers. He moved smoothly and selected the group of three that was closest to him as his first victims. While he wanted to tell himself these people were as bad as the criminals who owned the premises, the truth of it was they probably weren't. Still, the weapons they carried weren't merely for show. The way they carried them and their coordinated approach told him they weren't simply thugs picked up off the street. Not many people had proper trigger and muzzle discipline and evidence of tactical training.

Taylor decided the wise assumption was that their safeties were off. From what Vickie had told him, they were ready to shoot on sight, which brought about the cliché of shooting first, second, and however many times thereafter and once everyone was dead, only then trying to ask a question.

He raised his sidearm. The suit was powerful enough to hold the weapon and shoot it accurately with only the one hand. The reticle that appeared in his HUD was certainly a help and gave him a target to work with for every step he took through the darkened warehouse.

After a moment of thought, he lowered his weapon by a few inches and pulled the trigger.

The entire space lit up for a split second and gave the three men a brief glimpse of the hulking mass that now advanced on them. It wasn't much but they reacted immediately, pulled back even though they were blinded, and attempted to locate their adversary. One of them had already fallen and clutched his leg. Taylor reached him within a quarter of a second and kicked his weapon away with enough power to snap the strap slung around his neck and skid the weapon across the floor.

He adjusted his aim to the second man and pulled the trigger twice this time. Both bullets punched through his opponent's right leg. He would endure months of recovery and traction after this, but at least he was alive—assuming there were no complications like hitting an artery or whatever.

It was something he needed to consider when fighting humans. Killing cryptids never affected his conscience but it wasn't the same when dealing with humans, weirdly enough.

The last one finally saw who had attacked them, but he didn't turn fast enough. He still attempted to swing his weapon into position by the time Taylor reached him, and the weight of the powered suit of armor struck him like a car. The force drove him into one of the nearby empty shelves and the entire thing collapsed.

The noise was sufficient to catch the attention of the other men in the warehouse, who whirled in that direction and spoke rapidly into radio comms they wore in their ears. The gunshots were loud but difficult to pinpoint in the cavernous area, but a falling shelf was enough to provide a location.

Some attempted to turn lights on, while others retrieved flashlights—the kind that was likely issued to them as standard equipment by the company they worked for.

Their efforts wouldn't be enough, however.

Taylor shifted position into the shadows and remained low. The group converged on those who were injured and who groaned in pain on the floor.

"They're trying to call emergency services," Vickie alerted him. "There are people in the vehicles. Do you want me to cut their communications?"

He considered it but shook his head. "There's no need to keep these guys from getting medical treatment. They will need it."

The six members of the team who weren't guarding the doors gathered quickly. A hasty scan confirmed that two were positioned at each of the two entrances, which made a total of ten. They examined their teammates who he had attacked but held their weapons aimed outward in case he launched another assault.

"What the hell attacked you?" one of the newcomers asked the man who writhed in pain.

"A huge guy." He growled through gritted teeth. "Just... fucking massive. He shot me, then he shot Baker and threw Young into the shelf like he weighed nothing. The force was enough to topple that massive shelf."

"How is Young?" the first man asked the two who

attempted to negotiate through the wreckage of the racking.

"He's out cold. It looks like he might have broken a fair number of bones, but he's still alive. Hey, Crash, how's that ambulance coming along?"

"They said it'll take a few minutes to get here. What kind of injuries are we looking at?"

"Two gunshot wounds," the apparent leader stated. "And we have one unconscious with unknown internal injuries to be evaluated once the paramedics—oh shit!"

"Reeves?" Crash, speaking from one of the cars outside, asked. "Reeves, are you still with me?"

He was not still with them. Taylor had identified the man as the leader of the group, which made him the primary target. Disabling him would shake their morale and leadership a little. There was no other comparable option, and the man saw him advance on him with barely enough time to react with a reflexive curse.

Unfortunately, there wasn't time to do anything. He reached the leader in only a couple of steps after the exclamation of alarm, grasped the barrel of his weapon, and yanked it savagely upward. The man's finger found the trigger and he fired his submachine gun toward the ceiling twice before his attacker finally managed to pull it out of his hands. The strap caught across his neck and dragged him forward and into the butt of Taylor's shotgun. The blow to his mouth dropped him immediately and blood seeped between his lips.

The other five men spun to face Taylor, and he swung his weapon to aim it directly into the chest of the man in front of him. The blast when he pulled the trigger flared enough to show him the shock in his victim's face when he was knocked back a step, lost his balance, and sprawled awkwardly. He groaned a second later, which confirmed that they all wore body armor. It was undoubtedly the kind that would stop a round of buckshot, but it would still feel like being kicked in the chest by a mule.

He adjusted his position as a couple of rounds hammered into his armor. Although they didn't punch through, he could feel their impacts and the alarms already showed where they had struck. His armor wouldn't take much punishment but thankfully, it wouldn't need to. He selected his next target, held his aim on the chest area, and pulled the trigger. The powerful blast of the shotgun hurled another man off his feet while Taylor moved hastily from his position to swing the butt powerfully and crush another man's cheekbone.

This adversary also fell, which left only two. They had already emptied the magazines of the submachine guns they carried and looked surprised by the fact that they had simply pulled the trigger with the weapon set on full auto.

Taylor checked his suit alarms and located five impacts. Three had struck him in the torso and the other two in the legs. Maybe these guys had training, but they were not professionals.

They scrambled to reload and scrabbled desperately for the extra magazines they carried, but time was against them. He surged forward and closed the distance between them. The semi-automatic shotgun fired another blast that caught a man in the chest and flung him to join his downed comrades. Taylor grasped the second man's weapon and yanked it hard to swing him into another shelf. The heavy storage unit collapsed, the man half-buried by the wreckage.

He assumed they were all alive. All needed fairly urgent medical care that was already on the way, but they would live. Most of them were conscious and still able to move somewhat, even if it was to groan and curl in pain, which meant there were no spinal injuries.

It was about as good as he could make it.

With the six team members dealt with, he moved away from the wounded men and toward the door. The two guards at the front entrance had left their posts and attempted to discover what had caused so much noise and destruction. Taylor didn't want to engage them. Escape was the only reason he had fought in the first place.

That option was open now and he twisted to circle away from the two who advanced blindly. They wouldn't see him, and as long as they didn't hear him either, he was in the clear.

"Okay, I tried to hold them off as long as I could, but the shots fired alerts are lighting up all over the city. You have an army of cops headed your way," Vickie warned him over comms.

Taylor reached the doorway and paused, his shotgun aimed at the two who still moved away from him until he slipped out of the warehouse.

"Okay," he whispered. "I'm out of the building. Do you know where I can go to avoid the cops? How long until they get here?"

"If you enter the building across the street and get out of the suit, you should be fine," she assured him. "They don't know what they're looking for at this point. No one has provided even a vague description. Once you're out of the area, you're in the clear, Taylor. But get the fuck out."

"I'm working on it."

He increased his pace and sprinted toward the same building he had originally exited from.

A van was parked between him and his destination, and it was only a matter of time before one of the people waiting in it saw him. He needed to make sure he had already reached them before they could act.

The dim light worked for him, but he was still five paces away when the man seated in the shotgun seat saw him.

Taylor rushed forward as the door opened a sliver before he pounded into it and slammed it shut again.

"Fuck!"

Taylor looked through the window at the man who fell back in his seat and clutched a broken arm. His gaze, however, looked into the inhuman visor of his attacker's helmet. The driver looked as stunned as his partner, and neither made any attempt to reach for their weapons when he tapped their window with the barrel of his shotgun.

The driver locked the van doors hastily, more out of instinct than any actual thought that it might be effective against the man who loomed outside.

That was all he needed to see. He peeled away and maintained his pace until he slipped into the close confines of the abandoned building where he had spent most of the day. Habit and training kicked in to effortlessly pull the armor apart and settle it into the crate he'd brought it in. He had used a trolley to ferry it and he checked that the load was secure before he shrugged into his jacket and dragged the trolly behind him as he walked casually out of the back of the building.

By now, sirens blared through the silence. They were close enough for him to see the flashing red, white, and blue on the walls around him although no cruisers came down the back street he now walked down. They would be drawn immediately to the site of the shootings and expand from there. Now that he was outside of the immediate radius, he didn't need to rush as much.

It wasn't long before he reached the van he had parked in a secluded place for Vickie to work from. Once he was within five paces, the back door opened.

She gestured for him to hurry. "Come on. Get in here."

"Do we have someone on our tail?" Taylor asked but did as he was told.

"Fuck no. You're in the clear, but I don't want to wait around in this heat all day."

She had a point. It wasn't something he generally noticed, but he had sweated hard while in the suit and it had continued while outside in Louisiana's muggy heat. The refreshing cool air seeping from inside the van came as a relief as he used mechanical help from the van to lift the crate in and followed it quickly.

"How are you feeling?" she asked as he immediately made his way to the driver's seat.

"Like we need to get out of here. Strap in," he answered simply and followed his advice before he started the engine.

CHAPTER FIVE

It seemed like pandemonium had erupted throughout the city. Police cars raced in from everywhere, all headed to the same location. Roadblocks were set up, but the van was waved through quickly. From what they could tell, the police still had no idea of what they should look for and merely prepared themselves to act the moment they had any kind of description for their suspect.

The farther they got, the fewer reactions there were to what had happened. Police cars still raced in the direction from which they had come, but it looked like most of the available police force were already in the area.

"Vickie, do you have a finger on the pulse of what's happening out there?" Taylor asked. He kept his eyes on the road ahead of him to avoid drawing any attention from law enforcement for driving erratically.

"Yeah, it looks like they have a cop swarm in that area," the hacker called from the back. "Which I guess is a good thing. If these guys are involved in illegal shit, having the police arrive in numbers like that is probably their worst nightmare. I'm picking up the details on the guys you tagged on the way out. It looks like they're all alive and the paramedics have been called in to help. Did you plan to leave them all alive?"

"Well, I tried to inflict non-lethal strikes and aimed for leg shots and their body armor. Are they all alive?"

"It looks like it, although the police on the scene have tagged them as criminals too. From what I can see, the security company they work for appears to be a front for organized crime. Most of the guys you ran into were former violent felons with ties to the local Russian *Bratva*. They needed to show gainful employment to be released on probation, and this company was set up to give the appearance of employment while it enabled them to still perform their duties as muscle for the local chapter of the Russian mob."

"Well...I feel a little less bad about leaving them injured in that case," Taylor commented. "Still. If I needed to, I was willing to go for the lethal options, and honestly, I'm not sure all the guys I ran into will make it. But attempting the non-lethal option felt like the right idea."

"Hey, I'm not judging. I would have if it slowed you and you were caught or injured, but if only injuring fools on your way out didn't make you lose a step, we're all good."

Her response drew a smile from him. "Well, I could have been out of there much sooner if I'd simply killed them, but at this point, once we're out and in the clear, there's every reason to look back and study my form. It'll help to make sure that when next time rolls around, I'm ready and improved."

Vickie didn't answer for a few seconds, which made

him think she maybe hadn't heard him. It didn't matter since he was mostly thinking aloud so he didn't comment on it.

When the silence lasted for almost a full minute, he wondered if she was ignoring him. It happened sometimes since she tended to focus on her work. Her job, at the moment, was to keep them safe and make sure the police didn't pick up their current location.

It wasn't long before he heard movement behind him and Vickie clambered into the front. She didn't speak as she pulled her seatbelt on and sat cross-legged on the shotgun seat, her phone in hand. She was listening to the police line through the earbuds she wore, which explained why she hadn't said anything for a while.

They continued to move through the streets until they reached a location he had surveilled the day before—an abandoned warehouse beside what had once been a small port. It had bustled with activity in the past, but business had moved elsewhere and the property had been abandoned. Most of the windows were broken and the walls damaged by desperate folk looking to strip its copper wiring.

The abandonment and destruction had begun years before, though, and anyone who bought it would probably have to tear the entire building down and start from scratch. Even the structure's integrity made Taylor study it suspiciously, but it provided a good location for them to switch vehicles.

They spilled out of the van as soon as he turned the engine off. It was pure common sense to abandon the van there. Vickie had already begun to pull her systems apart and pack them, which left him the work of transferring the suit to Liz. They had nothing much to say to each other as they worked and moved as quickly and as smoothly as they could. Everything was dismantled and packed in less than five minutes, and Taylor helped her carry her devices to the truck.

Once that was done, he smiled as she pulled off the gloves she had worn and shoved them into a plastic bucket that had been placed there already. He peeled his gloves off smoothly and dropped them into the same receptacle.

"Are you sure this will work?" she asked and handed him a plastic bottle with fifteen different warning labels pressed onto the side.

"It's a proprietary design made up by Dr. Jacobs specifically to take apart all biological material," Taylor explained and donned a facemask before he removed the top of the bottle. "He was excited when he explained it to me, which means I have no fucking clue how it works. But he did say the fumes are dangerous if you're exposed to them for too long, so put your mask on."

Vickie nodded and complied before he poured the contents into the bucket. Jacobs had explained that it had been originally designed to clean every tool and object he intended to use while testing the goop he had obtained. They had something like it in most labs that worked with the goop, but he had added a couple of design modifications to make it more effective. These resulted in the acid quickly generating a corrosive fog when it made contact with moisture in the air.

In this case, it was more than useful. Taylor picked the bucket up and held it as far away from himself as possible before he placed it inside the van and shut the door quickly. The acid in its fog state would eventually scrub any physical evidence that they had been in the van. Of course, any police officer who found the vehicle would be suspicious but by then—in as little as twelve hours, in fact —most of the acid would have already dissipated and taken with it all physical evidence of the two having been there at all.

It was a fairly new invention, and Taylor knew Jacobs had probably not even thought about the possible criminal uses for what he had helped to make. His motivation had mostly been to keep his work safe from the Zoo goop. Maybe he had, which was why he had shared it with him during one of their trips into the Zoo as well as details of where to purchase it.

As long as Taylor didn't share it with the local criminal elements, though, he doubted they would ever discover the advantages of using it themselves. Very few criminals were the creative types who thought outside the box like that. Most would simply choose the obvious solutions like fire.

The exception was them, of course. Technically, Taylor and his team were at least part-time criminals if he had to be completely honest.

He and Vickie scrambled into Liz, strapped in, and drew away from the rickety warehouse. With relief, he turned the AC system on and took a deep breath as the cool air quickly filled the cabin of the truck.

"So," he said, once they were a few blocks away, "will we have any problems with local law enforcement?"

She shook her head, still listening in on the police band. "I covered our tracks well and made sure security and traffic cameras were on a loop in the area, which gave us space to work with. Sure, if the New Orleans PD has good IT personnel on staff, they might realize they're looking at recordings, but that won't help them find us any faster. As it stands now, though, they're merely sifting through the mess, arresting all the guys you didn't shoot, injure, or otherwise maim, and collecting statements. The best-case scenario for them is that they find the van a week from now, which will be another dead end since it's registered under the name of the original owner who died fifteen years ago. And the chemical trick is very innovative, so there won't be much left there for them, even if they do find it."

"So we're in the clear is what you're saying."

"Well, there's no such thing as a perfect crime but we're as close to it as possible. Even the spikes you left in the computers are self-cleaning, and I washed them before I gave them to you so there are no DNA or fingerprints there either. They'll know something happened but given that I pulled all the data from their servers, they won't be able to pinpoint what we were looking for."

"So, since we're in the clear, do you want to talk about what Niki wanted when she called you before?"

"Oh…shit, I forgot that you'd heard that."

"You left my line open when you were talking to her. I couldn't hear what she said, but I did hear that you spilled the beans about us being here in New Orleans."

"Yeah, shit, I did, but only because she said she was coming here and wanted you to be on your way already. From there, it kind of slipped out."

"Did she say what she needed me for ?"

"Not really, but it sounded important. Or at least like time was a factor."

"Time is always a factor."

"I know. I only meant it was more than a factor. Like she wasn't willing to wait given your need to drive everywhere so she was a little relieved to find out you were already in town. Of course, it was quickly followed by her suspicions as to why you were here."

"So what is she up to now?"

Vickie shrugged. "Hell, if I were to guess, I'd say she's heading to Vegas to give Bobby and Tanya and their suits a flight here since they don't have any problem with flying."

"Bobby won't come," he responded emphatically. "He hasn't fully recovered from his last mission yet. Tanya won't let him anywhere near one of the suits, at least not if she has any say in it."

"You weren't fully recovered but you went there and put your body on the line, didn't you?"

Taylor nodded. "Yes, I did, but there's a difference between Bungees and me. He's a smart guy and I'm not. Besides, when you have someone out there who cares about you enough to tell you to not do stupid shit, you put more of an effort into it, now don't you?"

She tilted her head and regarded him in silence for a moment. "Yeah, I guess. So if I were to ask you to not do stupid shit?"

"Then I wouldn't. It would be a little hypocritical of you, though, since you've made a habit of doing stupid shit. I would need to jump in there to make sure you live long enough to learn the errors of your ways."

"Okay, that's harsh but fair. You might want to keep in

mind that Niki will want to know what we were doing out here on our own. And if I know her, she'll probably be ticked right the fuck off that you didn't include her in any of this."

"Well, it's a no-brainer. She can't be." He scowled and focused his eyes on the road. "She's always talks about how she wants to have plausible deniability, especially when you consider how illegal what we did is."

"Come on. You know she lost her job with the FBI because she helped you during your trip to southern Italy. We're way, way beyond her not wanting to know and not wanting to help."

"Fair enough. Still, if she wants to know, she'll have to ask me directly. I won't play any more games with her."

"Any more? What is that supposed to mean?"

He opened his mouth and snapped it shut again quickly. "Nope, I'm not getting into that now."

"Oh, come on. You guys might as well be a fucking Mexican telenovela for all the will-they-won't-they bullshit you're putting yourselves through. Seriously. I'm not joking even a little. You need to find some kind of resolution because watching the two of you dance around like this gives me a headache."

"Well, I'm terribly sorry. The last thing I ever want to give you is a headache. Unfortunately, though, if you dug into my life at all, you'd find any number of things to give you an even bigger headache. For now, this is what it is. And yeah, I'm working on it. Believe me, I'd like a resolution even more than you would."

"You're an asshole," Vickie commented cheerfully. "And on that note, this is the part where I ask why the hell you're heading into the city and to where all the cops will be looking for us. You know, where we escaped from and put a literal ton of work into making sure they will never find us?"

Taylor still didn't move his gaze from the road. "Well, if Niki's coming out here with Tanya and her team, the chances are this will be the last opportunity for us to get a meal before she greases us with rancid chicken fat and tosses us into the bayou for the gators to eat. I decided it's about time you had yourself a decent taste of the Clover Grill burger."

"Oh, you have to be kidding me."

"I don't have to be kidding you because people have to taste the fare from the best and oldest burger joint in New Orleans before they die. I wouldn't kid you about that."

She sighed, drew her legs up under her body again, and shook her head. "Dammit, what the hell."

"That's the spirit."

CHAPTER SIX

Niki wasn't sure what she should expect as the plane came down to land. She didn't like the south of the country and especially the southeast. Not for any cultural reasons, though, unless the oppressive heat that seemed to permeate the whole area had anything to do with the culture.

There was also the persistent threat of the summer storms that had only become worse over the past ten years or so. Or that was what it felt like, anyway. She wasn't a meteorologist so she had no idea if the storms were any better or any worse. But there was still something to be said for the people who stuck it out in an area of the country where they had to reserve about six months of the year for preparation to protect themselves against the terrifying power of nature.

While other areas in the country had to deal with similar feats of nature, most of those didn't need to cope with the heat that hung over the whole area like a blanket. There were people who liked the heat, of course, or preferred it to the cold, and she could understand that it was a matter of taste.

Still, it wasn't her taste. She could already feel the heat seeping into the plane as they came to a halt at the airfield.

"It feels like I'm rolling into a fucking sauna," Niki muttered and willed herself to focus on what had to be done rather than her discomfort.

"I don't know. I kind of like the heat," Tanya responded as they began to move to the door that opened slowly to admit a wave of hot air. "The dry heat of Vegas is fine, but something about being here in Louisiana is comforting. I kind of like it and honestly, I miss it."

"Did you grow up around here?"

"Not really, but I spent time around here in my late teens and early adult years. I don't know…sitting outside, soaking in the late afternoon sun while drinking a cold beer feels like the perfect way to end the day."

Niki fought back the urge to tell the woman what she thought about it. It included something about how if she wanted to go to a sauna, she'd pay for it herself. Of course, she didn't particularly enjoy being in a sauna either and never saw the point unless she had sinus problems like her father did from time to time.

"So," her companion started as they stepped out, "what have you dragged us all out here for?"

Niki was suddenly reminded of another aspect of the area she detested—the insects. More specifically, those that were airborne and tried to suck her blood at any opportunity. She slapped one that tried to land on her arm quickly and shook her head. In the waning hours, she could hear the dull buzzing of hundreds of them as they flitted around in search of someone like her to latch onto.

Tanya shook her head. "You know, I never had much trouble with mosquitoes. They never liked me."

"There are several factors that play into what mosquitoes prefer, and as it turns out, O-type blood or universal donors like me are more attractive to the flying assholes."

"You haven't answered my question."

"That's because the whole team isn't here and I don't feel like explaining myself twice. Thus far—which you should be able to grasp from the data available—is that I need as many bodies in suits as I can get my hands on. This means you, Taylor, myself, and either Jansen or Maxwell."

Jansen, who didn't appear to have any problem with the heat or the flying insects, looked at his partner. "Maxwell did considerably better in Taylor's tests than I did."

"Well, this is an opportunity for you to better yourself," the other man countered quickly like he had anticipated the challenge. "How else will you improve if you don't put yourself in one of those suits and train in the abilities you need?"

"Well...sure, but in the end, you want to keep practice and operations separate."

Niki jogged closer to interrupt. "As much as I enjoy having you two debate which of you is the prettiest, I'm afraid I'll have to agree with Jansen on this one. We are going out into the field, and that's not the best situation to drill him in how to use the damn suits. You were a little better at it and I need my best hands on deck. Jansen will run intel for this operation."

Maxwell nodded and didn't seem overly heartbroken

by the decision. Niki wondered if he didn't enjoy playing with the suit he had been fitted for. She had already made the decision, despite the fact that Bobby had sent the suit set as neutral so it would work for either of the two. It merely made it easier that the crate had Maxwell's name on it—and seemed fortuitous, somehow, in that it would most likely be more easily and quickly calibrated to him.

"So, do you guys have any idea of where we're supposed to meet Taylor?" Tanya asked and scanned their surroundings.

"Vickie said he would meet us here at the airport when we touched down," she recalled. "I guess I should have known that was too good to be true. Do you have any idea of what he came here to do?"

"What about the—"

"I don't care about plausible deniability. The chances are you guys will need my help with the local law enforcement anyway, so the sooner I know the details, the quicker I'll be able to work through all the muck and mire and get to the meat of the problem."

The woman shook her head. "Honestly, all I know is that Vickie tracked the people who tried to have the shipment stolen in Africa. She narrowed it to New Orleans but stalled at that point. Suddenly, she picked up on something, there was a flurry of talking I don't think anyone but Vickie understood, and they loaded the lightweight biker suit onto the back of Taylor's truck and left. I didn't ask any questions so that's the limit of what I know."

Niki wasn't entirely sure she believed the woman, but at this point, there was nothing she could do. She wouldn't exactly call her a liar.

Then again, maybe she was hiding something. She probably felt a little more loyal to Taylor and especially Bobby than she did to Niki.

Still, it wasn't something she could fault her for. As she considered this, her phone vibrated in her pocket.

"It's Vickie," she announced. Maxwell had already begun to bring the car around, while Jansen directed the workers at the airstrip to take the suits out of the plane and into a nearby warehouse. They would need to be stored there until they could bring a van in or something to transport them with.

"Well, don't keep us all in suspense," Tanya muttered. "Where are they?"

"She wants us to meet at some dive burger joint," Niki muttered. "I guess she and Taylor decided to get something to eat instead of picking us up here."

"What's the name of it?" Jansen asked as he returned.

"Oh...some place called Clover Grill on Bourbon street."

The man's eyebrows raised. "Oh, well...we have to get all this squared away. We have somewhere important to be."

She scowled at him. "What the hell are you talking about?"

"Clover Grill is somewhere you need to visit if you ever end up in New Orleans," he explained and gestured at Maxwell to pick up the pace. "I wanted to suggest that we head there once the mission was over as a celebration, but I guess it works for a pre-mission pick-me-up too. So, let's get going."

Taylor wondered at the mixed feelings of both fascination and trepidation. It wasn't a particularly good sensation and he knew he was staring a little too fixedly at the hacker seated across the table from him. It hadn't been his idea to choose a booth, but Vickie said she wanted the full experience. He wouldn't cheapen it by making her sit on one of the barstools, even if there was something to be said about watching the professionals at work over the countertop.

Once the food was delivered, he didn't want to tell her what she was supposed to do. It wasn't like there was a certain way to enjoy the burgers merely because he had found his perfect way to enjoy them. Putting your own burger together provided an odd kind of satisfaction. She had asked for something fairly regular and left him to put his together on the plate.

"What?" she snapped.

He was staring again, of course. Taylor turned his gaze to the burger in front of him, picked up a couple of fries, and dipped them into ketchup before he scarfed them quickly.

She shook her head and lifted the burger off the plate. It wouldn't be much to look at. Given that the food had been in production for almost three-quarters of a century before Instagram came about, it wasn't meant to look the best. It was supposed to taste good.

The single look he got from Vickie while she chewed her first mouthful was all he needed to know. He had been half-afraid that he had over-hyped it to the point where her suspicion would diminish the taste, but he recalled how ridiculous the notion was.

"It's not fair," she muttered, her mouth still full. "It's not fair for something to taste this good and somehow be bad for you."

"How dare you."

"Come on. It's not exactly the healthiest of foods. Still, I could eat here for every meal of every day and die contentedly from a heart attack six years from now and it would all be worth it. Holy Mary, mother of God."

Taylor wanted to comment on how blasphemy wasn't quite called for, but it was his turn to take another bite of a burger—one of which he had already enjoyed earlier in the day—and sure enough, it still tasted as good as the first one had.

"Now do you see why I said it was the kind of food you would want to eat for your last meal?" he asked a second after swallowing his first bite before he dove into his second.

Vickie mumbled something while she nodded and leaned back in her seat like she was focused on enjoying the mouthful and keeping herself on the first wave of pleasure.

He grinned as he took a sip of his drink and shifted a little in his seat. "These guys have been open for a long time. You have to admit they know what the hell they're doing. I wish I could make burgers like this. You know—pick a grill up or something, set it up on the longer days where we don't have as much work to do, have it out there and ready to feed everyone working. I'd probably need a little while to practice, but it'd help to make it a little homier."

"It sounds more like you want an excuse to cook while on the job," she countered.

Taylor was about to answer when his gaze settled on a heavy SUV that had pulled up outside. A moment of paranoia made him think the FBI had somehow managed to track them despite all their work to make that impossible. A moment later, though, Niki climbed out, and he realized another and yet similarly terrible fate had befallen them.

"How...how did they find us?" he asked and shoved a couple of fries into his mouth.

"Oh, I let her know she could find us here," Vickie explained. "I said we would meet them at the airport but since you wanted to come here instead, I told them to meet us here. Maybe we'll get them some of this too."

"Yeah, but then we'll talk about work and Niki will rope us into another mission. I had kind of hoped it would come tomorrow after we'd had the time to sleep and prepare for it. But no, she'll jump us here instead. Thanks, Vickie."

"I don't feel too bad about it."

"Yeah, because you'll sit in front of a screen and make wisecracks while I'm out there being attacked by whatever new monstrosity she's hunted for us this time."

"Okay, that's fair enough, but it's too late now."

The hacker was right, of course, and she waved Niki, Jansen, Maxwell, and Tanya to the table. One of the waitresses was already waiting to help them to bring a table and chairs closer to allow the four new arrivals to join the other two.

"Jansen has built up the burgers this place serves all the way here," Niki stated and looked like she was a little tired but also as annoyed. "Here's hoping they live up to the hype."

"They will," Taylor asserted before anyone else could speak and Vickie agreed with a firm nod.

"So, what brings you guys here?" he asked, took a sip of his drink, and toyed with the fries still on his plate. "Something tells me you have another sob story about how a rich CEO needs you to yell at him before he realizes that creating monsters in a lab can only end badly."

She smirked. "We're looking at something a little different this time. It's still along the lines of people being stupid but not our usual kind of stupid. We're looking at an advanced kind of stupid."

"Okay, you have my interest," he muttered and turned his attention to his half-eaten burger as plates were brought for the others in their party.

Niki took a moment to assemble her burger before she continued. "To cut a long story short, we're looking at the story of a merger. One company was on the brink of bankruptcy and was about to be taken over by one of their former rivals in a massive buyout. Kensington Inc. is the name of this company. Their rivals, Burley & Harrison, ran an audit on their operations before they completed the purchase."

"Let me guess...the Kensingtons were running iffy experiments they wanted to keep secret."

"Correct, and they did a good job of it too. Such a good job that once the purchase was complete and money was distributed for projects, the iffy one received their funding again and everything continued and simply ran on autopilot until—"

"Something went boom?"

"Well…no, not really. Not yet, anyway. We have a whistleblower working at B&H who picked up on what was being imported from the Zoo, put two and two together, and realized that something was about to go pear-shaped. They activated the alerts that reached Jansen. You know the rest of the story."

"Wait, so if nothing's gone wrong yet, why do you need us?" Tanya asked, took the first bite of her burger, and closed her eyes. "Oh, holy fuck, this is a tasty burger."

Jansen and Maxwell were already halfway through theirs and could only murmur agreement. Niki scowled at all of them before she took a bite and paused to appreciate the taste.

"Okay, I won't lie. I'll dream about this baby tonight," the agent muttered, her mouth still full. "And it won't be a PG-13 dream either."

Taylor winced. "That's a little more than I needed to know. Anyway, Tanya makes a good point. You usually only need us when there are verified monsters that need killing."

"This case is more complicated," she told them around another mouthful of burger. "We're playing the prevention game here and for a particularly good reason. You see, Kensington's cover-up was so effective that when B&H reshuffled their operations for efficiency, they moved their goop-related research into a lab inside the confines of the New Orleans area."

"Oh...fuck me." He groaned and rubbed his temples. "How long have they operated here?"

"At least three months. Maybe longer. The data we have is incomplete. We need a fire team ready for action at a moment's notice while we continue to gather information and hopefully shut the whole facility down."

"Everything will be closed by now," he replied. "You probably won't be able to reach any of the folks who are in charge and you certainly won't get a warrant."

"I don't need a warrant," Niki countered. "I live in a fun new world where keeping the population safe from alien monsters comes with a couple of interesting perks. They'll have security in place who will be able to let us in or at least put us in touch with someone who will. Hopefully, the people in charge will only have been incompetent and not realized what they had under their nose and let us clean everything out for them."

"It sounds good. Should we get going?" Taylor asked.

"There's no need to rush," Niki responded quickly and held her burger a little tighter. "I don't see why we can't take our time. We should at least finish our meal before we get started."

CHAPTER SEVEN

They lingered long enough for the group to finally understand why Clover Grill still operated almost a hundred years after it opened.

But despite the pleasant interlude, they had work to do. Taylor didn't like taking part in so many missions so close together—two on the very same day, no less—but there was no way to avoid it. If there were in fact cryptids located in the middle of New Orleans, they could realistically anticipate a massacre at an unprecedented scale if things turned bad.

When it came to action, quicker would definitely be better.

He hadn't brought his heavier suit, so the smaller one would have to do. It was heavier than some of the lighter assault suits that were sent into the Zoo and had better gear than some of those he had piloted in himself. While he would never dispute the simple fact that his heavier suit was better, he could make do with something a little lighter if he had to.

Vickie was the only one he trusted to drive Liz to the address of the lab, which left Jansen to tap on a laptop he used to keep himself apprised of the situation. Despite the indications to the contrary, they still hoped it would not become a situation they needed to deal with.

Niki had decked herself out in her suit, as had Tanya and Maxwell. The man looked a little more uncomfortable in his and it seemed like he was still adjusting the power settings to something that felt a little more comfortable. It would take him a while, exactly like it had everyone else, but Taylor decided not to tell him the best way to do it. He had to use it, so it was something he needed to do on his own.

He grasped his sidearm a little tighter and tried not to tense every time he heard a police siren wailing around them. The chances were they were still investigating the crime scene he had left. He reminded himself that if there was a problem, Vickie would pick up on it in time for them to know and leave town.

It didn't ease the nervousness, though, although it did help him to look past it.

Vickie had driven Liz from time to time when they needed her to make deliveries or pick parts up and Bobby's truck wasn't available. She had become rather good at it and fortunately didn't need a commercial driver's license as this wasn't necessary to drive a truck of that particular size.

It didn't look like any of them were worried about the police pulling them over, and it wasn't long before the vehicle drew to a halt. From what he could see through the tinted windows, it looked like they were in downtown

New Orleans, although the building itself appeared to have been isolated from the rest. A wall separated it from the streets around it, and he couldn't make out any windows on what looked like a five or six-story building.

There didn't appear to be a sign of who might own it, and to the people who probably walked past it every day, it would simply appear as another structure like those that filled the city around them.

In this type of scenario, however, having all the security in the world made no difference. Cryptids always found their way out eventually. It was only a matter of how long it took them. In a situation where the nature of the tests wasn't even known to security personnel and the facility was smack in the middle of a densely populated area, it had all the ingredients of a catastrophe.

Once Liz stopped, Taylor was the first one out. They had parked in front of the entrance and a solid-looking steel gate barred their entrance. A guardhouse was situated beside it and interestingly enough, a police cruiser had already stopped in front too.

"You guys got here fast," the officer inside the car shouted and climbed out with more speed than the weight around his waist should have allowed. "I thought you boys were all occupied with the circus going on in the East Side and didn't think—"

He froze when he saw Taylor standing in front of him. The officer's instinct to reach for his weapon was under-standable, all things considered, but he stopped short of drawing his sidearm as Jansen jogged closer and the other members of the team dismounted.

"Good evening, Officer," the agent said and pulled a

badge from his coat pocket. "I'm Agent Jansen with the DOD. Could you inform us of the reason you were called here?"

The man took a moment to inspect the badge before he nodded. "I…sure, what the hell. The security here received a couple of alerts. They thought they were being broken into from the alarms that activated but later told us there are no breaches in their security. I've merely swung by to make sure. Why? Who called the DOD in?"

"That's classified, I'm afraid," Jansen responded smoothly and motioned for Niki to join him. "Suffice it to say we're operating under the Cryptid Act and will expect the full cooperation of the proprietors of this establishment."

"Cryptid….holy shit. Are you telling me there are fucking alien monsters in there?"

"That's what we're here to establish."

The officer's eyes widened as he suddenly realized why four armored suits had begun to advance on the gate.

"What was that about a mess on the other side of town?" Niki asked through their comms as Jansen marched forward to deliver a similar speech to the guard they hoped would let them in.

"Ask me no questions and you need hear no lies," Taylor muttered under his breath.

"What was that?"

"This kind of conversation can wait, don't you think?"

He was right and she knew it.

The security man was more skeptical than the officer, but after a quick call to a superior, he pressed the button to open the gates and allow the team through and motioned for Vickie to pull Liz in. She parked the truck outside the building and immediately began to set her computer systems up, likely tapping the surveillance inside the lab.

"What are we looking at here, Jansen?" Niki asked as the agent returned to her.

"It looks like movement alarms have been tripped in the lower levels that are supposed to be shut down for the night," the agent explained and gestured for the guard to join them. "A few of the security team were sent to investigate and—surprise, surprise—they haven't checked in. They also haven't responded to the attempts to hail them on their radios either."

"Vickie, can you see anything on the cameras?" Niki asked.

"I'm still setting up but Desk has already taken a look from her side. She's confirmed that they don't seem to have any surveillance in place on the lower levels. I'm trying to boot up the computers in that area to see if I can access a few webcams from here."

She didn't sound too hopeful and by the looks of things, the situation wouldn't improve much. The security guard looked like he was about to request a change of pants, but he still wanted to talk to his supervisor.

"These guys realize that we're here to help, right?" Maxwell asked and seemed to still have to make adjustments to move more easily in his suit. "Having to comfort the dumbasses who got themselves into this problem has to be the worst part of this whole situation."

"Your mic's hot there, bubba," Taylor noted and patted the man's shoulder.

Jansen returned to the group. "Our credentials check

out and he's only waiting for confirmation from his boss..." He paused as the security guard waved them frantically toward the building. "Which it seems he has. It's time for you guys to do your thing."

"All right, folks." Taylor spoke decisively through the comms, knowing it was his responsibility to take control of the mission from that point. "We'll go in careful and quick. No sudden movements, no jumping at shadows, and certainly no shooting at anything that moves. We still have two possible friendlies down there, and you must hold your fire until you have a clear target. I'll take point. Niki, you have my back. Tanya and Maxwell, take up the rear and make sure nothing sneaks up behind us, got it?"

The team responded with confirmations and he motioned for them to advance into the building. Vickie had already located the blueprints, uploaded them to the HUDs, and even marked the route they should follow to reach the area where the goop-related research was conducted.

The lights were still on, thankfully, and he nodded approval as the team fell in behind him. He trusted Tanya and Niki well enough but having a newcomer in their ranks made him a little nervous. Maxwell's inexperience made him something of a wild card, and it wasn't pleasant to consider the possibility that someone might accidentally shoot him in the back. The assault rifle the man carried would punch through his armor with ease.

"Vickie, do you have any eyes here yet?" he asked as he led the team to the correct floor. "Or any idea of what we can expect?"

"Unfortunately not. All the computers they work with

there were built sometime in the nineties, so it's taking me a little longer to bring everything up."

"That has to be a blow to your ego."

"Not really. I wouldn't be annoyed by the fact that I can't break through the firewalls of a typewriter, after all. But if you're looking for something to shoot at, you might want to go to the specific area where the motion sensors were tripped. I'll send you coordinates now."

Taylor waited a second until an area of the building was now highlighted as promised, and he indicated for the team to follow him through the narrow passages. His first thought was that it wasn't like any of the labs he had been called into before. It looked far more like an office building.

"This doesn't feel right," Vickie muttered.

"Is something wrong?" he asked.

"No, nothing like that. It's only that the security here is so lax, it feels like taking candy from a baby—one that's high on cough syrup."

"Who the hell gives a baby cough syrup?"

"Terrible parents, but that's not the point if you're there to steal the baby's candy. Stop complaining about my metaphors, Taylor. Taylor?"

He held his fist up to command the team to halt. His suit's motion sensors alerted him that multiple somethings moved around the corner and in the precise location where the alarms had been tripped. Most were too small to be the security guards they had been sent down, in part, to hopefully find still alive and well. One, however, was way too big.

"Not to sound like a sage, old space wizard," Taylor

murmured and advanced slowly, "but I have a bad feeling about this."

"I'm quite sure Han was the one who said that first. Or was it Luke?" The hacker sounded unimpressed by his possibly mistaken reference.

"Hush." He curled around the corner, his sidearm held firmly in his hands and aimed in the direction of the movement in the hall, and almost held his breath as he looked for a target. "Oh...fuck me."

CHAPTER EIGHT

The team was only a few seconds behind him. Taylor didn't want to put too much into a single curse, but it was still warranted in the circumstances.

"What the hell is that?" Tanya asked, her head tilted in obvious bemusement.

The question was warranted. As zoo monsters went, this one looked less inherently threatening than the other creatures they were used to dealing with. If he were honest, the critter bordered on cute. It was small, comparatively speaking, and reached to about his knee at the shoulder with distinct feline features. It was covered in black fur with small blue spots, something he'd not seen in his previous missions, either in the Zoo or in the States.

At least not in person. He'd seen pictures and artist renditions of a cub that had been taken out of the Zoo a while before that looked like that. The fur had acted like active camouflage inside the jungle, where the darkness was only slightly broken by tiny spots of brilliance where the blue goop could be seen flowing through the trees.

It wasn't a common sight, but it looked like the tiny creature was a cub. Powerful muscles had barely begun to show, but the panther-like mutant bared its teeth at them. This revealed fangs much like a snake's that dripped with venom while its long tail waved slowly from side to side as it backed away.

This didn't resemble any of the cryptids that had spontaneously evolved from being exposed to the goop in a lab. The fact that it looked exactly like a cub that had been extracted before and would probably grow up into one of the powerful panthers he'd dealt with in the Zoo gave him pause.

"It's...a cub," Taylor answered finally while he and the muscular ball of fur continued to stare at each other.

"A cub?" Niki repeated.

"Yeah, a cub. A young version of something far bigger and much more terrifying. It's kind of cute if you think past the whole lethal killer aspect."

"Wait," Vickie cut in over their comms. "Exactly how big do those things grow to? How young is this one?"

"I'd say...maybe a couple of months," he replied. "I haven't ever seen a cub myself."

"Then how do you know that it's not a fully-grown critter?" Niki asked.

"Because I've seen the grownups and I've killed my fair share of them too. They did have cubs and someone got one of them out for testing, but they keep them well-hidden. This is the first one I've seen directly, though."

The small animal reached its limit and turned quickly to sprint down the hallway. He made a note of the bloody tracks its large paws left.

"I hate to say it, but I think we know what happened to those security guards," Maxwell commented.

It wasn't a pleasant thought but it was unlikely that the blood was from something else in the lower area, and he doubted the cub was on its own.

"Vickie, were there any details on exactly what was being tested down here?" Taylor asked as he motioned to the team to continue moving with him. The tracks were fairly easy to follow, which indicated the amount of blood the cub had walked through, and he pulled his sidearm. He moved cautiously and chose to give it some distance. He didn't want to step around a corner and end up face to face with an angry mother.

"They did a thorough purge of all the data regarding the origins of the test subjects, but the chances are someone in charge would have kept notes."

"I don't think I would be able to kill something like that," Tanya stated aloud. "Yes, I know it's a dangerous critter, but it's not like anything else we've run into before. I don't think I've ever seen a cute cryptid before."

He didn't want to comment on the massive creature that had almost killed him and had wrecked his suit. It wasn't cute by the strictest definition, but it had been a gorgeous beast—the kind that under any other circumstances, he would have left alone to live its life like if he would if he ever ran into a grizzly or an elephant. Definitely dangerous, he'd admit that, but even when attacking him, it had felt like the creature was defending itself.

They reached a corner and he motioned for the team to stop. The cub's tracks weren't the only ones visible now, and a long smear resembled one left by a dragging trail and suggested that the bodies of the guards had been moved to a more private location.

After a couple of seconds to study the motion sensors—which told him this was where most of the other movement was coming from—he stepped around the corner. Ever-cautious, he held his weapon aimed at whatever waited for him.

The cub he had encountered fed on a very human-looking corpse, as did two others. All three were suddenly aware and alert when a rippling, rumbling growl of warning issued from the fourth figure in the hallway.

"That's more like it," Taylor whispered and leveled his weapon on the larger creature. She was clearly the mother of the youngsters. Her shoulders were almost as tall as his. The spots were gone from her fur, which was pure black with a hint of a gray stripe running down her spine. She was almost twelve feet long, and another growl spurred her offspring to run toward a hole in the floor.

The size disparity between the youngsters made him wonder if they were different ages and she'd simply had three in quick succession, or if there was a test that involved feeding the cubs different amounts to make them different sizes. Since they were in a lab, he accepted that neither scenario was impossible. He'd had first-hand experience with the lengths many researchers were willing to go to for scientific discovery, especially with the amount of money that surrounded the Zoo's industry.

The mother assumed a defensive position between Taylor's team and her cubs. She crouched in preparation for a possible attack and bared her teeth at them.

"In case you guys aren't aware," Taylor warned. "These fuckers have venomous fangs, so…you know, be careful."

"Should we start shooting yet?" Niki asked. She seemed enthusiastic to get into the action as she advanced but remained behind him and a little to his left.

He waved for her to pause and kept his weapon aimed at the panther. In close quarters like this, if they didn't make a decent first strike on the mother, she would attack and cover the short distance almost immediately. Her fangs could slice into a suit with ease. He wasn't willing to risk losing anyone to that kind of danger unless he had to.

"Oh, this will suck," Taylor muttered and fixed his gaze on the mother as she remained in place, frozen while she watched the team of humans who had invaded her territory.

"Vickie," Taylor called. "You can go ahead and tell the security guard up there that his friends are dead. Show him visual footage if you need to."

"I don't think that's necessary. I'm fighting the need to spew simply watching it from your feed."

"Well, make sure the building is secured. We're looking at a small breach, but I don't need to tell you how quickly a cryptid infestation can grow."

"No, you don't need to tell me, but I'll have to tell them." The hacker sighed at the admittedly frustrating prospect of informing the locals about what they should do. It involved the inevitable and unpleasant threat that things would get worse if they did nothing about it. "Do you have any suggestions?"

"Yeah. Be assertive but don't act like you're rolling these

people over. They need to listen to you, not feel like they're being attacked."

"See, it sounds like you think that's informative advice, but I have no fucking clue how to be assertive without rolling people over."

"You do it all the time when you talk to me about your interests. Channel that."

"Oh, that kind of assertive."

"Yeah. People respect being told what to do when those orders come with a casual tone and many big words they don't understand. They pretend to understand simply to keep from looking stupid."

"I can do that."

"Ahem," Niki interrupted. "Shouldn't we focus on the situation right in fucking front of us?"

"I am focused," Taylor replied. His gaze hadn't wavered from the mother. The cubs stood frozen at the hole in the floor and gave no indication that they would enter what he assumed was an access to another level or perhaps their den. He allowed himself a few seconds to look more closely at it and realized it didn't appear that they had dug it themselves. In fact, it appeared to be an older manhole with the cover removed. It meant the cryptids had a way out, but from the way they stood their ground, it didn't seem like they intended to abandon their kills.

He wasn't sure if the sudden display of natural instincts in animals that displayed them so rarely was comforting or distracting. What he did know was that the mother was not one of the creatures created outside the Zoo. Those were far more hostile. From what he remembered of the critters, they could be whipped into a frenzy in a variety of ways, but in many situations and especially when they were in smaller numbers, they only attacked out of self-defense or if they were hunting.

Stories were common of the smaller, locust-like creatures simply grazing as they watched teams march past them. The smarter groups and those he led only fought when they were attacked directly and preferred to keep moving at a decent pace. Something about seeing their fellow mutants killed drove the rest into a violent rage.

Taylor remained calm but watched the animals closely. "Okay, here's how we'll do this. We have to draw the mother away from the cubs and into a fight that doesn't include them. Don't injure the youngsters or they'll bolt the hole, and I'll go ahead and guarantee they'll move faster down there than we can."

He moved a little to the left and gestured for Niki to do the same while he waved Tanya and Maxwell to the right. If they positioned themselves as close to the corner of the intersection as possible, it would divide the attention of the mutant. The mother anticipated that their movement meant they were about to attack and lowered more aggressively in her stance as Taylor raised his pistol and pulled the trigger.

It was almost impossible to see her. The high-speed reaction meant that by the time the flash from the barrel of his gun had faded, the monster had already moved. A splash of blood confirmed that the bullet had struck, but he had aimed at the head and hit somewhere on the flank.

His teammates opened fire but by the time they managed their first shots, the animal had already closed the distance between them.

He moved forward and away from the jaws that snapped at his neck and attempted a couple more shots. The others in the team struggled to keep up with the creature's impossibly fast movements. They opened fire as the powerful beast roared and tried to sink its claws into Niki as its jaw opened to almost ninety degrees. As her two teammates tried to advance on it, the long tail swept into them with more power than either had expected and hurled them off their feet with ease.

Taylor steeled himself. He didn't want to turn his back on the pups since they had the venom-tipped fangs their mother attempted to sink into Niki, but he couldn't reliably put them down. Honestly, he didn't want to. At this age, they didn't pose the dangers the mother did. While it wasn't an option to release them into the wild, of course, something could probably be done. Maybe they could be shipped to the Zoo for the people there to study.

It didn't matter. The mother realized Taylor was now between her and the cubs and immediately turned her attention to him. She stared at him for a moment in an aggressive challenge and he could almost see her thought processes as she scrutinized him and the situation. He used the brief respite to yank the shotgun from his back and moved his handgun to his other hand a second before the creature surged forward like a big black blur. Fangs and claws lashed out at him and he twisted hastily and dove to the side.

It would have been difficult to do with the larger suit, especially in the tighter confines of the hallway they were in, but the smaller suit performed the maneuver without a hitch. He rolled over his shoulder, scrambled to his feet, and fired both the sidearm and the shotgun as he continued to race to the left and away from the fangs that were still bared at him.

Something caught him in the chest with enough power to knock the breath out of him. The whipping tail flashed across his vision before he impacted with the drywall. It crumbled under the weight of the suit and almost gave fully as he pulled himself up with the help of his suit's hydraulics.

The fangs looked massive up close, especially since the creature pounced on him and forced him into the wall again. This time, he plunged through to the other side and into what appeared to be the office of one of the researchers who worked in the area. His sidearm clattered and slid away from him, while the weight of one of the mutant's paws bore down on the arm that still held his shotgun.

The fangs looked positively huge at this point.

"Hey, Taylor," Vickie called. "How are things down there?"

Taylor freed his left arm and shoved it into the cryptid's mouth to stop it from clamping far enough to sink its fangs into his throat. "Not...the fucking...time!"

"Oh, crap—sorry!"

A volley of shots issued from the other side of the wall, likely Niki, Maxwell, and Tanya recovering from the attacks on them. It was about fucking time too.

Suddenly, the beast paused. She vaulted away from him and hissed and roared, not at the attackers but at the cubs.

He pushed up from where he had been pinned and winced at the pain radiating from his shoulder and wrist as he peered through the hole and froze. One of the smaller creatures lay on the floor and a pool of blood seeped from it.

Its blood, he realized in mere seconds, not that of the two guards' corpses.

"Oh, fuck," he grumbled and stretched to retrieve his fallen weapon. The mother changed tactics and made no effort to attack any of the four who were there with her. Instead, she turned away from them and used her body to block her other cubs as they huddled around the manhole they would try to escape through.

Taylor reacted purely on instinct. They couldn't be allowed to get out. He raised both his weapons and opened fire. The massive mutant remained in place and she snarled at the humans until one of the shotgun blasts powered through the side of her head and she fell onto her side.

The shotgun was empty but he stopped shooting with the sidearm as well. She was dead. The chances were she would have died in minutes from the wounds, but the one to her head had sealed it. The two youngsters that had survived were also on the floor. He didn't like it but given the damage they would have caused to any biome they interacted with, he'd been left with little choice. This was a situation that called for big-picture decisions. He hated them but they had to be made.

"Hey, Taylor, it looks like everything's cleared," Vickie called over the comms. "Is everything resolved? Are you dead? Please don't be dead."

"I'm fine. What's up?"

"I don't know what you did—maybe knocking into a computer sped things along. Okay, not realistically, but what matters is I have access to the hidden files on the testing. It looks like the creatures were being tested for their reproductive abilities. It's fairly in-depth and way out of my realm of expertise but from the little I do understand, it seems they were dealing with the parents and the cubs."

"Parents?" Taylor asked. "Plural?"

"That's how reproduction works, Taylor. I can't believe I need to tell you this. See, when a daddy mutant and a mommy mutant—"

"We only had one adult here!" he snapped and dragged the dead panther slowly from the hole she had attempted to shield. "Is there any chance one of the adults died before we got here or something?"

"They had an entry on both adults from yesterday, so I have to assume...no. And there were five cubs in there too."

"Fuck!" Taylor turned to the rest of the team. "Okay, we have to go down there and find two more cubs and another adult. At fucking least."

"That's a bad idea," the hacker told him. "Those sewer tunnels are barely large enough for a regular human. You guys in the suits won't be able to move in there."

"Well, it's not like we have many options."

"Thankfully, those sewers are isolated like they are in most labs dealing with hazardous waste, so there's a very straight line out of there and to the Bayou. The good news is that all specimens were tagged to make it easier to identify them during testing. Even better news is that these are GPS linked, although I don't think they even considered needing that. If you guys get up here, I think we can pick up the signal—even if we have to use a manhole to locate it

—and intercept them. That way, we can follow them while they're on the move."

Taylor looked at his team and shrugged. "Okay, we'll head up. Get the truck started and we'll get out of here."

"What about the rest of the facility?" Niki asked. "We can't leave it like this."

"I can call in some of our people with the DOD," Jansen suggested. "I'll stay while you guys go hunting."

CHAPTER NINE

The heat that hung over the city, even at night, remained unbearable. It was worse while wearing a suit that was the pinnacle of weapons technology but lacked a great deal in terms of breathability.

It felt much like the Zoo, Taylor realized morosely. Their present surroundings mimicked the jungle's tendency to lock the heat of the Sahara in, which made the whole area a stuffy nightmare.

The recognition of that wouldn't make things any easier but at least it wasn't outside of his realm of experience. He could only imagine that Niki, Tanya, and Maxwell had similar difficulties with adapting.

"Okay," Vickie announced from the front of the truck. "The tracker indicates that they are heading toward the exit. It is supposed to be sealed with heavy filters, for obvious reasons, but all things considered, I think we can assume they will find a way out."

"How far away from the exit are we?" he asked.

"Still a couple of minutes. You'll arrive behind them, but only seconds apart."

"How the hell are we able to GPS track something moving through a tunnel?" Maxwell asked. "I thought that was still impossible."

"Well, yes...technically, it is, but people have to work in these sewer tunnels, so they've installed wiring that allows connectivity with the outside in case... Well, you know, if something happens. Anyway, that's how I'm able to track them through it. It's not the solution I would have gone with, but as low-tech options go, it's fairly ingenious."

The hacker was rambling. Taylor had learned to listen for the dull monotone that indicated her mouth was talking but most of her brain was somewhere else. It usually meant she was either working or worrying about something. In fairness, he was a little concerned himself. Monsters heading into a swamp on the outskirts of a major population center was the kind of nightmare Niki was probably supposed to avoid.

The fact that Vickie followed the cryptid's movements underground while they navigated the streets of New Orleans probably meant she was both worried and working. He had suggested that one of them track the beasts physically as well, but she had insisted it was unnecessary work given the chips the lab had implanted in each specimen they studied.

Taylor thought that it was probably because she didn't want any of the team to be alone in the tunnels, where they would be extra vulnerable due to the limitations of movement. For all her snark, the hacker was fiercely protective and especially of him. She no doubt knew he'd be the one to volunteer.

The truck suddenly came to a halt and Vickie motioned for them to climb out quickly. The team complied without discussion. They were at the edge of the city and in a section of the Bayou that probably didn't see too many tourist boats. A few smaller shrimping vessels were visible, but the area thankfully seemed largely abandoned for the night.

They had a couple of hours before the sun began to rise, when it would bring more of the population with it than he was comfortable with.

"I'm transferring the trackers to your suits," Vickie told them. She looked tired and stressed in a way that made him want to tell her to get herself something to eat and have a few hours of sleep.

Hell, he felt like he needed a couple of hours himself, but that would have to wait.

"They're out in the open now, so you should catch up with them. Of course, I imagine the swamp won't be that easy to navigate, but it looks like they are sticking together. You'd better get going, though."

He nodded. "We'll move fast. Stay behind me and alert the rest of the team if you see something moving. If you see them, shoot to kill. The chances are we have better vision in these suits than they do, so stay calm, stay alert, and stay together. Let's go."

It wasn't his first time to move through a swamp. He remembered his second job with Niki when she had sent him to find what looked like a cryptid killing humans and turned out to be something considerably less palatable. He wasn't necessarily proud of what he had done when he discovered the truth but it had been necessary. It had felt right in that moment and he hadn't changed his mind about it since.

He checked his weapons to ensure they were all fully loaded before he led the others through the wetlands. The darkness wasn't much of a problem. The sky was clear and they were fortunate to have a full moon. Its light was such that they almost didn't need the night vision, but it made things a little easier and enabled them to navigate through the swamp and avoid sections where they might be more heavily bogged down.

The mutants continued their progress but at a slower than expected pace, which perhaps suggested caution. They were in a new environment and one that was home to one of the oldest and deadliest predators in the world. The animals would probably be able to stand against the average alligator, or at least the adult would. The cubs wouldn't be as effective, although the venomous fangs would possibly give them a fighting chance.

"Oh, fuck," Taylor muttered to himself as the thought of the Earth predators settled in. "Right, team, keep your eyes open for any alligators. Not specifically in relation to our quarry, but because…yeah, we don't want to fuck around with alligators."

"Come on," Maxwell replied and chuckled. "These suits were developed to kill the biggest and baddest killers in the world, alien or not. I could kill a fucking building in one of them."

"A building doesn't shoot back. More importantly, it isn't lurking in the water waiting for you to get close. I'm serious. Even in a suit of armor, do not underestimate these fucking things."

"Taylor," Niki interjected, "are you trying to tell us that on top of a fear of flying, you have a deathly fear of alligators?"

"It's more an existential dread of facing a predator that's been around and at the top of its food chain for the past thirty-seven million years in its particular habitat. If you're smart, you should feel the same way."

"So, do you have an alligator phobia?"

"It's a natural and well-founded survival response." Taylor didn't want to talk about it. If they wanted to be dragged into the water to do the aquatic tango with an alligator, that was on them. He hefted his shotgun and held it steady as they advanced on the cryptids with no clear indication of their target location. The creatures still didn't move in a distinct direction, which made it difficult to predict where they might go next.

"We should split up," Maxwell suggested over the comms. "Okay, not split up but spread out. That way, we can make sure to stretch a wide enough net so none of them can escape. How many of them are there again?"

Taylor paused to think about it. "One of the parents and a couple of cubs. The cubs will most likely stick as close to the parent as possible, so I don't think we need to spread out, at least not until we engage. The GPS will show us if any of them try to break away from the group and we can decide how to deal with that if and when it happens."

"Yeah, the chips were a lucky break," Tanya commented. "The alternative would have been to follow them through the tunnels."

"I'd have done it if I had to, but even I have to admit that sometimes, the old-fashioned method leaves much to be desired. I wouldn't have given myself great odds in an underground battle if they attacked in limited space like that." Taylor gestured around the swamp they were in. "And even here, the thought of having to track them without the help of the GPS signals is borderline nightmare."

She nodded and every movement jolted her suit until she recalled the powered systems and stopped. "Yeah, I have to agree with you there. I'd like to live in this area but I don't think a swamp is a pleasant experience for anyone, let alone when you're hunting killer mutants."

The signals a little ahead of them indicated that they were approaching the group and that the creatures remained together. He adjusted his weapons to avoid maintaining the same position for too long and kept his head on a metaphorical swivel. The motion sensors should have been of greater assistance, but with so much movement around them, things were a little more difficult. Hundreds of animals were present in the area although most were insects. A few birds and smaller creatures were identifiable as well.

Also, almost constant ripples shivered through the standing water despite a complete lack of wind, which told him something moved beneath the surface— it could be snakes, alligators, or almost anything. Large expanses of standing water had been one of the few things he hadn't needed to worry about in the Zoo.

Then again, he had needed to deal with hundreds of small things moving around him and determine what was merely something tiny that posed no threat and what could attack him without a second thought.

Still, having to worry about what was under the water as well as what he could see through the motion sensors was unnerving. It wasn't that he had an alligator phobia. Or maybe he did. There was a natural benefit to wanting to keep as much distance between himself and them as he could.

Then again, he was the kind of guy who charged head-first into an engagement with alien monsters of all types and shapes, but he drew the line at alligators. A phobia element was undoubtedly involved.

Taylor raised his hand with a closed fist to bring the team to a halt. The swamp was far from silent, but as they stood completely motionless, he could faintly detect something moving ahead of them. The dense undergrowth made it difficult to see anything, but the sound was present. A light splash was accompanied by what sounded like the combination of a mewl and a growl. It immediately conjured an image of something large and feline-like moving through a terrain it was uncomfortable with.

The mutants would learn quickly, though. That was what made the Zoo and the creatures it spewed so terrifying. Everything was adaptable. Hell, it had turned the Sahara Desert into a jungle.

He motioned for them to push forward but at a slower pace and it wasn't long until physical evidence began to appear. Bushes were damaged where something had tried to climb them, tracks led away from the team, and they even noticed a few broken branches with claw and teeth marks on them.

"Taylor, you'll want to see this," Niki called and gestured for them to move a little closer to where she stood. Taylor joined her quickly and grimaced as he looked at what she'd found.

From what he knew about alligators, they liked to remain in the water at night and only came out during the day to bask in the sunlight. Yet one lay torn to shreds and partially eaten and the tough, leathery skin had been ripped open.

"How did they get it out of the water?" Maxwell asked and lowered himself to inspect the corpse more closely.

"It probably attacked quickly, dove into the water, and injected its venom immediately—that would have killed it within minutes," Taylor surmised. "You know, jaguars in the Brazilian Pantanal strike the local alligators from behind and break their skulls with a single bite."

"I'm fairly sure they have caimans in the Pantanal, not alligators," Vickie interjected. "Although it could be considered purely semantics."

"How—"

"I like alligators, crocs, and caimans. It's something of a hobby of mine."

"Of course...of course you do," he muttered quietly. "What kind of family am I involved with?"

"What was that?" Niki asked.

"Nothing. We should push on. They're still on the move after their quick meal, so we'll need to...oh, fuck."

"What?" Tanya queried.

Taylor studied the tracker on his HUD and scowled as the signals began to circle on a wide loop that would bring the mutants to where they stood.

The dead alligator, only half-eaten, didn't look like it had simply been left behind, now that he considered it. The kill had been deliberately displayed in an open area. The logical assumption was that it had been done to catch their attention and both slow them and distract them while the creatures moved behind them.

He turned his attention to the low-hanging trees around them, his senses alerted by the utter silence and the fact that he didn't notice any movement.

A few moments later, however, he caught the hint of a rustle in the branches above them.

"Get back and keep your eyes on the trees," he warned and narrowed his gaze on something dark that slunk through the shadows before he could focus enough to establish a target.

He dragged in a breath and as he exhaled, everything went to shit.

Water churned behind him and Taylor shifted his attention as an unidentified creature surged out of the swamp. His initial instinct made him think one of the cubs had hidden there, but the power of the bite and the lack of any fangs sinking into his leg told him it was something else entirely.

"Fucking—help!"

The savage jaws locked over the limb and the reptile began to drag him into the water. In response, the team rushed forward to help. The distraction was perfect and the panther in the branches above was quick to take advantage of it. The low growl became a roar as it plunged toward the team and impacted with Maxwell's shoulder.

Tanya spun hastily and opened fire on the mutant as Niki rushed to help Taylor.

"I bet this doesn't help your deathly fear of alligators, huh?" she asked and stretched her arm behind him.

"Now? Really?" he snapped, yanked his pistol clear of its holster around his hip, and turned to see his assailant. In the dark, it looked far bigger than it probably was. Most of the 'gator was already in the water, into which it attempted to drag him. Still, it looked like it could easily be a ten-footer and it twisted and heaved in its effort to break his resistance. He'd seen all the videos of how they killed and ate their prey and he made up his mind he would never be one of those.

Taylor turned as the creature yanked hard but he made no effort to fire as yet. He gritted his teeth and heaved himself away from the water before he opened fire on the massive reptile. The first few shots went wide and struck either the water or the dirt, but the third hit the creature in the head, quickly followed by another one. They were glancing shots but enough to distract the beast from his leg. He could tell he hadn't killed the hulking monster, but at least it had begun to retreat into the swamp.

Niki stepped in and kicked as it turned and slid beneath the surface with a splash.

"Are you all right?" she asked and fixed him with a concerned look.

He scowled. Emptying the magazine at his attacker and only managing a couple of glancing shots at a distance of under five feet was probably not his proudest moment in the world. That said, it had been effective. It wasn't dead but it had given up the fight.

"Yeah," Taylor lied and slapped a new magazine into his weapon. "It only...twisted my leg a little. I'm fine, we need to—oh, shit, Maxwell!"

"Fuck, right!" she shouted and whirled toward their teammates.

The situation on the other side of the fight was deteriorating rapidly. The panther had hold of the man's shoulder and its fangs dug around the pauldrons on the other side while Tanya attempted to try to disengage them. It wasn't long before the massive mutant dragged him down and tipped the suit into the swamp with a massive splash. A flurry of movement from the other side of the water made him shudder. More alligators, he assumed.

Tanya attempted to pull him out but she was attacked from behind too.

"Stop—" Taylor cursed, raised his weapons, and opened fire on the cubs that tried to drag her away. "Shoot them, goddammit!"

The woman nodded and faced them as she raised her assault rifle. The shadows cast by the overhanging trees together with the splashing water made it difficult to see clearly what was going on in that particular area, and she hesitated. Logically, she didn't want to take a shot at Maxwell by mistake.

"Fucking...damn it!" Taylor snapped but her hesitation was well-founded. At least Niki had a better shot and she focused on the cubs while he advanced on the parent's position and remained as low as possible and pushed into the water. He could almost make the panther out where it continued to dig its claws and fangs into Maxwell's suit while it tried to leave the swamp.

Something splashed through the surface and into Taylor's shoulder and almost knocked him off his feet. The slippery surface beneath his feet did little to aid him, but he managed to retain his balance. It required all the effort of the gyros in the suit to maintain it, but he finally lunged forward to drag the beast away from its ongoing struggle with Maxwell.

He managed to find a tenuous hold on the back of the panther's neck, and with a firm yank, jerked it free from his teammate. Tanya and Niki were immediately in position and lurched into the water to pull the agent out. This close, it was possible to see the water leaking into the man's helmet.

The women were already helping him, which made his task only too clear. His hold on the beast slid free and it retreated a few paces, which gave him barely enough time to yank the shotgun from his back. He aimed both his weapons at the massive panther but it simply stared belligerently at him and flashed its teeth as it tried to wade out of the water so it could attack him.

It was an easy decision to not give it the option and he pulled the triggers on both weapons. The semi-automatic shotgun was mostly full and the firepower played to the temptation to turn the beast into chum. He managed to resist, however. The last thing he wanted was to draw the other creatures to an easy meal churning in the water. God only knew what the combination of Zoo panther and alligator would be.

CHAPTER TEN

Taylor didn't like the idea of leaving the bodies for the local predators and scavengers to gnaw on. There was no telling what the goop in their systems would be able to do with a whole swamp area to work with. The risk, he had once heard, was almost negligible, but he had heard many Zoo myths that were contradicted by actual events. This seemed like an err-on-the-side-of-caution situation, and he had no intention to leave the bodies out.

The corpse of the parent was considerably more difficult to recover than the cubs. The blood had mixed with the water already but in the bigger scheme of things, the amount was negligible and it would already be diluted. Its existence wasn't too much of an issue, but he didn't want to deal with the concept of an alligator mixed with the goop. That was not something he would risk.

It was a little challenging to manage the corpses, but they finally had success with some tarp that was a part of the regular suit's gear. Most of the standard items included little extras like that, usually things that were easy to carry and useful for a variety of things if they needed them.

Thankfully, Maxwell's suit hadn't been completely ruined. There was some damage where it had been bitten and clawed, but the fangs hadn't penetrated completely through the armor, and the man himself, fortunately, hadn't been subjected to the venom.

Taylor's suit had damage around the legs from where the alligator had latched on in its attempt to drag him into the water. They would have to spend a fair amount of time repairing it, but it wasn't as bad as it could have been. He was in his secondary suit, which was simply put together, and the agent's could always be replaced by the one they had reserved for his teammate. It would be Jansen's turn to accompany them next anyway unless they agreed to something else.

All told, things could have gone very differently and far more poorly. Even so, they had needed to remove Maxwell's helmet to clear the water out of it and make sure none of the electronics were ruined. Taylor had a feeling a couple of circuits would need replacing but again, it could have been much worse.

Tanya jogged ahead of the group and carried one of the corpses in her tarp. Taylor lugged the larger corpse, while Niki assumed the responsibility to help Maxwell navigate without the HUD to his suit. She also hauled the last of the cubs. Taylor suggested that he help the man, but she brought up the very good point that he would have challenges navigating the swamp with the damage done to his suit. Sure enough, a few steps after they set off, water seeped in through the gaps.

At first, it was merely an unpleasant feeling and a little discomforting. Before long, though, he began to receive warning signs that certain circuits had to shut down to avoid burning out or electrocuting him, which left him with a very distinct limp on the right leg.

"Hey, Taylor." Tanya hailed him on a private channel.

"What's up?" He shifted the weight from the tarp to his off-shoulder, which allowed his free hand to draw the shotgun should any more alligators emerge from the water.

"Not much. I wanted to have a quick word with you in private."

He snorted. "Niki will be able to see you're in a private channel if she pays attention or if she sees us like this, so you might want to get that over with quickly if you don't want to include her."

"Well, yeah, but the problem is that she is the one I want to talk to you about."

This would be more uncomfortable than the water squishing inside his suit, he realized unhappily.

"More specifically," the woman continued, "about you and Niki—you know, together. Everyone knows you guys are crushing hard on each other, and it's painful to watch. As in physically painful. Therefore, you guys need to settle this somehow for the comfort of all the people around you. I don't know how and don't care, but settle it."

Taylor narrowed his eyes at her. "Well, I'm very sorry my personal life is such an inconvenience to you guys."

"Like it or not, you've become a huge part of the lives of the people around you. Ditto Niki. And when you two are uncomfortable, we are too, so you need to find a way to resolve it between yourselves. And given that you guys have made yourselves such a large part of our lives, we do feel a certain responsibility to help you find a solution since you're too close to have a decent perspective."

"My perspective is fine, thanks." He didn't mean to sound as grumpy as he did. "And regarding myself and Niki…well, I have a plan."

"A plan?"

"That's right, a plan."

"What kind of plan is that?"

"A plan to work the whole thing out in a manner that will make it easy for everyone involved."

"So, this plan to work everything out…does it involve finding the guts or balls to ask her out on an actual fucking date?"

"Something like that, yeah."

"And at what stage of the planning for that are you in?"

"Deliberative."

"Oh, okay. So, talking about it. With whom?"

"You, obviously. It was previously in the contemplative stage, so I think we've made considerable progress for one night."

Tanya laughed and looked at the sky that had already begun to change from dark-blue into a lighter blue, with a hint of pink sneaking over the horizon. "Well, moving on from that, I didn't realize we're looking at sunrise in a couple of hours. And that's after a nice long flight before and a long day at work before that. The adrenaline kept me up for the most part, but I think I'll crash in under an hour. Do you think I could find a hotel and get food before I crash for about a week?"

"Maybe not a week, but why don't we take the day off?" he countered. "We can head home the day after. Make sure to keep your receipts since they all go to Niki in our invoice."

"Right."

"Hey," the agent called over the shared comms. "What the hell are you two talking about?"

"You, obviously," Taylor replied quickly. "Do you have people heading in to clean up?"

"Jansen is…well, Vickie told me he told her they've almost finished cleaning the lab, and we'll have people waiting for us at the truck to help with these corpses so we don't have to carry them through the town. Oh, and I'll need everyone to clean their suits before we pack them. I don't want the plane to smell of dead mutants and mossy swamp, and it's easier to clean the suits than a whole fucking aircraft."

"Do you see what I mean?" Taylor asked Tanya, still in the private channel.

"Yeah, yeah, whatever. It simply means I'll have to put my food and sleep off to clean this baby."

"Rest assured, the pay will make it worth it."

"Nothing's worth having to stay up."

"Not even a nice hotel room and a couple of meals for free on top of what you'll be paid?"

"Close, but no cigar. Sorry."

"So, should I hold off on calling you for future missions?"

"Fuck no. You dumbasses would get killed without me."

"How are you feeling?"

Taylor looked up from the platter of food that had been placed in front of him. He still felt like he could sleep for another week or so, but there were places to be and people to see. For one thing, he had a business to get back to. Even if Bobby held the fort at the shop, he didn't want to leave the mechanic to handle all the work on his own. If he ended up doing any more of that, he would have to consider giving the man a hefty raise.

"Hmm?"

Vickie laughed, leaned back in her seat, and stretched luxuriously. "I asked if you're okay. Given that you will drive me to Vegas, I thought I should make sure everything still's working beforehand. You know, for safety reasons."

He looked at his leg. The heat was a perfectly good explanation for why he wore shorts, but the fact that he had an ice pack wrapped around the limb was even more of a reason. Getting his pants over the pack had proved to be a little too challenging in the afternoon, especially since his whole body felt like it had been hit by a train.

"I guess I'm fine. A little sore, but once we reach the interstate, there shouldn't be much trouble. The AI will take care of the driving. I can nap or watch something while you...I don't know. Do as you like, I guess."

"Oh my, aren't we feeling gracious today?"

"We've had a trying couple of days. I feel like both of us have earned the right to not push ourselves too hard for any particular reason. It should take us a couple of days to drive back to Vegas, and since Tanya's going on Niki's plane, there's no one but us chickens to tell each other what we need or want to do."

"And the fact that you're the boss of it all means…"

"Nothing. I may be the boss in name but I reserve the right to be bossed around by my employees."

"Yeah? So, you would let me boss you around?"

"Did you do anything but that all night?"

"That…came out wrong, didn't it?"

"Sure, but you did boss me around."

"Well…yeah, okay."

Taylor took a sip of his coffee. It wasn't the best beverage with the steak, fries, gumbo, chicken, and sausage, as well as a healthy portion of white rice to tie it all together. In his defense, he had started the day off with a light workout in the hotel's gym. While not enough to put his bruised and battered leg under any kind of strain, he had still worked up a decent sweat that earned him the massive "breakfast" around four in the afternoon.

Of course, he was working to build up more of his muscle mass, and that came with an added amount of calorie consumption. Vickie, for her part, looked more than happy to have breakfast foods, which included bacon, toast, easy-over eggs, and OJ. They shared the same pot of coffee, which allowed them to cream or sugar their cups as they pleased.

"I don't know when the last time was that I've pulled an all-nighter." She groaned and stretched gently. "I know I work long nights fairly often, especially when I need to focus on studying and work, but it's been a while since I was up early, worked all day, and continued all night too. It puts a strain on the body. But Taylor, you have to know your physical state was not what I was referencing."

Taylor scowled and tilted his head. "Fucking hell, will

everyone be involved in my personal life now? Is that why you chose to stick with me instead of flying with Niki?"

"Uh...I...okay, yes and no. Well, no, that's not right. I don't want to talk about your personal life but there is the fact that Niki is my cousin and you're my boss, so it kind of makes me feel like it's my business. And I don't like it."

He shook his head and continued to eat, then washed it down with one of the caffeine-infused sodas he'd also ordered. On top of the coffee, it would probably provide enough of the energy he needed to keep an eye on Liz while she did most of the work of driving them to Vegas. They would drop the suits at the airport for Niki to ferry for them, so that was at least one item he could tick off his list.

It wasn't long before they were set up for the trip. There wasn't much luggage for them to carry except for the fact that Vickie didn't enjoy the idea of other people handling her gear. Still, it was quick work to load it on Liz and for them to set off. Starting deep into the afternoon probably wasn't the best way to begin a cross-country trip, but he had no desire to increase the hotel bill, even if he didn't have to pay for it himself.

More importantly, he had no intention of remaining in New Orleans. Even in an air-conditioned room, the heat seemed to weigh heavily on him. He closed Liz's windows and blasted the AC along with enjoyable music while they cruised out of the city as the sun began to slide toward the horizon. It was definitely a more preferable way to spend his evening.

Vickie had elected to settle into the shotgun seat next to him. Liz was large enough that there were no tight spaces involved in the drive. His companion had an odd way of sitting with her legs under her body while she studied her phone and her earphones masked the music he played.

It was only once they were out of the city and on the way to the little airport Niki liked using so much that he turned his music down and gestured for her to remove at least one side of her headphones.

"How are we doing regarding the local law enforcement?" he asked. "The fact that we weren't stopped on the way out of the city was as good a sign as any, I guess, that there's no one looking for us, but—"

Vickie held her finger up to stop him and he waited silently while she checked the details on her phone. "From what I've been able to pick up on the local police band, they're still very confused and have made no progress with the investigation. There's no sign that they've picked up my intrusion in the local cameras, and they haven't even found the van yet. All they have is a few witness statements from the security personnel, who mention a huge guy wearing a black biker outfit and a helmet. A couple of them call you the Stig. I don't know what that is."

"Haven't you looked it up?" Taylor asked.

"I only read it now. Why? Do you know who this Stig is?"

"Yeah, it's a character on a TV show in the 2000s and 2010s about cars."

"Like…with car characters?"

"No, it was only three guys talking about cars."

"And the Stig was one of these guys?"

"No, the Stig famously never talked. He always wore a

driver's outfit and a helmet and drove all the cars—like a stunt driver."

"So, the guys who talked about cars never drove them?"

"They did, but it was mostly to try them. When they wanted the cars tested under extreme circumstances—like taking lap times and driving at maximum speed—they brought in the silent professional. There were a couple of running gag jokes between them. Anyway, the joke was always that the Stig was never able to talk and all he could do was drive cars extremely fast. And he had a group of family members wherever the show ended up driving to."

She shook her head. "It sounds weird. And this was a popular show?"

"I assume so. It ran for a while—over twenty years, now that I think about it. Mostly with the same cast of three guys."

"Huh. And you liked it?"

"The three guys had damn good chemistry, which made it much better than the sum of its parts. It's fun but probably not for everyone."

Vickie nodded slowly. "Well, you built this truck and named her, so I guess it makes sense that you would enjoy it."

"And how were you able to get all the info from the police? I didn't think you could do much hacking from your phone."

"It wasn't only me. Since I was busy tracking you guys and the creatures, Desk stepped in and helped with everything else."

"And your cousin was okay with Desk helping you like

that? I thought she worked for Niki. She probably wouldn't want her to assist us with our less than legal enterprises."

The hacker narrowed her eyes at him for a few seconds. "I guess she merely knows Niki needs her to help us even when we're not technically busy on one of her missions. At the end of the day, the operation was a success."

Taylor smiled. "So, why did you decide to come with me instead of taking the plane?"

"I..." She paused and finally shrugged in an offhand way. "Honestly, I'm a little scared of Niki. And she would grill me on the plane. If she continued for long enough, I would probably admit to anything, up to and including shooting Kennedy. I was the shooter on the grassy knoll."

He laughed. "Yeah, I get that."

"And she has someone in her sights now." She leaned closer and patted him gently on the chest. "So...good luck with that."

"Oh, God, I'm thoroughly fucked," he conceded and shook his head. "I guess it remains to be seen how well that will work out for me."

She groaned softly. "I did not need that mental image, thanks."

CHAPTER ELEVEN

"Hey, Taylor!"

He looked up from the truck. They had a long drive to look forward to and Vickie took a moment to have a quick chat with Tanya before they left.

While he wouldn't say hearing Niki shout his name from across the hangar was the last thing he wanted to hear, it came damn close. He liked being around her, but it took a fair amount of energy, especially as she sounded like she was well-rested—or as close to it as she could be.

"And now this is happening," he muttered under his breath.

"What was that?" she asked as she reached him.

"Nothing. How is the weather for your flight to Vegas?"

"Not too bad. I had a look at the kind of invoice I can expect from you. Jansen writes these kinds of things up and if you want, you could check it and see if you like it."

He nodded and glanced at the paperwork before he took it from her hand. "Uh…sure, I'll have a look. I do trust

Jansen's work but if it'll make you feel better, I'll give it a once-over. Was that all you wanted to talk about?"

"Well, a hotel stay for the night for three members of your team would have been a hard sell for the FBI, but Speare said he wouldn't pay attention to the bills I sent him as long as the results were in the bag. And so far, they have been, so if you keep up the good work, I'll keep up your expenses. Or the taxpayer's dollars will keep up your expenses."

Taylor laughed. "Speaking of which, do you like French food?"

"Okay, wow…that's expensive. It would be difficult for me to justify that on a budget, even my new one."

"No, I mean…do you like it? French food?"

She shrugged. "Like I said, it's expensive. It's not always my kind of fare, but I guess I could say I don't dislike it. As long as there's nothing like…snails or slugs involved. A good chef can probably make almost anything taste good, I suppose, but even the thought is enough to put me off. Why…why do you ask?"

It seemed she might have begun to grasp what it was about. He could only hope that was the case. "Well, yeah, it's the most expensive restaurant in Vegas. And the second most expensive in the country—not that I thought it was a competition or not the kind of competition most restaurants want to win, at least. And it's not my usual scene either, but I've come to realize that some things I think aren't my scene might have their benefits if I were to give them a chance."

Niki smiled. "It sounds like you did your research. You must want something."

"Yes, and at the same time, a very resounding no. I only want a woman to know I want a chance if there is one. It's a small price to pay as an entry ticket to a different future. She is special, at least to me."

She quirked an eyebrow. "Special like you would deal with her armor personally special?"

His cheeks heated suddenly and he scratched his chin idly. "Son of a...Bungees?"

"Nope."

"Vickie?"

"Also no. Answer the fucking question."

Taylor scowled. He was too tired to play these kinds of games but it was probably too late at this point to back out. "Yeah. For this woman, I would go through every rivet of that suit twice simply to make sure she'll go into wherever with the best possible protection money can buy. Because she's worth it."

Niki groaned. "Oh, fucking hell—that last was as cheesy as fuck. Not that I mind. But you do know I've been called psychotic in the past, right? In situations where that might even have been warranted?"

"Sure. It takes one psychotic to know another, right?"

"Coming from you, that's practically romantic."

A silly grin slid across his face. "I try. I've been called determined in the past, you know, as well as psychotic."

"I hear the two are very similar once you peel away the veneer society wants to put on us. But I look forward to trying the French place."

"You should know I'll probably not wear flannel when the time comes. Mostly because places like that have a dress code, but also because...you know."

She wore the same kind of silly grin as she gave his arm a gentle squeeze. "Yeah, I do. Anyway, I have to go. Jansen probably already has the plane waiting to go. I got him to hold off until you guys were ready to travel too. Send me the invoice when you're finished, okay?"

He nodded, having almost forgotten about the piece of paper in his hands. "Will do. It'll probably come the day after we get back, though. I'm reasonably sure I'll hit the hay for the night when we arrive."

"It sounds good." She smiled and waved as she walked to where her SUV was parked outside the hangar.

Vickie and Tanya offered each other similar farewells as the plane's engines turned on and started the dull whine that hurt his ears. The hacker wasn't an idiot, though, and he had a feeling she had probably picked up on the arm-touching by Niki. His suspicion was confirmed by the way she smirked as she walked toward him.

"About time, you psychos," she said as she scrambled into the truck.

"Shut up," he retorted as he slid behind the wheel.

The state of the warehouse wasn't quite as he'd pictured it. The crime scene photos had been covered in blood. The reports had been of a madman dressed like a fetishist biker who dealt all the damage, and while it had been considerable, none of the wounds inflicted had been lethal. That wasn't the kind of thing you expected from a madman. Not only that, but most of the guys who were put in the hospital were also all "reformed" criminals with the kind of files on them that strongly suggested they worked as muscle for an organized crime element. All that combined seemed to indicate that whatever had happened there was not merely a spontaneous eruption of violence.

That kind of shit did occur, but Officer Benson had been to those types of crime scenes. The mess there was much harder to clean and inevitably finished with the people responsible being caught since they usually slept it off in a nearby dumpster. He didn't want to say it, mostly since the term was frowned upon by most of his bosses, but this looked like the work of a professional.

But, his opinions notwithstanding, he wasn't a detective. He was a recent arrival to the local force, and the fact that he was on the fast track to sergeant meant he wouldn't make any assumptions on such a high-profile case. He would be especially careful if they might derail his promotion.

Benson wasn't the only one in the area. A handful of officers remained to keep the location sealed as a crime scene, and one of the detectives in charge had chosen to visit the scene again. The fact that these guys weren't seated at their desks and looking at the pictures meant that despite it all, they effectively faced the sour sight of a dead end in their investigation. While that was common in many criminal investigations, he assumed the bitter taste never became any easier to swallow over time.

"Benson, right?" the detective asked as he approached. "You were one of the first on the scene here, weren't you?"

The officer nodded. "I sure was. It had been a quiet night until the calls came in and I heard the shooting. I feel like I've been fucked over for that since I've been assigned to keep an eye on the area, but it's been much quieter since then. I guess all the criminals have realized the cops have set up camp and headed out. Not that I blame them."

The other man chuckled and took a pack of cigarettes from his pocket. He offered one to Benson, who declined, then tapped one out and lit it for himself.

"You know," the detective stated after a few seconds of silence. "I've seen shit like this before. People arrive and blow the absolute crap out of each other and vanish without a trace. It wasn't even that long ago. It may look like something straight out of a Scorsese flick, but when you really, really pay attention, the details don't add up. All the cameras were conveniently down and some kind of malfunction made us lose the data. The brass are happy to write it off as yet another episode of gangland violence, but everything my gut has to say tells me it's something else. It's far more professional than merely gang-bangers having it out over the going price of heroin or some shit."

Officer Benson studied the man closely for a few seconds and tried to decide whether he was serious or not. He certainly didn't look like he was joking. His expression looked both irritated and intrigued as he breathed out a lungful of nicotine and poison and stared into the warehouse.

The crime scene cleaners had already been through it to remove all the blood, bone, and mess that had been left behind.

"What did the witness statements say?" the detective asked and frowned as he tossed the cigarette butt into a nearby trash can.

He scowled as he tried to remember. "The witness

statements from one of the so-called reformed criminals we pulled out of here after everything? They said they and their comrades had been called in when an alarm in the warehouse was tripped. They've been authorized to protect this property with all the firepower they have, so they went in fully armed and ready to shoot. Someone attacked them first."

"Hence the mess inside."

"Right. But the guy in there didn't even attempt any kill shots."

"I thought he caught a couple of them in the chest with a shotgun."

"Well, yeah, but they wore body armor. Those who came in first were hit in the legs, away from the arteries. I guess he knew they wore body armor and he wanted to put them down quickly without killing them. Either that or he was lucky. I don't know much about this kind of thing. But the guys who held the fort outside had a better look at him. Those inside only saw darkness and then something big, but the others who did get a good view said he wore a motorcycle helmet of some kind, was decked out in leather, and that he was huge. Like...linebacker huge."

The detective grunted and reached instinctively for the pack in his pocket before he stopped himself. It was typical behavior for someone limiting his intake of the little cancer cylinders. "He didn't try to shoot them?"

"According to them, they tried to get out of the car and he slammed the door and aimed the shotgun at them while they were inside before he simply walked away. They decided not to pursue him and I can't say I blame them.

But wait a second—you said you'd seen this kind of shit before, right? In New Orleans?"

"Not specifically, but it feels similar. There was something else they noticed at this crime scene—USB devices plugged into the computers. They were erased before the tech guys could see much about who was involved or what had happened, but it's clear that engaging the security team was not intentional. Whoever it was probably didn't mean to. Either way, it was high-tech."

"Something military, do you think?"

"I have no idea." The detective shrugged. "All I know is that our tech team was impressed and stumped at the same time. That's not common with your standard B and E, you know? One of the tech guys talked about military-grade software."

Benson did know but he didn't want to talk about it. "So what do you think the brass will do about it?"

"Honestly, they'll do what they did last time. Call it gang violence, pin it on a high roller with *La Cosa Nostra* or the *Bratva,* and pass it on to the FBI. They didn't get to where they were by putting the hours in. Too much time is spent kissing asses at City Hall."

"Hey, Bobby?"

Elisa was the only one at the shop, but the mechanic sometimes forgot she was there. She still took calls and had the kind of voice that carried, but after enough hours during which the two of them simply did their own thing together and yet apart, it was almost like he worked on the suits on his own.

He didn't mind help, of course. Spending time with Tanya was always a treat, and Taylor was one of those guys who was a decent student of the human condition and knew how to work in silence in decent chemistry. Even when Vickie was around and wanted something to do, it was nice to have a younger mind present that he could teach while working.

Even so, being productive on his own did have its benefits. It was something he enjoyed.

"What's up?" he asked finally but didn't look up from the suit he was hunched over.

"Taylor and Vickie aren't supposed to arrive until tomorrow, right?" the reporter asked. "And you'll pick Tanya up at the airport later this afternoon?"

The mechanic finally pulled away from the suit and his eyes narrowed. "Yeah. What's the matter?"

"It's…well, it looks like the security feed has picked up a car as it circled into the camera range—a limo. Did we order a limo?"

Bobby stood, walked to where she was seated, and leaned closer to the computer screen. He frowned as the vehicle came to a halt outside the shop door. Once it had stopped, two men stepped out and looked around for a way in. He had come to recognize the signs—the flashy clothes and the veritable dragon's hoard worn around their necks and on their fingers, a watch so big that they needed to pull their sleeves back a little so that it could fit, and ridiculous spray tans despite the fact that there was sun in Vegas every day of every year.

These men were criminals. The higher-end kind, admittedly, but not those at the top of the food chain. No, they worked for those who were at the top of the food chain. They might have clawed into positions close to the top of the ladder but they still weren't quite made men yet.

"I'm not sure what these fuckers are here for," he muttered. "But it would probably be best if they don't see you."

"I won't leave you here alone."

"I didn't intend to suggest that. In fact, I planned to suggest something you're quite familiar with. Climb into one of the suits and wait there to see if I need backup. That way...well, it's the kind of backup that sends a powerful message."

Elisa nodded and scurried to climb into one of the suits they had suspended from a harness. They were made to be accessed easily like that, and it wasn't long before she was hidden inside.

The men outside had grown impatient and one of them began to pound on the doors of the shop. Bobby scowled and wondered if they would simply leave if he left them shut. He doubted it, though. The mafia was nothing if not persistent to the point of idiocy. With a sigh, he pressed the button to open the doors.

They hadn't even rolled up all the way before both ducked under the barrier and used the small space available to enter. They were armed, that much was clear, but the fact that they didn't come in with their guns drawn despite looking annoyed and ready to start a fight was a good sign.

"Can I help you, gentlemen?" he asked and folded his

arms in front of his chest.

The men oozed sleaze and he didn't want them to wander freely. He was convinced they would try to steal something on their way out.

"We're here looking for an individual by the name of Taylor McFadden. Our boss would like to have a chat with him. You should know Mr. Marino by now, right?"

Bobby nodded. "I do. Unfortunately, McFadden isn't here at the moment. If you like, you can leave a message with me and he'll get back to you as soon as possible."

"You wouldn't happen to know where he is, would you? This is a matter with something of a time component to it."

The mechanic shook his head. "I have no idea. But once he gets back, I'll let your boss know."

The second man—the larger of the two and obviously brought in as the muscle—stepped forward. "Look, we won't leave this piece of shit strip mall without the guy, so you tell him to come out of whatever piece of shit closet he's hiding in and we can be on our way."

The man walked forward like he thought he was intimidating, but Bobby didn't back down and simply smirked instead. "Look, you can go see your boss with a fat lip and maybe a couple of teeth missing, or you can leave the way you are now. I honestly don't care which."

The two seemed to suddenly remember that they were there on a peace mission. They were used to intimidating almost anyone they ran into, but once they were up against someone who didn't buy into their bullshit, they needed a second to rethink their approach.

The first man to speak placed his hand on the bouncer's shoulder and pulled him back. "Look, we don't know why you need to act all aggro like that but since you're not in the mood, why don't you tell McFadden to contact Mr. Marino at his earliest convenience. Make sure to tell your boss there's a profitable proposition waiting for him, all right?"

Bobby nodded. "I'll be sure to pass the message on. Now get back into your little limo and fuck off."

Neither of them looked happy about the unequivocal invitation to leave, but he didn't want them in his shop any longer than was necessary. Once they were out and their limo was driving away, he motioned that it was all clear for Elisa to climb out again.

The woman looked a little pale when she clambered free of the suit.

"A little PTSD from being back in one of those?" he asked and pressed the button to close the doors.

She paused for a few seconds and finally shrugged. "I guess I was too in the moment. I wasn't about to let you face two of those bozos on your own. As big as you are, I'm sure even you would have had a little trouble with them. Plus, I'm sure they had guns too so...something to think about."

Bobby couldn't help a deep chuckle. "How is it that Taylor finds the people with the most piss and vinegar to surround himself with?"

"Why do you care? Aren't you in a relationship with one of those people?"

"Sure, and Tanya will be the first to tell you she's a little off the deep end herself. Hell, I had hoped that you would be a sensible one—the kind who would be something of an anchor for this place so I didn't have to be all the fucking time. But no, oh no, it's all back in my lap."

Elisa narrowed her eyes at him. "You thought I would have done that?"

"Yes. Yes, I did think."

CHAPTER TWELVE

Detective Pembroke was back in the daily drag of his routine and tried to stop himself from being numbed by the sheer amount of bad shit that happened to people.

The conversation with Officer Benson hadn't revealed more than what he already knew about the incident. He had hoped for a little more. The first man on the scene sometimes noticed shit that was gone by the time the techs got there. But the man wasn't imaginative and he wasn't great at the observational aspects of the job either. He was a decent enough officer and would probably rise steadily in the ranks over the years. Maybe he would even reach Captain before he retired if he made friends with the right people. Commissioners liked having their yes-men in the captain positions.

Thankfully, though, it didn't seem like he knew what he was there for. Not many people wanted to deal with the organized crime operations in their divisions since they tended to work closely with Internal Affairs. There was a reason why most of their detectives and officers weren't officially listed in most of the reports.

He knew there would be little chance for him to rise in the ranks and in all honesty, he hadn't joined the police to be a lifer in the force. Not that he did it for the fuzzy feelings or the thought of making the community he'd grown up in a better place, although that did help. The chances were, he would retire in eight years with half his salary, but it wouldn't end there. He was already talking to people in the private sector who were willing to pay through the nose for younger retired police officers, especially those with experience on the front lines, as it were.

All they wanted from someone like him was a solid career with a couple of big busts to bring up during the job interview and a history of delivering the goods without any citations for bad behavior or anything like that. He had mostly managed to keep himself out of trouble. A couple of retirement options were also involved if the private security option didn't pan out.

But while he was with the police force, he intended to do as good a job as he could. That determination was the source of his current frustration. Two cases had come across his desk and both would stick with him the longest. This one showed every sign that it might be the third in that list.

He rubbed his eyes and resisted the urge to bang his head on his desk. The techs continued to sift through the evidence and tried to find something they could use to link it to anyone before the commissioner called it a gang-on-gang case and passed it to the FBI like he had with the other two cases. He didn't feel hopeful, though, and reading through the witness statements of the survivors didn't help him. The men had been scared out of their wits and as talkative as hell—which was unusual with career criminal types—but they proved as useless as Officer Benson had.

His attention was dragged away from his computer screen when a shapely ass in a grey pantsuit dropped onto the side of his desk. His gaze moved to the woman it belonged to and knew before he reached the cold, steel-gray eyes that it was one of his fellow Organized Crime detectives by the name of Sasha Underwood.

"Detective Underwood?" he asked and leaned back in his seat. She had a gloating look about her that told him she had good news, which probably meant he now owed her a favor or maybe a couple of beers once they were done for the day. Either was possible depending on her mood.

"Nice to see you again, Detective Pembroke."

"Is there anything I can help you with?"

"No, but I think I can help you with the hunch you came to me with yesterday. I did a little checking with my CIs, and as it turns out, your hunch that this might be military could have legs to it. It turns out one of the people on my roster has their ears on the smaller local airports—you know, the kind the rich and the powerful use to park their jets. It's important, though, as one of those airports has a whole section shut down because—get this—the DOD commissioned one of their hangars and needed operational security. I don't know what it's about but it smells of black ops to me."

She placed a file on his desk, which included a couple of

pictures taken with a phone's camera. It was too blurry to see more than the figures who vaguely looked like three women and three men, all surrounding a smaller private jet. In the background, a forklift was used to ferry heavy crates from a truck to the plane.

"What's in those crates?"

Underwood snapped her fingers. "You know, I had the identical question. I looked and asked around. It turns out those crates aren't exactly the standard equipment for transporting anything you'd see in shipping containers. A guy I know in the military recognized them immediately as the crates they use to transport the suits of power armor they use in the Zoo."

"I…huh."

She nodded. "Right? I thought it was interesting because there aren't too many DOD operations active in the US that have the authority to use weaponry like that. And since some of the witness statements mentioned a huge guy with a helmet, I thought it might have something to do with that."

Pembroke shook his head. "I've seen one of those suits in action and I don't think there's any way for anyone to mistake one of them for a biker with a leather fetish."

"Still, it's worth looking into. If the DOD's involved, we might have alien shit on our hands. There have been reports of that lately."

He scowled. "I think I'd prefer that it was only the DOD doing clean-up. I'm still waiting on the techs to tell me what that warehouse was used for. If there's something to do with the military in there, we could get the commish to stop it from being sent to the FBI."

"You don't want to fuck with these black ops assholes, Pem. Take my word for it."

"Yeah, you're probably right," he conceded. "I owe you one."

"You owe me two." She held two fingers up. "Two rounds tonight. You'll go, right? It's Travis' retirement party."

"Yeah, yeah, I'll be there."

Niki knew who would be waiting for them the moment they touched down in the little airstrip outside Vegas.

Taylor wouldn't have arrived yet since he would take his time with a cross-country drive home. But Bobby would be there, of course, waiting outside his truck with his massive arms folded across his chest.

If he was about five inches shorter and lacked about a hundred pounds of muscle mass, he would have been the spitting image of Jet Li with his hair cut short like that. She had no idea why that association came to mind, but it felt like the two could have been brothers. Or, more likely, Bungees was the guy's long-lost son or something.

Tanya was the first off the plane and jogged to the man, and they embraced quickly. He checked her for any injuries and she waved him off and insisted she was fine. The operators at the airstrip had already opened the lower compartments to get the suit crates out.

She decided to give Tanya and Bobby a moment together in the fading Vegas sunlight before she exited, approached the man, and proffered her hand.

"Another successful mission?" he asked and shook energetically. "With no injuries, by the looks of it."

"Taylor was roughed up a little by an alligator," she commented. "A regular one, not anything to do with our mission. Oh, and there are a couple of holes in the suit Maxwell was riding, so there are repairs to be made. Still, everyone got clear mostly safe and sound. No one's dead, and no one needs any extensive medical treatment. Taylor limped around with an ice pack on his leg, but he was probably milking it to add a little to the invoice later."

The mechanic barked a laugh before he could stop himself and pretended to clear his throat. "I wouldn't put that past him. But he's not the kind of guy to fake injuries either."

Niki shrugged. "I guess not, but still. With the suits that were damaged, how soon until you think we would be back at full capacity?"

He narrowed his eyes. "I'll need to take a look at them before I make any kind of sweeping declaration, but given that Taylor was out with his smaller, secondary suit and we already have one for either Jansen or Maxwell to use, you should have enough for myself, Tanya, Taylor, you, and one of your boys to head in if we have any immediate trouble. It should take us a couple of weeks to get everything up and running again. Maybe a month, depending on what the workload looks like."

The agent made a face but nodded. "I don't know. We've never really needed it, but after that shit-show in Wyoming, I've always wanted to have a full team ready if there was ever an emergency. But that's on me. I have issues. Still, if you guys need a little extra incentive to have the suits ready with priority speed..." She shrugged.

Bobby nodded his understanding. "I'll talk to Taylor and we can see what our schedule looks like. He can talk to you about it later. I'm only the mechanic."

"Bullshit. Everyone and my mom know that titles aside, you and Taylor are equal partners in this whole business. Hell, I'd be willing to bet Vickie is an equal member by now too."

"I'm not so sure about that." He scowled and watched the forklift carry the last of the crates to be loaded on his truck. "Taylor knows how to run a team. That comes with a fair amount of delegating and letting other people make calls you might be a little too ignorant to make. But that doesn't mean he's any less in charge and it doesn't mean I'll make any calls about his business for him while he's away."

Niki raised her hands quickly. "That's fair enough. I didn't mean it like that anyway. I'm sorry."

He shook his head. "No apology necessary. You know how to run a team yourself, as well as delegate when you need to."

She couldn't help a small smile. "I appreciate that."

Tanya moved closer and draped an arm across his shoulder. "Are you two playing nice? Do I need to put anyone on time-out?"

"Bobby was educating me on how Taylor runs his business," the agent replied.

"Not that it was needed," Bungees said. "Anyway, do you know when he will be back? I have a message from Marino for him that I'd rather not keep on my chest for too long."

Niki shook her head. "He's driving, so I assume you

won't see him until tomorrow afternoon. Is there any trouble? Anything you need me to look at?"

He shook his head. "Not really. The guys who delivered the message said it was a business proposition."

"I'm still not sure how Taylor got in business with the sleazy fuck in the first place," Tanya declared and looked like she'd bitten into a lemon. "I don't like it."

"I'm sure he doesn't either," Bobby countered. "And I don't think Taylor would call it being in business with the guy. It's more a tenuous truce between our two parties that he fully expects to break any day."

The agent nodded. "Let me know when it does. Okay, you guys are loaded. I won't keep you."

Bobby shook her hand again. "Nice seeing you again, Niki."

Tanya wrapped her in a hug. "Don't be a stranger."

CHAPTER THIRTEEN

There honestly seemed to be no end to the tedium. Taylor had done a couple of drives across the country before. He liked driving, and hitting the open road was one of the few treats left in the world. It had almost no downsides—sitting and bobbing his head to good music as the miles sped by. It was hard to find a bad thing to say about it.

But damn if the open expanses of Texas hadn't begun to tell on him. He had been through the state before and he wasn't sure why it bothered him like this now when he didn't remember it doing so before.

Vickie didn't look perturbed, of course. Liz was a big truck and gave her enough space, and the new-fangled setup even provided a decent Wi-Fi connection. He assumed that was something of a requirement for her. As long as she had a decent enough Internet connection, she would be happy.

He opened his mouth to say something as the song began to wind down, but she cut him off quickly.

"France and most of Switzerland," she stated without looking up from her laptop.

"I...what?"

"You could fit France and most of Switzerland into the landmass that is the Lone Star State," she explained, her gaze fixed on the screen in front of her. "I looked it up three hours ago. I assume you're as bored as I am given that we've been driving through the same state for what feels like years and you might want to put an actual, comparable number to it like I did."

Taylor nodded with a hint of pride. "I sure am. That's good."

"Thanks...and not only for the compliment."

He took his gaze off the road for a second to scowl at her. "What else for?"

She shrugged and looked a little uncomfortable, but her eyebrows were drawn low over her eyes, which told him she was committed to whatever she planned to talk about. "You know...everything. All the fucking reasons."

"I hate to say it but you'll have to be a little more specific than that."

The hacker sighed and rolled her eyes. "Fine. For starters, for not being a shitty boss. And for letting me do things the way I think they should be done, even if you have your reservations. Let me see, what else? Oh, taking me in when even my own family had a hard time with it. Giving me a job and a place to stay, even if it was at a shitty strip mall under construction. Working with me, trying to keep up with me, dealing with me when I'm not the easiest person to deal with, delegating, and trusting me. I can keep going if you want. I'm all about listing shit."

Taylor laughed. "Was there a point in there somewhere? Or is this merely a cleverly disguised way to get me to listen to you? Because I won't lie, complimenting me on my leadership skills is one hell of a way to do it. Kudos."

Vickie didn't look amused and ran her fingers through her cropped hair. "No. It's only… I guess it's my way of saying I appreciate everything you've done for me. I know Niki handed me over to you and no one could have blamed you for half-assing a job that shouldn't have been yours in the first place. While no one would have tapped you as being a good dad, you have been fantastic. You were the person I needed to step up in the world. If I get mad at you, know it could be me being scared and angry—lashing out, okay?"

He immediately regretted his attempt at levity. She had shared something important to her, and voicing it made her look a little vulnerable. Her discomfort seemed to manifest physically, although he wondered if that was only him projecting his unease. He wasn't used to having conversations with deeper emotional relevance, much less talking about him being some kind of father figure.

The seconds ticked past and another song came on and finally, he took a deep breath and lowered the volume before he responded. "Honestly, I don't think having a daughter—or any kids, for that matter—has ever been a part of my overall life plan. Which isn't to say it wasn't a possibility that ever occurred to me. You should know, though, that I couldn't be prouder of who you decided to be and what you can do. You're a level-one kickass, and it's been an absolute pleasure to work with you over these past… Hell, it's going on a year now, isn't it? Anyway, I don't mean I want to take your dad's place or anything—"

"No, truly, you can."

Taylor shrugged. "Be that as it may, it's not like I'd be offended if I'm not your second choice to walk you down the aisle at any possible or eventual wedding that might occur. I might be a little offended if I weren't the third choice, but only a little."

She didn't answer immediately, and after a few seconds passed, he turned to see that she was looking away from him. Even so, he could see her face reflected in the window, wet with tears that trickled down her cheeks.

"Hey," he muttered. "Come on over here."

Vickie didn't move but also didn't pull away as he dragged her to his side of the truck, slid his arm around her, and squeezed gently. She turned her head and pressed her face into his shoulder for what felt like a couple of hours but was only a few minutes. It was difficult to tell with the scenery unchanging from the dry shrubs and grasslands.

Finally, she raised her head, took a deep breath, and wiped her eyes with her shirt sleeve until he retrieved a tissue box from the glove compartment.

"Thanks," she whispered in a hoarse voice and wiped her cheeks carefully but didn't move away from where nestled against him. "Why the fuck couldn't you have been my real dad, huh, Taylor?"

"First of all, I think you're too old. I would have been fourteen when you were born if I have my math right."

"Fifteen," she corrected quickly.

"Right," he replied. "Secondly, it took me eighty-three

missions into the Zoo to earn the right to be in your life, so there's that."

"That's….some profound shit, Tay-Tay."

He nodded. "It doesn't make it any less true, Vay-Vay."

A moment passed as both exchanged a glance and she shook her head. "No, no Vay-Vay."

"You know, it felt wrong when I said it. Simply not right."

"I'll give you points for trying."

"Thanks, I'll take the points and maybe cash them in when I need your help with something."

Vickie took a deep breath and moved to her corner of the truck. "Did I overdo it with the mushy?"

Taylor held a hand up with his thumb and forefinger less than an inch apart. "A smidgeon. Maybe we should change the topic of discussion. Do you think you need any new computer bits or pieces? I thought I could probably justify any new expenses on that side for tax benefits since they would be for business, after all."

She grinned suddenly. "You know, I hoped you would ask me that sometime. I've been meaning to go on a shopping spree. Mind you, most of the shit I'm interested in won't be at your average Best Buy or anything like that. On the plus side, it probably means it'll be much less expensive than it would be on a production line. Do you want me to write you a list?"

"Why don't you do market research to find what you need and get me the details and the pricing." His attention was now fixed on the road again. At least they were still able to talk to each other normally. He had worried that the real conversation would somehow change something but it seemed things were back to normal.

Taylor's leg still throbbed a little when they pulled into the shop. It had been a long trip, and while most of it had been with the AI inside Liz doing the driving, he still needed to put effort into it once they reached the city limits.

It wasn't hard work and certainly not something he would have noticed if his leg had been fine. The bruising was closer to black now, and it ticked painfully whenever he didn't have the ice pack on it.

Besides, even with the car doing most of the driving on its own, he couldn't leave it entirely to its own devices. It had meant that sleep was mostly relegated to dozing so Liz would wake him whenever she beeped to tell him she needed something. Usually, this involved routine issues like checking the tire pressure or filling up with gas. Vickie had been able to settle into the cot in the back and catch her metaphorical Z's, but he felt he needed a nice long night of sleep once he saw the doors to the shop open.

Bobby and Tanya were still there and so was Elisa, although all three looked like they were packing up for the day.

He stopped Liz in her assigned parking space and climbed out slowly. Bobby already waited for him with a bear hug. He'd almost reached the point where he felt he was running out of oxygen and saw a couple of white spots in his vision when the mechanic released him.

"Shit, I missed you too, man." Taylor grunted and took a deep breath.

"Niki told me a 'gator did a number on your leg," the other man grumbled and studied the visible bruising. "I saw the damage to the suit. Are you sure that the critter wasn't a cryptid or something?"

"I don't think so, but I killed the fucker anyway." It wasn't true, of course, as he and Niki had simply given it a good reason to retreat. Still, it sounded good so he let it be.

"Well, the way I see it, you're lucky to still have that leg. From the damage on the suit, I thought it had at least broken something while it hung on and did its thing. You need to be more careful out there."

"Your concern for me is touching, as always."

"For you? Please. You head out in my suits and I expect you to at least take good care of them."

Taylor grinned. He recalled the man talking like that when they were in the Zoo. It was his way to show he cared without showing it too much.

Tanya and Vickie were already hugging, followed quickly by Elisa, who looked like she was about to head out.

"Don't let me keep you guys," he told the team and looked around. "It's been a long drive, so all I'll do is order something to eat that I didn't buy at a gas station and get some sleep. Maybe we can take a look at the suits tomorrow and work out that invoice for Niki?"

Bobby nodded. "There is something else you might want to think about first, though. Some of Marino's cronies visited the shop yesterday."

"Shit." He grunted with displeasure and narrowed his eyes. "Is everything okay? What happened?"

"Everything's aces. The two who came here looked like they wanted to play some kind of alpha-male bullshit, but they were sent by Marino himself. He wants to have a word with you and said it had to do with a business proposition. Now, telling him to shove the offer where the sun don't shine is probably the right call, but it seems like the kind of message to send back in person if you know what I mean."

Taylor nodded. "Okay, I'll get in touch with him. You guys head off for the night. Thanks for holding the fort while I was gone, Bungees."

The mechanic grinned and took his extended hand. "That's what I'm here for, boss. I'll see you all tomorrow."

Vickie retreated quickly to her car, which she had left parked at the shop when she and Taylor headed to New Orleans. Elisa had her vehicle and she waved to the rest of the team. She hadn't spent very long at the strip mall and had soon found a small apartment nearby that wasn't the best but was still better than what Taylor had to offer.

Tanya and Bobby both left in his truck. Taylor couldn't help a small smile as they all headed off to their own homes. Vickie probably needed a solid night's sleep as much as he did, and so did the rest of them, even those who had worked in the shop while he had been away helping Niki.

And making sure they didn't have any trouble with future shipments. It hadn't been a guarantee, but with the data Vickie pulled from their servers, things were looking up.

For a long moment, he wished he could simply order something—pizza probably—have a bite to eat, and collapse on his cot, but the world was a cruel place. Unfortunately, it meant he had business to attend to first.

He pulled his phone out, pressed the quick dial on a number that he had already saved, and held it to his ear.

"Rod Marino's office, how may I—"

Taylor cut the secretary off. "I'm sorry, I need to have a word with your boss right now. Tell him it's Taylor McFadden returning his message."

The woman paused, likely a little insulted by his rudeness, but he was too tired to abide by any societal rules of politeness at this point.

"Of course, Mr. McFadden. I'll transfer you immediately," she said quickly and her voice was replaced by the telltale clicks that accompanied the process.

"Taylor!" Marino called once the line connected. "Long time no see, my friend."

"I'm not your friend and can you tell me why your boys came to my place of business and tried to bully my mechanic?"

"I'm very sorry about that. They only had instructions to find you but became a little too aggressive about it. I have no idea why. If you want something done right, you do it yourself, right? Anyway, I wanted to have a word with you about helping me with a small problem I have, and I'll more than make it worth your while. What do you say to having breakfast with me tomorrow morning? Shall we say eleven?"

More than anything, he wanted to tell the man to shove it, but he was suddenly out of energy. He could say it to him in person the next morning and make him pay for a decent breakfast to make up for the trouble he had put Bobby through.

"Where should I meet you?"

"There's a nice little restaurant at my casino. Show up and I'll have people there to meet you. I'll see you tomorrow."

The line cut and he took a deep breath and shook his head. He would deal with all this tomorrow. The past few days had been too long and intense for him to give any shits about it now.

He opened a food-ordering app and selected a pizza and a soda from a venue that would deliver in under an hour. It was essentially all he was capable of at that point. He dropped into one of the office chairs and pulled up something for him to watch while he waited.

Tomorrow was a whole other day and he would worry about everything then.

CHAPTER FOURTEEN

The fact that Marino had his breakfast at eleven in the morning was probably something Taylor would have been annoyed by under any other circumstances. Of course, a casino owner's responsibilities might mean the man worked all hours of the night while the business operated. It was a logical assumption.

Still, he doubted that the man did much work outside business hours. He merely didn't seem the type.

After a solid night of sleep without any unexpected interruptions, he resumed his habit of time in the gym before he took a shower almost before he remembered he had a breakfast meeting. It soured his buoyant mood somewhat and he spent most of his workout and the time he took to prepare wondering if it was too late to cancel.

Finally, he ordered an Uber Black on his phone and shrugged into a blazer to make himself look a little more presentable after combing his bright red hair and beard. The temptation to simply call the man and tell him to drop dead became more appealing by the moment.

It even lingered persistently as he climbed into the SUV that arrived to pick him up. At that point, he accepted, the jig was up. There was no point in pretending he could deal with this in a way that wasn't in person.

It left a sour taste in his mouth but it wasn't long before he steeled himself against his inner protests. He merely needed to get it all done quickly—order breakfast, hear the man's proposal, turn him down, and return to the shop for a decent day of work. The thought of work reminded him that he also needed to finalize the invoice for Niki. The woman probably wouldn't be happy that she'd been made to wait as long as she already had.

The SUV pulled up to the casino entrance, where he stepped out, straightened his blazer, and made sure to leave a generous tip for the driver since the man hadn't said a word for the duration of the ride.

Sure enough, as Marino had stated, someone was already waiting for him. The brief thought that the mob boss would leave the job to someone who didn't know him dissipated quickly when he realized how impossible it was. His size, his hair, and his beard made him a fairly easy person to identify.

A younger man who appeared to be an employee of the casino rather than one of Marino's goons jogged quickly to where he stood.

"Welcome, Mr. McFadden," he said and stepped a little closer than was necessary. "Mr. Marino wanted me to take you to where he's having breakfast. If you'll follow me?"

Taylor didn't bother to reply as the kid had already turned, anxious to fulfill this responsibility before he returned to what was most likely a valet station. He had a twenty-dollar bill waiting for his guide when the young man led him to a small restaurant deep within the casino itself.

Breakfast seemed to have already been done and served, and everyone was most likely now geared to serve lunch or begin pre-dinner preparations. Despite that, it was held open for the owner, who was seated in a corner with a window overlooking the casino floor.

Taylor clenched his teeth against the foul taste in his mouth triggered by the sight of the young, successful mob boss. His entire demeanor was of a man in control as he sipped coffee from a porcelain cup and nibbled at a piece of toast that had been heavily smeared with butter and strawberry jam.

He stood when he saw his guest approach and motioned for the taller man to take a seat. "I'm so happy you chose to accept my offer of breakfast. And I'll be honest. I thought you would cancel at the last minute."

"That's funny because I thought about canceling at the last minute," Taylor replied and sat, his expression neutral.

"Do you want anything to eat? I instructed the kitchen to stay open for breakfast in case you hadn't eaten yet."

"I haven't, and I would love breakfast."

Marino gestured and a few seconds later, one of the waiters hurried to the table. He tried to look happy but it came off more as polite tolerance of their presence.

"If you guys have it, I'll have a stack of pancakes with butter and maple syrup, a stack of bacon, and about as many scrambled eggs you guys can muster. Oh, and OJ and coffee."

His host's eyebrows raised at the order and the waiter nodded quickly, turned away, and headed to the kitchen.

"You certainly have an appetite, Taylor."

He shrugged in response. "You don't keep a body like this by cutting carbs. Plus, I've tried to recover the muscle mass I've lost and since you're picking up the bill for this, I thought I would take all kinds of advantage of your generous hospitality. Call it me getting back at you for inconveniencing my friend."

"Ah, well, I suppose that makes sense. And the meal is on me, of course. Now, while we await your feast, what say you I lay out the business proposal I had in mind for you?"

The coffee was the first to arrive and Taylor leaned back in his seat. "Far be it from me to keep anyone from speaking their mind."

Rod smirked. "Well, the fact of the matter is that I need a small favor from you. As I recall, I did do you something of a favor before—"

"And charged me full price for it too, if I remember correctly."

"You do. Naturally, I would pay dearly for the execution of this favor that requires a…deft touch."

He shook his head. "I'm not here to be another one of your work-for-hire lackeys."

"Of course not, but I do consider the possibility that you might perhaps become a merc for hire."

"I'm not in the family, Marino, and I don't aspire to become a made man or some shit like that. Also, I don't like the feeling that I'm being led into a deep, black hole from which there is no return or even a chance to turn any unsavory work from you down."

"There is no black hole," the man insisted as he leaned forward and kept his voice low. "Usually, I would send my people on this kind of mission, but as I said, I require something a little more efficient. As you are well aware, my people are enthusiastic but lack the professionalism I require for this job, given that it involves an ex."

"An...ex?"

The conversation paused when his meal came out of the kitchen. Taylor had no idea how they had all that food ready but he wouldn't complain. He hadn't eaten anything since the pizza from the night before and after his work-out, his body was starved for a substantial meal. The bacon, in particular, made his mouth water, and it wasn't long before he bit into one of the strips and cut into the stack of pancakes.

It was delicious, but he hadn't expected anything different.

"It's fantastic, yes?" Marino asked and sipped his coffee.

"It's no Il Fornaio, but it'll do in a pinch," Taylor conceded, his mouth still half-full of syrup and butter-covered pancakes. "You said something about an ex?"

"My ex, to be exact. It's the age-old story of boy meets girl, boy loves girl, girl loves him but loves another guy too. And then another guy. And another one after that. Honestly, I kind of lost count after a while. When I finally looked beyond my focus and need to grow my business, I realized she wasn't the woman I had married back in the day. I blame myself, honestly."

"Sure."

"To make a long story short, a divorce followed. I cut her off from my money and sent her packing with a chunk of change her lawyer managed to wrangle out of me. Unfortunately, it wasn't cold enough on my part and there are certain elements out there who feel I might still hold her in some kind of affection. They called my bluff, to use a term familiar to me, and have essentially challenged me to prove I don't care."

Taylor was almost halfway through the stack of pancakes before he paused to look at the man. This was a side of Marino he'd never expected to see and he didn't believe a single word of it. Still, there were certain benefits to making sure people knew not to mess with those close to him, even if they had been cut off.

"You have to know this isn't something that'll go away," he said and began to pile eggs onto the plate with the pancakes. Some people turned their nose up at the thought of maple syrup with scrambled eggs, but he felt the salty and sweet flavors were made for each other. "If this is a weakness they see you react to, they'll exploit it again. And again. And—"

"Not once they get the message I want to send about messing with people I care about."

He shook his head. "I won't kill idiots from a rival gang simply to send their bosses a message about your business dealings."

"I never thought you would." Marino growled under his breath and began to sound annoyed.

Taylor had the feeling the man didn't often have people saying no to him, but he didn't care. The mob boss had made too much of a nuisance of himself for him to give a shit about what annoyed him. He didn't respond and simply proceeded to enjoy the food piled on the plate in front of him.

Rod took a moment to calm himself again before he drew a deep breath. "I merely need professional hands to get her out of the situation she is currently in. Once she's free, I can send a message."

His nod was non-committal and he took a moment to finish chewing the food in his mouth, then washed it down with orange juice. "And what kind of compensation do you think would be appropriate for professional involvement?"

The mob boss smirked and took another sip of his coffee. "Are you asking me what I think my slutty ex-wife is worth?"

"In so many words. I did try to be a little more professional about it, though."

"Naturally. I thought a hundred thousand dollars would be a reasonable fee for this kind of operation."

He tried not to show any surprise at the figure. He knew Marino probably spent that much money on an average Tuesday night for entertainment. People like him had no concept of what money was worth, at least not in the way those like Taylor did.

"For a rescue op? No killing except in self-defense?"

Marino sighed and looked like he fought to resist the urge to roll his eyes. "Agreed. Do we have a deal?"

Taylor looked at the plate in front of him. Somehow, all the food was gone, along with the hunger pangs that had annoyed him. The coffee had similarly disappeared, and all that was left was a half-glass of OJ.

"Fine." He grunted and drained the glass. "You can send the details of where, when, and all that shit. And I'll probably need about ten grand in advance for my expenses. In cash."

Rod withdrew an envelope from his inside jacket pocket. "Here's twenty, to be safe. And the hundred on top of it once the job is done."

He took the envelope without so much as a glance at it and tucked it into his pocket as he stood from his seat. "Oh, and one more thing. Your thugs who showed up at my business. They tried to throw their weight around and they annoyed my friend. If I had been there, I would have sent them back to you with a sound thrashing and I think I'm still owed that opportunity. Ten minutes, only them and me. They need to be taught a little lesson."

Marino laughed as he stood and adjusted his jacket. "I'll talk to them about it, but you should know I won't put them against you in a mech. That wouldn't be right."

"No armor, no suit, and no weapons. Only me."

The mob boss hesitated and studied him carefully. He frowned as he tilted his head with what appeared to be reluctance. "I suppose it would be your funeral. You might be one hell of a kickass in one of those suits of yours, but those two have fought in dark alleys since they learned to walk."

"Only ten minutes. If I don't walk out of there, I'll owe them an apology."

Rod thought about it for a few seconds and nodded. "Deal. But I won't bring it up to them until the trollop is safe, do you understand?"

He raised his hands. "That sounds fine by me. I'll let you know when it's done."

The man smiled as Taylor stepped out of the restaurant.

He hadn't expected to accept the job offer. Then again, he hadn't expected Marino to be the kind of guy who had ever been married, much less be willing to put however much money on the line to make sure his ex-wife wasn't threatened. Helping to rescue someone for the man didn't sound quite so dirty a job.

Besides, he did owe him for helping them with the plane. It was best not to leave him thinking he was in any way indebted to him, though. Helping the woman did seem like he would walk away from this cheaply and with an added hundred and twenty grand in his pocket for his trouble.

No valet attendant waited to show him the way out, but there was no need. He took his time to find the route out of the labyrinthine casino. The details would come in soon. If the woman was kidnapped and a professional's hand would be needed, he couldn't simply arrive in a tank of an armored suit and charge in. That would risk getting her killed.

Marino was right in his assumption that he would have one hell of an advantage with a suit of armor, and it occurred to him that he might rely on the power of the suits a little too much. He had been a ferocious fighter in his own right once, but he wondered if he would be able to do something like this without his armor.

He could talk to Bobby about it when he returned to the shop. The man probably wouldn't like the fact that they were embroiled in Marino's messes again, but the mechanic didn't need to do much except maybe repair his smaller suit for the rescue. That would be all the advantage he needed to get in and out of a house with a mob boss' kidnapped ex-wife in tow.

The more he thought about it, the more the concept appealed to him. The only thought that did worry him, ironically, was getting into a cage with the two goons. He didn't doubt that he could handle both, but it would take something he wasn't sure he had since he'd been butt-fucked by a helicopter during one of Niki's missions. He needed to somehow make sure he still had it.

Sparring wouldn't cut it. He had never been able to unleash fully during training, and that was what he needed to do for this to work in his favor.

He would have to find a solution. Besides, it was a matter for later because he had more pressing matters to attend to.

"Taylor McFadden?"

He looked up and realized he had stepped onto the street, where another black SUV waited for him. He looked at his phone and grimaced. Vickie had messaged him.

I have you covered, Tay-Tay, her message read with a winking face added. He assumed she meant ordering the Uber Black for him.

"Yeah, that's me," he answered finally and slid into the back. The hacker needed to learn a thing or two about boundaries.

CHAPTER FIFTEEN

"You did what?"

Taylor nodded his head slowly. He could understand why Bungees and Tanya would both protest the decision he had made over breakfast and hadn't even vaguely expected them to go along with it.

On the contrary, he'd anticipated that they'd be vehemently against it.

Even so, he hadn't been able to prepare himself for their disappointment. Tanya was the most vocal of the two, but he could see the dark expression on Bobby's face. His large arms were folded in front of his chest and he looked for all the world like a disapproving dad.

That stung almost more than the foul language from Tanya as she circled the shop in an effort to calm herself. Elisa didn't look at him. The only person who remained more or less neutral was Vickie, and while she didn't look very happy, she didn't manifest open displeasure either. He assumed it was because she had somehow listened in on his conversation with Marino and had already vented her curses to get them out of the way.

Bungees sighed again and still looked disappointed in his boss. Finally, he shrugged and shook his head. "Well, okay. It looks like we'll save the hussy, and for a solid hundred and twenty grand, I guess you can always make the excuse of catching more bees with honey than vinegar. Kind of like Elisa's sales tactics."

"I heard that," the former reporter called from across the room.

"Will you deny that you use your feminine wiles to make sure those men spend more money than they might otherwise?" he replied over his shoulder.

"Well, I won't deny that I sell more than Taylor might if he tried to flirt."

"He might be the guy to do the selling if most of our clientele were female," Vickie pointed out. "I'm not sure how he does it, but I have studied his success rate with the opposite sex and while it has dropped of late, it's usually right up there."

"I think that has more to do with the quality of what I sell than my tactics," Taylor countered. "You, for instance, are on top of all the best technical gizmos on the market, so when the best of something comes out, you don't need much of a salesperson to convince yourself it's what you want."

The hacker nodded, but Bobby didn't look persuaded.

"What you're selling here is your body, right?" the mechanic asked, his head tilted. "Whereas she uses herself as a tool to sell something else."

"It sounds wrong when you say it like that, but sure," Taylor conceded.

"You mean the 'change your tactics because it's in a morally grey area' description of it?"

"I guess it means you're pushing your views of right and wrong on other people."

Bobby paused for a few seconds and shrugged. "Okay, it does sound wrong when you say it like that."

"Sure, and while sometimes people who do that might be in the right, they go about it the wrong way," he explained. "You run all over people with your morals, which sees your ends justifying your means. In doing so, you use a position of strength to convince others that they're doing something wrong in a kind of twisted might equals right pattern."

"So I'm wrong in pushing my opinions on the two of you?"

"It seems more like you're wrong to make the assumption that everyone would share your morality system. Then, you get annoyed when they don't feel the same guilt you would if you were to do the same thing."

"You'll start making an argument about how prostitution is okay if you keep this up," the man retorted.

"Is it?"

"No!"

"Think about it. If you look at it that way, you have to consider that people getting married bring a financial bargain into their romantic lives. Hell, if you think a woman willingly engaging in prostitution is wrong and a guy willingly putting his body at risk in a coal mine is okay, you might want to rethink your morality system."

"Oh, please fucking stop it!" Vickie called from the other side of the shop and rubbed her temples. "You've obviously thought this through and this is what made your brain think having meaningless liaisons is an example of healthy behavior."

"Is it not?"

"No," the hacker insisted. "And if you go into a relationship with my cousin with a mentality like that, it'll end with someone hurt, more than likely her. While I adore the shit out of you, Taylor, don't think I will hesitate to end your life if you hurt her in any way. And not a quick ending, either—a very slow and agonizing kind of ending where you're left penniless and have to pay off the pizzas I send to wherever you end up living."

Taylor nodded. "It sounds like you've thought this through."

"I have. So you'd better not slip, Tay-Tay."

He paused for a few seconds and sighed. "Okay, message received. And if there's anything Tay-Tay doesn't do, it's slip when he's determined to get something done."

The hacker grinned. "Well, well, well. We'll see if Tay-Tay has it in him."

"Tay-Tay might want to stop talking about himself in the third person," he added.

"That sounds about right," Vickie agreed.

"Wait," Tanya interjected. "Are you guys really on board with getting into bed with Marino again? What's the matter here? Have we simply forgotten the fact that he's tried to destroy your business from day one?"

Taylor shook his head. "Gaining a better idea of how his dealings are run while we're paid for it seemed like a good idea to me. There isn't much about us he doesn't know by now, and getting into the "know thy enemy" side of Sun Tzu's writings gives me the feeling that an inside look into an organization we're likely to go up against does feel like the smart thing to do."

"Have you considered that you might simply be strengthening his position?"

"No more than he would be already. Besides, if we don't help him, it means he'll call someone else. Having another team in our city might encourage him to think he'll be better off in a city without us to embarrass him. Anyway, the decision's made and I'll make sure to tell him I want to consult you guys before I dive into any other situations with him. Does that sound like a decent enough compromise?"

Tanya raised her hands in a frustrated manner and shook her head. "Honestly, my whole issue is that we're dealing with him in the first place. Still, I guess you're right in that we probably shouldn't put ourselves at odds with the man yet. But let it be a part of the record that I'm not a fan of the arrangement."

He scratched his beard. "And I appreciate the input. If I'm honest, I'm not a fan of the arrangement either."

Vickie sighed deeply. "Well, now that we've established that none of us think Marino is anything other than a large-diameter dickhole, we can move on to how we will help the woman even he thinks isn't worth having around. According to the details he sent us, she was kidnapped two days ago by certain members of the Russian *Bratva* in our city.

"I could go into a whole slew of high-tech solutions like

tracking the people through traffic cameras and face-recognition software, but this is one of those cases in which simpler is better. I picked up the known members of the gang, who have used their credit cards to consistently order food for delivery to a house that doesn't belong to them, and viola. The deliveries started two days ago and they've ordered an average of seven pizzas a day since they got there."

"Seven pizzas?" Taylor asked and folded his arms. "I'm fairly sure that accounts for three or maybe four guards, plus a prisoner."

"You'll have to show me your math later," she retorted. "That aside, it looks like they have entrenched themselves in a house that doesn't have any owners aside from the bank that picked it up after the former owners defaulted on their mortgage. It might be that this bank is owned by the *Bratva* since many of its members have accounts with them. What it does mean, though, is that no one will break their party up any time soon."

"We'll see about that," he muttered. "Four guys, plus a prisoner, means this is probably a one-man job. Well, one man in a suit of armor and Vickie running support. Given that I want to sneak in and not break through the walls to do it, I'll probably need my civvie outfit. How long do you think we'll need to bring it into fighting shape?"

Bobby startled and realized that the question was directed at him. "I've already replaced all the damaged armor plates since there weren't many of them to begin with. I only have to test the electronics, fix anything that needs to be messed with, and it should be good to go. Maybe by later this afternoon?"

"Which gives you all the time you need to get surveillance on these assholes," Vickie pointed out. "We all know how you prefer to have eyes on people instead of cameras, and I'm done being annoyed by it."

Taylor nodded. "I'll get on it. Give me a call when everything is ready."

"And you will give me a portion of the profits from this job, right?" the mechanic asked and raised an eyebrow.

He smirked, withdrew the envelope Marino had given him from his pocket, and handed it to the other man. "Think of that as your cut. To be sure, though, I would think twice about depositing it in a bank."

"Yeah, that's a good call," the mechanic agreed, took the bills out, and pretended to count them. "Doesn't that mean I'm running support on this one too?"

"In that case, I want my twenty grand too," Vickie grumbled.

"Yeah, yeah, but you'll get it when Marino pays me the full balance," he muttered. "I'll see you guys later. Vickie, I'll take an earbud to stay in touch with you when I get there."

"I honestly don't see why you don't simply use my skills to give you a comprehensive view of the location," Vickie told him through his earpiece. "That way, there's much less chance that you might have your ass spotted. You're not the toughest guy to notice when you're out there, you know, and when things start to go sideways, I assume you'd want to have your suit closer rather than farther away. I'm not saying you can't handle yourself without one, mind you, but it's still better to have than not, right?"

Taylor leaned back in the seat of his four-by-four, closed his eyes for a few seconds, and enjoyed the music. Traffic wasn't heavy in the area but people were still out and about. It looked like it had once been a development project that quickly ran out of money. Some of the houses were complete, others were in various states of disrepair, and many lots had no buildings at all.

It wouldn't be long until someone rolled around and tried to take advantage of the cheap real estate and began development. Of course, they'd hope the coding issues that had plagued the people who had tried it previously would simply vanish. Sometimes, a little money in the right hands could do significant good.

The parking lot he had found was directly across the street from the house in question. A small strip mall almost like his had been propped up by smaller mom-and-pop businesses, all of which provided sufficient foot and car traffic to leave him more or less invisible.

In the end, there wasn't much to see. The area was more urban than suburban, which meant the house he watched had perimeter walls, mostly maintained by two buildings on either side of it. Not many houses in the US had that kind of closed-wall system and a steel gate that opened electronically. He had only seen it open once when four men had arrived and others left again almost immediately. Logic suggested it was probably a change of the guard.

There were still enough potential problems for him to examine. If he had set up security on the location, he would have two men to patrol the outside and two men inside, connected via radios to keep each team informed of the situation with each of the teams on an ongoing basis. If they had done this, gaining entry would attract the kind of attention from the men inside that would probably end poorly for their hostage.

Taylor rubbed his cheek as he considered his options. Assuming he could enter the house without anyone seeing him, the most likely result would be that the men inside raised the alarm. If so, he would have to face four men, which left no way to avoid combat. He also didn't know what kind of weapons they carried. If one of them had armor-piercing rounds—not entirely unlikely given that the *Bratva* didn't mind engaging the police from time to time—even the suit wouldn't protect him from being punched full of holes.

"Here's what I wonder," Vickie said into the silence as she tended to when no one was there to stop her from rambling. "Like...when I think about it, they've ordered seven pizzas on average for teams of four, plus one prisoner. Given the woman's recent Instagram pictures, she probably isn't taking more than one or two slices, so why that particular number? One team eats more, obviously, but they only order them twice, one at lunch and one for dinner. Do these guys simply not eat breakfast or something?"

"It's reasonable to assume both teams will have at least one or more likely two meals while they're away from the house. The breakfast equivalent is probably on the way and dinner on the way out. I'd say they're only given enough money by their bosses to order one meal and don't feel it's worth it to try anything else until it's time to go. Speaking of that, do you know more or less what time these new arrivals will order their food? Are they consistent with their timing?"

The hacker paused for a few seconds, which indicated that she was probably looking the data up to be sure. In turn, it told him she hadn't even thought of it. "Oh, yeah. The first order is usually delivered between midday and one in the afternoon and the second order—the one with four instead of three—generally arrives between seven and eight at night. Why, what are you thinking?"

"That I could probably intercept whoever delivers the pizzas," Taylor said, thinking aloud. "Stop him or her, take their vehicle, and use the pizza delivery as my way in. That way, I could get as many of the guys as possible at one time."

"Well, I guess…but I kind of feel bad for the pizza guy. He didn't do anything wrong."

"I'd leave him a generous tip, of course," he assured her. "More than enough to compensate for this kind of thing."

"I'll bet you he won't feel that way."

"He might. I'll probably leave him enough to pay his rent for the month, so that should alleviate his woes."

"And if he goes to the cops?"

He shrugged. "He won't have seen my face and will only know where I was going. Even if he does talk to the cops, the chances are the *Bratva* guys won't say too much so at best, they'll simply hunt a big, hulking dude in a motorcycle helmet."

"You have to be careful. If it is somehow connected to what happened in New Orleans, we might have the FBI breathing down our necks. Niki doesn't work with them anymore to help and keep them at bay."

He bit the inside of his cheek and scowled. "That's a good point. Either way, though, this still feels like the best way for me to get in there so I think we'll have to cross that bridge if and when we get to it."

"Short-term solutions might result in problems for the long-term."

"Let's be honest. The chances are I won't survive that long."

"Don't even say that, Taylor. I'm not kidding. Not even as a joke."

He paused, tightened his hold on the steering wheel, and resisted the urge to inform her that he wasn't joking. "Sorry. Is Bobby finished working on my suit yet?"

"Yeah, and I had the brilliant idea to tell him to drive it to you to save time. Look at me, being proactive as your support. I think I deserve a raise."

Taylor smirked. It was almost six in the evening, which meant he would have about an hour before they placed their order. He had enough time to suit up and move into position to intercept the driver.

A short while later, the tell-tale thrum of Bobby's truck rumbled to where he was parked. He motioned for him to meet him behind the strip mall in an alley with little traffic and no cameras that would enable him to suit up without being seen.

"Good luck terrorizing innocent delivery boys," the mechanic stated once he was ready and tested the new armor.

"Oh, for fuck's— Vickie told you?"

"Of course she did. Now, speaking of delivering, do you think I should charge delivery fees for this kind of thing?"

"I'm very sure the twenty grand I gave you should cover that," he retorted and lowered the sensitivity on the leg as the new hydraulics were a little more sensitive than the old ones. "I'm surrounded by money grabbers. Seriously."

His friend laughed as he climbed into his truck.

CHAPTER SIXTEEN

Vickie was right. Taylor did feel bad for the kid who would deliver the pizzas. The chances were this was someone barely out of his or her teens who used their recently acquired driver's license to make money. They were either saving for college or wanted to buy more weed from their dealer.

With that in mind, his plans didn't feel like the kind of thing someone like that would want to be involved in, no matter how much money they were paid for it. All things considered, the kid would likely not see any repercussions of what happened unless they went to the police, but that didn't justify what he set out to do.

Unfortunately, it had to be done.

The hacker had brought up the route he would use, and tracked him—she had somehow determined it was a him— on the delivery app to make sure. Taylor was already waiting on the route, three blocks away from the house. He'd decided it was best to not leave too much distance between him and his destination to be safe.

It wasn't long before the motorcycle circled the nearest corner. He noticed immediately it wasn't a scooter, thankfully, although it would remain to be seen if it could take the full weight of his suit.

He turned the four-by-four on and edged in front of the motorcycle to block him but still leave him enough time to stop. More importantly, the driver had no room to try to circle the larger vehicle.

Still, it was best not to leave anything to chance.

Taylor stepped out of the car in a half-second, his sidearm already in hand. It was a motion he'd practiced a couple of times beforehand to ensure that the suit could handle it, but it still felt like a clunky maneuver.

Fortunately, he was dealing with an unsuspecting pizza delivery driver so it was quick enough. He stood beside the vehicle with the barrel of his weapon aimed at the kid's head before the motorcycle had even pulled to a full stop. In the circumstances, he made sure to keep his finger off the trigger. He had no intention to hurt the kid, even though he would make him think that was the case.

"You lose." He delivered the statement in a growled tone and the suit masked his voice slightly. "You lose so don't make any stupid mistakes, get off the bike, and pull your helmet off. Now!"

The last word was enough to snap the kid out of any thoughts of resistance or flight. He slid off the bike in a heartbeat and dropped to his knees.

"Please, man," he said, his voice muffled by the helmet. "I don't have any cash on me. I'm only here to deliver pizzas."

"I know." He used his free hand to yank the youngster's helmet off. "I'll borrow your bike and do that delivery for you. How much do you make a month as a delivery boy?"

"Ten...ten bucks an hour," the kid replied. He looked both terrified and a little curious as to why he had been asked that. "Plus tips, I guess."

"Not enough to get killed over, right?" Taylor retrieved a pair of handcuffs, pulled the young man's hands behind his back, and clicked the cuffs on. "I have five thousand dollars in cash for you once this is over so calm down. I'll be back in less than fifteen minutes with your bike and honestly, you might even get to keep the pizzas for yourself. So stay calm, don't do anything stupid, and you'll walk away from this with more money than you'll make all month. Got it?"

He nodded in response as Taylor lifted him to his feet, heaved him into the back of the four-by-four before, and snagged his phone out of his pocket. The chances were the kid would try to call the police. Cuffs would only work for a very limited time.

Hopefully, the promise of the money and the threat of the massive gun held in his face would be enough to stop him from doing anything that wrecked the whole plan.

"I'll be back," he promised and realized that the muffler made the comment sound vaguely like a former California governor before he closed the truck.

Once his unwilling and entirely innocent accomplice was successfully locked inside, he moved the vehicle into a parking space not far from where the bike was, then returned to his new mode of transport. A quick inspection told him there was no way he would get it to move with him seated on it.

He put his back into it and pushed the bike the rest of the way. It was faster than regular walking and he doubted anyone who wasn't a natural sprinter or an athlete could keep up with him. Still, his muscles burned and sweat built inside the suit. Thankfully, night had already begun to fall and brought the temperature down with it.

It was less than three minutes until he stood at the door of the house he had surveilled for most of the afternoon and pressed the doorbell.

The late arrival was likely noticed as it was only a few seconds before the door was opened for him. He lifted the pizzas out of their compartment.

"Sorry," he grumbled. "The bike broke down three blocks away and I had to push it here."

The two men there to greet him looked more annoyed than suspicious, shook their heads, and indicated that he should hand the delivery over while they cursed in Russian. The one who took the pizzas turned away and gestured for his friend to pay for the food.

Taylor took the distraction as an invitation.

It was almost too easy to step in and power his armored fist into the head of the man who had his back turned. The pizza boxes fell, although thankfully, the contents weren't strewn across the floor.

The second man dropped his wallet and fumbled for the weapon he carried tucked in the back of his pants.

It wasn't the most accessible place, and Taylor didn't have to rush to have his sidearm out and ready. He held his finger on the trigger this time and aimed it squarely at the man's chest.

"Don't do it," he warned and held his aim steady. It was

weird that the modulator still sounded like it had an Austrian accent. He would have to talk to Vickie about it. Maybe she had something to do with the alteration.

The man considered not doing anything for a second. It was easy to tell that the idea of simply giving up and living to fight another day flitted through his mind, but it didn't last. His hand continued to inch toward his weapon.

Taylor moved before he could complete the action. He did not intend to take any chances with these guys. He'd told Marino he would try to avoid killing them, mostly because he didn't want to deal with the heat of a murder investigation hanging over his head. It didn't mean, however, that these guys wouldn't know they'd been in a very one-sided fight.

Despite his initial surprise, the Russian was fast. The .32 revolver was already in his hand by the time Taylor reached him, but he wasn't fast enough. He barely had time to position his arm to aim before a heavily armored fist struck him hard in the jaw. A couple of teeth broke with the impact but the man didn't fall. His eyes almost closed and he lost his footing, but his gun hand continued to move into position.

Even so, it was easy work to catch the mobster's hand by the wrist and jerk his head forward. The crunch of a broken nose against his helmet was all Taylor needed to hear. The man lost all control of his body and fell heavily, his whole body as stiff as a board.

"Vickie," he called through the earpiece. "You might want to get paramedics on the way."

"What should I tell them?"

"Sound confused and a little scared. Say a fight is

happening and some people are on the ground unconscious. Maybe tell them a couple of guys are involved in
the fighting, not only me."

"How long will you be there?" she asked. "Shouldn't we
be concerned about the paramedics arriving before you
leave?"

He grinned, pleased to see that she was learning to look
for potential problems. "I don't know if it's possible but you
might be able to check where the nearest emergency
vehicle is and calculate their response time."

She paused, although he couldn't tell if it was because
she didn't think she could do something like that or simply
hadn't thought of the possibility herself. "Okay. How long
do you need?"

"Fifteen minutes should be all the time I need," Taylor
asserted without hesitation. "It's safe to say these guys will
be unconscious in under a minute—assuming I don't break
anything serious or…kill them, I guess."

"I thought you said you wouldn't kill them?"

"I said I would try. I'm not Batman, though, and I won't
lose much sleep over putting a couple of Russian mobsters
out of business."

He scanned the area to check for any sign that the
people inside were aware of what was happening. It had
only taken him a couple of seconds to disable them, and it
appeared they hadn't made any attempt to use the radios
they carried on their belts. They had chosen to go low-tech
for their communication options and probably relied on
the idea that they wouldn't have to worry about people
finding them, much less interfering.

Taylor took their weapons away and threw them into

the grass where they would be impossible to find until the sun came up again. There was always a possibility that they might try to get up and join the fight again.

He grasped his handgun but left his shotgun where it was still holstered on his back. Hopefully, he wouldn't need to worry about using the heavier weapon as anything other than a club.

The house itself wasn't large. Only one story, it was sandwiched between two of what appeared to be smaller office buildings which served as the side walls. He wasn't sure why it hadn't been torn down and turned into an office building as well, but maybe that was why the bank still owned it.

Even so, Vickie had fitted his HUD with blueprints that gave him a good view of what he was looking for—the master bedroom, one of two bedrooms in the house and the only suite. They had probably barred the windows to make sure their prisoner didn't try to escape and left her to her own devices. Logic suggested that if they held her for ransom, they didn't want any more trouble than was necessary. Keeping her fed and more or less happy would be the general idea. He noticed no sign of a Wi-Fi connection in the residence, which meant no one had put any work into keeping it livable.

The door was locked from the outside with a chain system, most likely in case she needed something. It would enable her to open the door and call for someone nearby without being able to leave the room itself.

The small joint manipulation on the suit made managing the chain lock a little more complicated than he liked, but it wasn't long before the door opened. He stood face to face with the woman he had been sent to rescue.

She was already standing when he entered and her eyes widened as he stepped through the door. He could understand her fear, all things considered. She had likely adjusted to the situation she was in over the four days she had spent in captivity. Change, for someone like her, inevitably meant things might get worse. A big man in a motorcycle helmet was probably not something she would think would end well for her.

The woman looked like she was a model, even after days without her usual selection of clothes and makeup. Her short blonde hair, long eyelashes, high cheekbones, and a tall, lean, yet curvaceous build suggested she would be perfectly at home in Venice or wherever the classy fashion shows happened.

Taylor sighed, shook his head, and extended his hand. "This is the part where I tell you to come with me if you want to live."

"Who…are you?"

"A guy in a motorcycle helmet who wants his identity to not be revealed in any of this until we're far away from this house," he responded brusquely. "Suffice it to say your ex sent me, and he wants you safe before he tears all these guys a couple of new assholes. He wants you out of range before that happens."

She paused for a few seconds and her confused expression faded quickly before she shook her head. He assumed she had been around Marino and his family for years. She likely knew what the man was about, even if he hadn't been the head of the family when they had been married, and couldn't have been blind to the kind of enemies he had. Or his friends, for that matter.

It was a good thing, in the end. There was no need to explain anything or convince her he was on her side. He was a friend of Marino's. End of story. Well, not a friend but an associate would work in the circumstances.

Taylor motioned for her to join him at the door while he peeked out to make sure no one had noticed his arrival. Someone spoke a mixture of English and Russian in one of the other rooms—probably a living room since most of what was said was obfuscated by the sounds of sports played on a television.

He froze when a shadow moved closer and guessed that one of the guards approached the main door, likely to check on the status of their pizza. It was probably something he should have made a mental note of at the time, but he wouldn't be able to get back into the room. Hell, even if he did, they would still see the door open and he didn't like the idea of being left with his back to the wall.

The man circled the corner as Taylor moved in front of the woman. He still didn't know her name and had no real desire to find out.

"*Cyka!*" the Russian shouted, drew his weapon quickly, and aimed it at him. He scowled at the defender, although the expression was pointless behind the helmet.

They had to know the woman was behind him and they would risk injuring or even killing the person they were supposed to keep alive and well in captivity. These men were amateurs, which meant they were far more dangerous since they would react unpredictably, make stupid mistakes, and most likely leave collateral damages.

Taylor shifted his position slightly to form as solid a block between the woman and the bullets as he could. He pushed her against the wall so he could hopefully avoid the chance that one would accidentally hit her.

The second man had entered the hallway now and both fired what sounded like MP-443s. If he remembered correctly, they either had fifteen-round mags, or seventeen. Either of those would damage his suit if he simply let them maintain their barrage.

Finally, one of them stopped. Clicking sounds told him it had jammed, while the other man was distracted by his comrade's problem and fired a couple of shots into the ceiling above his target.

Something about the carelessness of their assault irked him. Professionals could have destroyed or disabled his suit by aiming at the weak points, but these two apparently hadn't even considered that. Worse, they had no notion of muzzle or trigger discipline.

Taylor readied himself with his shotgun now in hand and hoped the woman had the good sense to cover her ears when he opened fire. The tight confines of the hallway would make it all very loud, very fast.

The man who was able to shoot was still distracted, but his attention focused quickly when he registered the sawed-off barrel of the semi-automatic shotgun he now faced. His eyes widened and he even managed another shot. It ricocheted off his shoulder pauldron and he once again decided the man wasn't a very good shot. It explained why, of the fifteen or so rounds they had fired between them, only five or six had struck him.

He had a mind to show him exactly what came from being able to shoot straight in high-pressure situations.

The shotgun boomed through the hallway and the buckshot tore through the man's chest. A second shot reverberated through the space. A double-tap with a shotgun wasn't completely necessary, but he had no desire to take chances. These amateurs weren't the kind he wanted wandering the streets of Vegas after he was finished.

The second man struggled with the simple action of pulling the bolt of his gun back. It wasn't complicated, but the adrenaline pumping through his body was bound to make even the simplest of actions seem complicated. Killing him with the shotgun didn't seem right so he moved forward and holstered his weapon as the guard tried to back away and tripped over his own feet.

Taylor caught him before he could land, wrapped his fingers around his neck, and lifted him off his feet. The man wasn't terribly large, although a host of tattoos told him his opponent was a long-time member of the *Bratva*. He tried to break his hold but shook his head and coughed as his grasp tightened. The hydraulics across the suit reacted as he lifted his captive a little higher. The man tried to kick and fight it but his assailant shifted and twisted his arm until a crack signified his neck breaking.

He released him quickly, and the mobster crumpled, his body limp and lifeless.

"Was that really necessary?" Vickie asked through the comms as he turned to where the woman stared at him and still looked a little terrified.

"Kind of," he said, deliberately vague before he set his

voice to the external speakers. "Are you all right? Did any of the rounds hit you?"

She shook her head. "Who the fuck are you?"

"Never mind that. We need to get going—now."

The two men outside were still alive and awake, thankfully, although they appeared to only be able to roll on the ground while they groaned and held the places on their bodies where they had been struck.

"How are we doing with those ambulances?" Taylor asked through the comms.

"Ten minutes away," the hacker replied rapidly.

That gave them all the time they needed to escape. He collected the pizzas hastily and put them into the motorcycle's trunk before he began to push it away. The woman followed him, but even she couldn't keep the confused look from her face as they increased the pace.

"It's a long story," he offered by way of a very inadequate explanation. She merely nodded, a little out of breath by the time they reached the vehicle again.

To his relief, it looked like the kid hadn't moved from where he'd left him, and it took only moments to unlock the cuffs and hand the bike and pizzas to him. The young man looked like he'd all but convinced himself he wouldn't return.

Before the youngster left, Taylor retrieved a wad of bills he had made ready before he'd started and handed them to him, but shock registered and the driver almost didn't want to take the money.

"Suffice it to say that if the cops or the press ever hear about this, you and I will talk again," Taylor warned and thrust the money in his hands. "Do you understand? Take the money, take the pizzas, and have a nice evening."

All he received in response was a wide-eyed nod as the kid mounted up with an expression that clearly said he didn't believe his luck and swung to accelerate away.

"Let me guess," the woman said with a hint of a French accent. "Another long story?"

"You know it." Taylor gestured for her to climb into the four-by-four as he did the same and they eased out of the lot as the first faint signs of approaching sirens intruded on the night silence.

CHAPTER SEVENTEEN

W ith Vickie's help, it took mere minutes to track Bobby to where he had parked his truck. He had waited there in case things went sour and Taylor needed backup. While his help hadn't been necessary, it was good to get out of the suit and not have to drive to the other side of the city while wearing it.

For one thing, if they were pulled over, there would be all kinds of hell to pay.

There were other reasons too. The operation was over and had been a success, but he couldn't help feeling a little dirty. He'd lost his cool there, and while it was justifiable— for the most part, at least—he still didn't feel right about it. It wasn't like him to analyze the thought process behind that too closely as he didn't want to press for too many details, but there was still a little something in him that was irked by how unfair the fight had been.

He returned to the four-by-four, which he'd parked far away from Bobby so the rescued woman wouldn't see his comrade. The fact that she would see him also didn't feel quite right but in the end, Marino would probably spill the beans on his identity anyway.

She looked surprised when he returned to the vehicle and her eyebrows raised as he climbed into the driver's seat.

"What?" he asked and turned the engine on.

"I assumed the suit added much more bulk," she told him. "That was a mechanized suit, yes? The kind I've heard are involved in robberies in Vegas? Although I thought you were stealing from my bastard ex-husband, not working for him."

"Well, now," Taylor replied. "I wouldn't rush to add two and two and get nine and a half. For one thing, there are other suits out there and not everyone who uses one does so with criminal intent. Besides, if I could steal from him in broad daylight using a mechanized suit and get away with it, why would I need to work for him? I merely have the skills to help him get you out of...whatever the fuck situation you were in. What's your name, anyway?"

"He didn't tell you?"

"He didn't. Imagine that."

"Genevieve. And you?"

"Taylor. Gene...vieve? Am I saying that right?"

She nodded. "Or as close to saying it right as you can with your accent. Where are you from?"

"Nope." He shook his head. "This isn't a getting to know you party. This is me getting you to safety. Your ex said he would send a couple of messages once you were safe. Speaking of which, Overwatch, do you mind connecting me to Marino?"

The woman narrowed her eyes at him and shook her head.

"Not you," he muttered and gestured to his ear.

"Oh shit," Vickie responded. "Are you talking to me? Am I Overwatch?"

Taylor nodded. "Yeah, I assumed you wouldn't want me to use your name while in the presence of a mobster's ex-wife. Some offense intended. Put your seatbelt on."

"Some taken," Genevieve muttered but did as she was told before she folded her arms.

It wasn't long before he heard a dialing tone on his comm line.

"Who is this?" Marino asked when he finally answered.

"The guy who has your wife in his car after leaving the kidnappers in his dust," he answered smoothly.

"You'll have to tell me how you got this number."

"I don't. All you have to know is that your package is safe and whatever you intend to do had better be done quickly because I won't wait around or babysit."

"I need you to take her out of the city," the mob boss stated. "There's a little town called Indian Springs. Get her there and you'll be clear from the fallout of what will happen next."

"Right. I won't do all this extra work for free." Technically, he'd already received extra but he was irritated enough to push his luck.

"I already—" Marino didn't sound like he was in the mood to haggle. "I'll add an extra two thousand for your work. Does that sound reasonable?"

"Sure. Let me know when it's over."

The line cut and he shook his head before he turned the four-by-four to head out of the city.

"That was him, yes?" Genevieve asked and still looked peeved. "You know, I don't think I've ever heard anyone talk to him like that. Too many people know who he is and are fearful of what he might do."

"You make it sound like you're scared of him."

"I am."

"Then I guess you know what my next question will be, right?"

"He told you I cheated on him, yes? With many men?"

"Was that…untrue?"

"Not really, but I assume he neglected to mention he was sleeping with a different woman every night. I counted and he didn't even bother to hide it."

"He didn't mention it," Taylor conceded. " But I assumed that was the kind of man he was. It made me wonder why he got married at all."

"I think we convinced ourselves we were in love when it was only… I don't know, physical attraction, plus the fact that I knew he was a dangerous man. That all faded a few months after the wedding. We cheated on each other until he had enough and sent me away, and I got the divorce papers soon after. He was willing to part with considerable money to get me out of his life, so I took it."

He nodded slowly. While he hadn't asked for the woman's life history, he had a feeling she hadn't had much opportunity to tell her side of the story to someone involved with her husband. Still, she had known what she was getting into and made a mistake. It sounded like she realized that and didn't blame anyone but herself. And Marino, of course.

Still, having someone to rant to about her past problems had to be cathartic.

"How did you get in bed with him?"

He shook his head. "Not in bed, not really. I resisted his attempts to try to sell me *La Cosa Nostra's* version of insurance and he wasn't happy about that. After a couple of months of dealing with the muscle he sent to persuade me, my team and I conducted a few operations to make sure he knew messing with us was a bad idea. We've had a tenuous peace since then and he calls me and my team occasionally to provide him with creative solutions to problems. Oh, and he helped us on one occasion as well."

"Not to sound contrary or anything, but that does sound like being in bed with the man. And you know he won't stand by and let someone challenge his authority like that. The chances are you will end up at odds with him in the future."

"Believe me, I'm well aware," Taylor muttered.

The drive to Indian Springs wasn't long, but they were a few minutes out when his phone buzzed a few times to advise him that a message had been sent.

It wasn't safe for him to look at the phone while driving, especially at night, but his gaze drifted to the screen anyway.

The car's auto-drive took over as he pulled his phone out, saw who the message was from, and scowled.

"Is it something important?" Genevieve asked. She'd tucked her legs under her body for the drive. Vickie had done the same thing when the trip was a little longer and he couldn't help but be reminded of it.

"Yeah," he confirmed and kept a hand on the wheel if only to feel like he was connected to driving. The newly developed software would warn him if he had to pay attention to something on the road. It wasn't as sophisticated as the AI in Liz, but it was a nice thing to have in the less technical cars. Although he'd never seen if it worked, he'd heard it was supposed to reduce car crashes too.

"Well, what does it say?" she asked once he tucked his phone into his pocket again. "I assume from the look on your face that it was probably Rod. People always get that annoyed, disgusted expression when they hear from him."

"It's good news, actually," Taylor replied and drew a slow, deep breath. "You can relax. No one will hurt you now, not anymore. It looks like he sent his message after all."

"He wouldn't ever let much of anything get in the way of that," she retorted. "Not even me—not for very long. Still, I guess the fact that I'm still alive is a good sign. Right? What'll happen to me next?"

He shrugged. The message had told him he could leave her at the bar he'd planned to go to anyway, but he didn't feel right to simply drop her off somewhere for Marino to get his hands on her.

"You'll probably want to have a chat with your ex," he said and shook his head. "He'll want to make sure you're safe and hopefully assign you someone for protection and shit."

"You?" she asked and sounded a little hopeful.

His scowl deepened. "That's doubtful. Besides, I have

my own business to attend to. No offense, but I do have better things to do than…"

"Babysit?" she finished his sentence when the words trailed off. "Yes, I have ears, and some offense is taken. Still, it seems you would be the one to call for protection if he wanted to…you know, make sure."

Taylor pulled the four-by-four to a halt when he noticed the bar ahead of them. "I don't think your ex will pay for that."

"He's not the only one with money."

"I don't think you can afford me."

She opened her mouth to reply but finally shook her head. "Okay, fair enough."

"I'll stick around until his guys show up. You can go in and have a drink or something."

She nodded, climbed out of the car, and walked into the bar. While she probably didn't have money on her to buy any drinks, she didn't seem like the kind of woman who ever let a lack of finances stop her. Someone was bound to offer to buy her drinks for her or failing that, Marino's men would have to pay any tab she owed.

He remained parked in front of the bar and watched the people who walked in. There wasn't much turnover, and he wouldn't have to push in and start a fight unless something changed drastically.

It didn't feel right to simply leave her to Marino's whims and whatever he wanted from her but once again, it wasn't his business. If the mob boss wanted her hurt or dead, he wouldn't have bothered to drop so much money on the rescue. There were others who were much cheaper and more trustworthy who would have dealt with the situation with less tact than he had.

A short while later, a familiar-looking SUV drew up outside the bar and four men exited. Taylor stepped out of his car, ready in case there was any trouble. He still had his shotgun inside the door.

They weren't inside for long before they emerged with Genevieve in tow. She looked tired but a little more mellow after a couple of drinks. After a brief look at him, she slid through the door that was held open for her.

One of the men broke away and approached him. He held a briefcase in his hand, which he put on the ground beside him.

"Mr. Marino instructed me to thank you for your service," the man stated, his expression neutral. "And he looks forward to doing business with you again."

"Yeah, whatever," Taylor responded brusquely. "If it's not the full amount he promised in there, he can expect another call from me."

"Naturally."

The man turned and headed to the car. It had already been started and pulled away as soon as the door closed again.

Taylor folded his arms and regarded the mechanic with what he thought was exceptional patience. Bobby hadn't been happy about the damage done to the suit, of course, even if he understood that it had been a matter of life or death—someone else's life or death, not his. But it still meant more work on a suit he had barely finished working on. He couldn't say the man was wrong for being annoyed, although it still irritated him. Nor did it help that he shared his feelings a little.

Still, it had been a long week by this point and he sensed that they were all tired of dealing with big problems. It was best to handle the little ones and move on. They had a business to run after all.

Bungees moved over to where he sat and put a beer on the table next to him.

"How are you feeling?" the mechanic asked in a hushed tone.

He shrugged. "Dirty. Like I ate a sandwich someone rubbed in the mud beforehand."

"Good. Remember that feeling next time you're tempted to take money from that asshole. Speaking of which, what will you do with the money now you have it?"

Taylor shrugged. "Well, I assume it won't be dirty money but still, I think it's best to keep it away from banks. My thought is to make it a rainy-day fund, something to have tucked away if we ever need it. Which we don't for the moment, but still. Circumstances can change."

Bobby nodded. "You think we might need it when Marino doesn't want us around anymore."

He nodded and his attention had already drifted to the center of the shop. Most of the area had already been cleared, which left them an open space where Elisa, Tanya, and Vickie stood. Tanya helped Vickie pull on the various pieces of one of their functioning suits—one of those that were put together and were ready to be shipped out but only scheduled to be sent in a few days.

It was slow work and the kind of process that Taylor and Bobby had both been drilled in what felt like forever ago. The mechanic had taught Tanya in turn about the various pieces, what order to follow, and what to check before adding the different parts. It was a forgiving process, meant to be put on quickly and to deliver the least amount of problems that would develop if they didn't do it perfectly.

Still, there would be small problems if you didn't do it right, and Taylor did remember being told to get used to doing it right and knowing what the problem was if something did go wrong. Of course, back when he'd started using the suits, they were still being tested. The hardware was far less forgiving, which made the steps he took every time he assembled his suit more natural than they would have been for Tanya or even Bobby.

Watching Vickie move while the suit was still being assembled around her felt like something he would have instructed against, but he kept his mouth shut. Instead, he simply watched them learn and laugh along the way.

"You know, Vickie wanted me to roofie Genevieve and hand her over to Marino's men while she was still unconscious?"

Bobby chuckled darkly. "Yeah. I don't know what it is about that family, but they do appear to have a problem tendency to produce psychos."

Taylor couldn't help a small smile as he watched Vickie pull her helmet on and fully activate the whole suit. She moved a few steps to the right, then to the left, and looked at her arms. Every tiny movement she made was exaggerated and almost knocked her off-balance before the gyros kicked in and kept her on her feet.

"I think I'm getting the hang of this!" she shouted as she turned.

The movement was picked up by the rest of the powered functions, and as she struggled to regain her balance, the suit's legs continued to stumble until the gyros weren't able to keep pace. The hydraulics kicked in and drove it forward at full steam until it collided with one of the walls.

Both Taylor and Bobby pushed to their feet and hurried to where she tried to push against the floor to force herself up. Tanya joined them and all three of them worked to haul her to her feet.

"I think that's enough training for now," Bobby told her, turned the suit off, and began to pull her out of it. "Now you know how to get it on. Next time, we can work out how you can put it all to good use. How does that sound?"

Vickie nodded and looked a little pale as she climbed out. "Sure. That sounds good. I think it's enough for today."

Taylor grinned and ruffled her short hair as he turned to check on the dent she'd left in the wall. "It looks like your family, along with its propensity for psychos, has something against these suits too."

"Shut up," she grumbled. He grinned in response.

CHAPTER EIGHTEEN

"You'll have to talk to her."

Vickie scowled and narrowed her eyes at the screen. Taylor had checked to make sure she hadn't suffered any bumps or scrapes from her collision with the wall, and he said there was nothing wrong with her and that she would be fine.

The problem was, she didn't feel fine. Her stomach was a little unsettled and her head ached a little. He'd given her an ice pack to deal with it and she felt bad about needing help like that. The guy's leg was black and blue from where he'd been bitten by a damn alligator, but no, he walked around like he was fine.

Then again, he was kind of a badass. Not necessarily the kind with electronics like she was, but the physical kind.

"Did you hear me?" Desk asked through the comm line she had set up.

"Yes, yes, of course I heard you," she mumbled, shook her head, and moved her mouse pointer across a couple of windows to check on the systems she had set up. There were still many people out there who intended to do her harm, and there was nothing wrong with wanting to know if they ever came to Vegas. Thankfully, the FBI kept track of them too, which made it easy to know about their movements.

"What do you have to fear?" Desk asked and sounded genuinely interested. The hacker sometimes wondered if Jennie hadn't done too good a job designing the AI.

"You've met Niki, right?" she countered. "Honestly, I wouldn't put it past her to send me to the Zoo to teach me a lesson about what suits are made for."

"That is fair, I suppose," the AI conceded. "But you don't intend to talk to her about your mishap with the suit, do you?"

"I don't, but if Taylor tells her about it, she will definitely raise it with me."

"You've monitored his communications all day."

"Technically, you have. You're merely doing it for me."

"Exactly, and I can tell you he hasn't talked to your cousin yet, so there's no need to worry about Niki knowing what happened—not yet. I suppose this is the instance for one of those sayings...we'll cross that bridge when we get there?"

Vickie scowled. Much too good a job, she decided balefully. She would need to talk to Jennie about the coding that had gone into Desk.

"Right."

"Should I set a line up?"

She nodded, knowing the AI could see her through the cameras of the shop, which gave her a bird's eye view of everything. She wondered if it wouldn't have been a better idea to make sure Desk didn't tell Niki. But that was something to consider later when her head no longer ached.

"Vickie, is that you?"

She drew herself closer to the computer and pulled her headphones on. "Yeah, I'm here."

"Did you have the time to check those documents I sent you?"

"You didn't send me any—"

"I mean the location of where you could find the documents I wanted you to look at."

"Oh yeah, all that work," she mumbled under her breath. She didn't want it to seem like she was complaining since this was exactly the kind of work she had signed up for when she left all the customer relations to Elisa. "There's nothing on the surface to indicate that you would need to step in and do your thing. At least, nothing I can understand. I think you probably have some kind of egghead on call to help you if you need it, though, so if you want a second opinion, I've already sent all the data I collected to you for someone else to look at."

"That's some nice work, Vickie."

"Thanks, but I didn't do it alone. Desk offered to jump in and help me with the heavier tasks."

"Really? I didn't notice any jump in activity on our servers."

"I think she's still operating from the FBI servers too," Vickie explained. "They haven't removed her, so it gives her more operating space when she needs it. And when she doesn't, she finds more shit to do, apparently."

'Huh. I'll need to talk to Jennie about that."

She laughed. "It sounds like a good idea. While you're at it, you might want to ask your sister why the fuck this AI is so damn human."

"You two know I can hear you, right?" Desk asked.

"I had a feeling you would lurk around our conversation," Niki told her. "And I won't even mention your... extracurriculars. I'm merely happy that you're still looking after my family."

"That was what I was programmed for."

Niki drew a deep breath as the call came to an end. Jansen and Maxwell argued outside about where they would go for dinner and ordinarily, she would have been annoyed by their childish behavior, but not this time. She genuinely missed the times when the only concern she had on her mind was what she would have for her next meal.

They were there to support her and she was grateful for their help, but they did have the kind of mind that could put it all behind them for a little while. Compartmentalization, she thought it was called.

Maybe she needed that. And maybe a little time away from the job, assuming fires stopped popping up every five minutes all over the country. Maybe Speare would need a few more teams running from other locations to help out. She honestly didn't think she could do it all on her own. They wouldn't push her to the edge for nothing.

Still, she did have help, and not only Maxwell and Jansen. Taylor and his team were there for her, the people on the front lines while she was simply holding the back line for them.

She pulled up the documents Vickie had sent her. Sure enough, there wasn't much she could understand unless she suddenly acquired a Biology PhD overnight. Then again, she didn't have a mind for this kind of thing and it was time to call in the people who did.

Opening a comm line was easy, but she needed to be patient a while. Jacobs was an active fellow and not likely to wait at his computer for her to call him.

Still, all she could do was wait for him to respond.

Thankfully, she didn't have to linger all night. It wasn't long before the connection was made and an answer appeared on the comm line before it opened a video call with the man.

It looked like he was in a machine shop, which made sense. They did have to use and maintain their suits unless they were damaged to the point where they needed to be sent to someone like Taylor. She wondered if they used him for their repair needs. And if they didn't, maybe she should recommend his services—assuming he didn't already know.

"Uh-oh, girls. It seems Sal is looking around the market," said a snarky female voice from behind him.

"Shut it, Connie!" Jacobs shouted before he turned to the screen again. "Sorry about that. We have a somewhat troublesome AI."

"I know the feeling. Did you pick up the data packets I sent you?"

"Yeah, and I'm looking through them now. I don't want to say you're a little out of your depth, but—"

"Why the fuck else would I call you, right?"

He shrugged. "I would have said it was because you missed my winning charm but hey, if you want to hurt my feelings like that, I guess I had it coming."

Niki smirked as another figure entered the screen. The tall woman with the look of a fighter was decked out in combat gear. Her dark hair was cut a little shorter than she would have considered for herself but it still looked good. She muttered something to Jacobs that the agent couldn't hear before she leaned closer and placed an affectionate kiss on his lips.

"How did the other project go?" he asked and tilted his head.

"The interrogation didn't quite go as planned. We ended up shooting the fucking scientist."

"Damn it."

The woman nodded, realized there was much about this line of conversation that Niki wasn't aware of, and kissed him again before she left.

Jacobs looked like he was blushing a little when she moved away. "That…that was Madigan Kennedy, the heavy hitter of our team."

"A little more than that, it looks like."

"Well, that's our business, but yeah." He grinned cheekily before he returned his attention to the files she sent him. "Okay, this makes for intriguing reading. I'm always interested in what they do with all the goop we send to them. I'm kind of glad, in a way, that it doesn't all go to the youth serum companies."

"Why's that?"

"Well, personal experience tells me that exposing this to

biological matter will end badly for everyone involved," he explained. "I have, in fact, put considerable personal study into what kind of effect it has on the human body. While the effects weren't the same as what came with applying it to your average plant or animal, the effects were still present."

Niki wanted to ask him exactly what kind of tests he had done on humans since that was still mostly illegal. Well, maybe it wasn't illegal in the Zoo, but she had come to think he was better than the kind of person who would experiment on humans. Even the legal testing had literal miles of red tape to navigate, and there was no way to cut that without someone like her being involved.

Before she could say anything, another woman entered. She was shorter and leaner and lacked the warrior characteristics Kennedy had shown. Still, there was much of the fighter in her, even if the white lab coat she wore said she was in the same line of work that Jacobs was.

"Who's on the line?" the woman asked.

"Someone I'm consulting for," he replied. "Agent Niki Banks, working for the DOD in the US, killing Zoo monsters that have appeared there. Niki, this is Dr. Courtney Monroe, one of the leading specialists in the field of Cryptid Biology."

"I thought that was more your schtick," she responded.

"Sure, but there are many leading specialists like there are many areas to be a specialist in around here."

"Right," Courtney cut in and shook her head. Niki wondered if there wasn't more to the topic they had discussed previously that had left the woman a little exhausted at even the idea of talking about it. "Did you see what Madie did? She shot the fucking scientist."

"I know, but I have a feeling it was warranted," Jacobs replied, quick to defend Kennedy.

"Sure, whatever you say." Once again, Monroe sounded tired. She was likely already on her way to take time off but leaned closer and placed a kiss on his lips as well. "I'll see you inside?"

"Yeah."

Niki stared for a long moment. There was no way that was a cultural thing since all involved were American. And there was no way Jacobs was having an affair with both women on his team without either of them knowing about it.

"What?" he asked when he saw the expression on her face.

"Nothing...uh, I merely wondered if there's something in the water there that prevents people from having a normal relationship."

Jacobs shrugged. "It's complicated. When you live this close to this much destruction, things like civilized behavior are kind of thrown out the window."

"Yeah, McFadden already gave me that speech."

"In fairness, I have a feeling he would know better than almost anyone."

In an instant, Niki shared Monroe's unwillingness to discuss the topic further. "Anyway, about what I'm paying you for?"

He grinned and turned his attention to the documents again. Vickie had done a thorough job of taking as much as possible from what had been available, which meant that if there was anything to be found, he would probably pick it up.

"At first glance, this all looks fairly standard to me," he stated and rubbed his eyes gently before he leaned closer. "I'm looking at details of the micro-testing, which involves inert organic matter being subjected to under one milligram of the goop, all while keeping anything that comes in contact with it in complete and utter isolation. They can't even wash it. From the looks of what I see here, they've abided by those parameters."

"Well, if they were breaking the law or doing something dangerous, don't you think they would keep it hidden?"

"Honestly, the right kind of researcher would make sure that as many people as possible know about what's going on. That way, if something goes wrong, someone has already begun to find a way to address it. But you're right. These guys won't simply leave everything out there for anyone to see. I'll take some time, look through it all thoroughly, and get back to you if I find anything."

"Thanks," she said. "Once you're finished, be sure to send me your invoice. I wouldn't want folks at the front lines of this fight going without their proper pay."

"I run a business. Of course I'll charge for my services. Still, given the fact that if I miss something, people will die, I'll be sure to be extra careful."

Niki smiled. "I look forward to working with you again, Jacobs. Have a good one."

The line cut and she leaned back in her seat and rubbed her temples. Her mind should have been on the matter at hand, but she couldn't help but think about Taylor. She'd always thought he was unique in his viewpoints of the world and it had been his coping mechanism. The fact that it wasn't only him made her wonder. She thought of Jacobs now too, but more as a matter of perspective. Maybe they were both that way?

While the area wasn't particularly large, Taylor thought it could be enough if they were able to plan well. They wouldn't be able to work in a fair amount of the mall, which made it interesting to deal with. Vickie had been a little afraid of the suit after she had barreled into a wall, and he had a feeling Niki had probably felt the same. The way the agent had managed to achieve the right mindset to continue training was through a change of scenery.

He didn't think a training area out in the desert was a good idea. People tended to be a little anxious when large weapons of destruction were used in the open.

Still, it didn't mean they had insufficient space of their own. Most of the strip mall was untouched, and he had been forced to be a little more creative in his effort to find ways to fill the areas with little infrastructure. Maybe this was a viable option.

Footfalls approached and from the weight behind them, he could tell Bobby had come to check on him for some reason. There was far more the man could focus on.

"What are you doing here?" the mechanic asked when he reached him. "Besides exploring the unused areas of the building you own?"

Taylor pointed at the open room. "I don't know exactly, but I thought Vickie and Elisa probably need an open area to train that won't result in damage to our shop."

"Right. I talked to a couple of friends of mine about that. They said they can probably come in tomorrow and patch the dent Vickie left in the prefab for a good price."

One of the benefits of using cheap material was that it was cheap to fix too.

"I thought we could set up a little obstacle course here for them as part of the training to familiarize themselves with the movements they'll have to use if they are ever in a combat situation. It's all about practice, so if we get them moving without the worry that they might cause any damage, they'll soon adjust."

Bobby nodded. "I remember the course they set up for us when we trained in the suits. I hope you're not looking to buy that much barbed wire."

Taylor shook his head. "Some, sure, but mostly sandbags, barrels, and shit they can climb, punch, and move over."

"Where will you get all this from?"

"Well, we do have the cash from Marino on hand."

"I thought you wanted to save that for a rainy day."

"Well, I'd rather spend it on this than have to rack up the bills to repair the shop."

The other man nodded slowly in response. "Yeah, I guess. Do you think you can do it on your own or will you need help?"

"Honestly, I thought you guys could help me. All of you and especially Vickie and Elisa since they'll run through the gauntlet the most."

"It'll probably be a good idea for Tanya to go a couple of

rounds too," Bobby added. "Honestly, we could all use a bit of training to keep sharp. It could form part of your daily workouts. Or have you been at it twice a day? Don't think I haven't noticed that you've pushed yourself extra hard lately."

He scowled in response.

"What?" Bobby asked. "Do you expect me to not pay attention to what my friend is doing?"

CHAPTER NINETEEN

Marino wasn't used to situations like this. It wasn't that he didn't like waiting. Usually, he found something to do while he waited to make the passing of time a pleasurable experience. But in this case, he was so distracted by everything that was happening that finding someone to drink or fuck with simply wouldn't do anything to keep his mind occupied.

This was his first proper conflict since he had taken the business over. Too many people had decided he would do it badly, and while the start had been exactly how he had wanted it to go, he now waited for the results of the work of people who were a little less professional or effective than Taylor and his team had been.

No, he reminded himself. In reality, he had sent the same people who had failed against Taylor and his team to finish the work. Rod felt like his mistrust in them was warranted.

It wasn't long before his caporegimes began to file in. They had kept track of the attacks his men had conducted.

Most of them were outsiders, mercenaries who didn't have problems with loyalty and whose only concern was the number of zeroes on the checks they received.

All of it was intended to keep Marino and his group out and away from what was happening. If anything went wrong and the police proved to be a problem or anyone was captured, there were three or four levels of insulation that would have prevented them from even reaching the capos.

Still, it was the kind of thing he wasn't sure he would be able to handle until it occurred. He had been raised with stories about the wars fought in his father's time. These weren't the kind of wars people generally thought of and mainly comprised a handful of fights out in the open, a significant number of bullets, and very few deaths. Most of the deaths came from bombs left in cars and houses being burned down. As it turned out, many of the people who fell in with criminal families didn't have great aim.

Most of the capos were already in the building with him. Their reports were encouraging. There had been a few casualties here and there, but the consensus was that they were pushing the *Bratva* back. Of course, Vegas wouldn't be a battlefield like it had during his father's wars. The message was sent that his family was stronger than the Russian brotherhood, and they would have to live peacefully with them from here on out.

It was a matter of establishing boundaries and so far, it looked like every single one of the Russians was being pushed out of his territory. Those who remained would wake up to their stashes being raided by police who were in his pocket.

The idea had always been to keep them in check, not drive them out. Marino had learned all about manageable growth during his time in college, and there was no point in pushing them out of the city if he wasn't able to expand to fill the vacuum. If he didn't, someone else would and the chances were they would be worse and less predictable than the Russians.

Colombian cartels were what he feared the most. They tended to treat any city they entered like a battlefield as a matter of course. It was best to not give them any opportunity to spread into Vegas. They were already sinking their claws into Southern California.

"Mr. Marino?"

He looked up from his desk and to the door of his office. His secretary stood there and waited for his response. He couldn't recall her name, but she was a new one, a redhead who had been hired after the previous one moved to the position of secretary for one of the other CEOs. He didn't remember that one's name either.

"Yeah?"

She looked behind her. "They're all here. You asked me to tell you when they had all arrived. They're waiting for you in the conference room downstairs."

"Thanks..."

"Felicia."

"Thanks, Felicia. I'll be right down."

It was very likely he would forget the name before a couple of hours passed, but he assumed she was used to it. It was probably not the first she had reminded him of her name.

He only needed to make sure she was well-compensated.

Later, though, he thought irritably. He pushed out of his seat and walked to the elevator, adjusted his clothes as he stepped in, and descended to where his people were assembled.

A small but generous buffet had been set out for them, and they partook enthusiastically while they laughed and shouted at each other as they ate and drank.

Marino chose not to interrupt them. It was a victory celebration, for the most part, and he wouldn't stop them from enjoying it. Thankfully, they sensed his mood, raised their glasses, and called out greetings and salutations in Italian. They didn't expect any kind of victory speech from him. This had all started with the *Bratva* overstepping and ended with a message from him that made them regret their actions.

He moved into a closed-off section of the conference room, his phone in hand, and called a number he had used often over the past few days. He couldn't honestly say he disliked Taylor McFadden. On the contrary, there was something about the guy he liked. If nothing else, he always had an appreciation for his style, even if it put him at odds with the man more often than not.

And it was good that they were more or less on the same terms now.

"What?" Taylor answered and already sounded annoyed. "No—over there. You need all the sandbags in one place."

"Doing some construction work, are we?" Marino asked.

"Yeah, which means now isn't the best time."

He smiled. "I have the feeling you would feel that way any time I called."

"True enough. So, how can I help you?"

"I wanted to talk to you about the second part of your demands," he told him. "You consulted for me regarding the security of my ex-wife, and I think now it's time for you to test a couple of my men in their hand-to-hand fighting abilities. In a cage match, if you like."

"It sounds like you have something you want to say. Out with it."

"I have much I'd like to say, but first, a question. I've thought about your request and raised it with my people. While I haven't unfortunately had the time to discuss it further, the more I think about it, the more I realize I might be willing to include a closed-caption option in this. Something I would be willing to pay you for to the tune of...shall we say, fifty thousand dollars?"

"So...fifty large to film and transmit me beating a couple of your goons on a private network?"

Marino laughed softly. "Well, I do appreciate your confidence in this, but yes, something like that."

A fairly long pause followed before Taylor finally answered. "You have something up your sleeve, Rod."

"Of course I do. If my boys win, I have the bragging rights and no small personal satisfaction since you have cost me considerable money over the past couple of months. If you win, I still have bragging rights and people talk about how I know you and how you're involved with me. I'll deny it all, of course, but I don't think it'll do much to dissuade the minds of those who ask the questions.

Anyway, it doesn't matter. Let me know if it's something you're interested in."

Another pause dragged on a little, although Rod couldn't tell if it was because Taylor was considering his offer or if the man still issued instructions to whoever did the construction at his strip mall.

Finally, he answered. "What kind of odds will we be looking at?"

He smirked. "What makes you think there'll be bets involved in this?"

"This is Vegas, Marino. Everything here has betting involved."

"Fair enough. There will be a few bets made by choice characters but know that I'll run it cleanly and honestly. There's no real point to making anyone think I don't run an honest casino here, right?"

"Make sure that you leave time for me and my contacts to have a chance in the betting pool. There's no point in only letting your people make money on this, right?"

"Once again, fair enough. The only things allowed in the fight will be a cup and some spandex, tape with nothing on it, as well as the person and his skills. Agreed?"

"It sounds good to me. No hanky-panky or whoever does it will, I'm sure, regret the fuck out of it later. You come in with your knowledge, skills, and fortitude. The last person able to stand wins."

"Agreed." He laughed and shook his head. "I told you I would make all my money back on you, McFadden."

"As long as you bet on me, I'm sure you will. We'll set a date later. I have to train for a couple of weeks. You might want to give your guys a heads-up to do the same."

"I will. Be well, McFadden," Marino responded and smiled as the line clicked. Yes, there was something he liked about the man.

"Do I even want to know who that was?" Bobby asked as Taylor hung up.

"Probably not, but I think you already know and I'll talk to you about it later. We should rather talk about the possibility of picking up training suits. I think I saw some in the catalog. Those are a little easier to handle with far less power behind them, right?"

"They are still fairly expensive," Bobby told him and frowned as he thought about it. "Fifty grand apiece if I remember correctly, but I didn't look to hard and it was a while ago that I saw them. Honestly, I'm fairly sure it would be cheaper in the long run to pick up one of those new simulators. It's a much larger investment, sure, but in the end, it means fewer repairs and we can plug the specs of different suits in to make sure they're everything we'd need."

"I agree," Vickie called from where she used the forklift to carry the different obstacles around. "Besides, I'm already used to nicer suits, so if you think I'll drop back to what's like a Yugo when I already know how to drive, you're out of your damn mind. It's embarrassing."

"It's not about being in a Yugo when you already know how to drive," Taylor explained.

"And it's not like you know how to drive a mech properly either, anyway," Bobby added.

"It's about you have to fix it if you fuck it up," her boss continued. "I don't want you to have to learn on very complex mechs. Instead, you need to be able to screw it up, fix it up, and get out into the course. You and Elisa—"

"And Tanya," Bobby interjected.

"Wait, what?" Vickie asked and turned to look at them.

"Yeah, I agree." Tanya growled. "Wait, what?"

"Yeah." Bobby grunted and showed no signs of backing down. "You have some skill, there's no doubt, but in the end, everyone needs a foundation. You need to go back to the basics, solidify your foundation, and grow from there instead of picking up a host of bad habits."

Taylor nodded. "Well, fuck. I guess we need to create a two-week training program like we had in boot camp. That would be something for Niki's team to work through too, you know. It would make them understand in case they're in a bad position and need someone to do expedient fieldwork."

"That's a good point," Bobby conceded.

"Okay, I'll have a chat to Elisa and see if she can help me with the negotiations."

"Hey, why not me?" Vickie asked and fixed him with a challenging look. "Well, yeah, I was a bitch on the phone but not because I didn't have any other options available. I merely did it because it was fun."

The two men exchanged a quick look and Taylor shrugged.

"Nope," the mechanic said finally. "We don't buy it."

She smirked. "Assholes."

Both men chuckled in response.

Taylor shook his head. "Look, I'll talk to Elisa and we'll

decide how to get a set for you two, Niki, Maxwell, and Jansen, plus one for me and Bungees. That way, I can show you how to move in the field and he can show you how to fix shit using his busted version after he bites it on the course."

Bobby grinned. "Vickie's right. You are an asshole."

"I never claimed to be anything else." He chuckled and nudged one of the sandbags with his foot.

"I can talk to Elisa," the hacker suggested and looked beyond the group to the woman who still examined the course they were building. "Maybe between the two of us, we can get you supremely good prices."

"I know one thing," the former reporter called and walked over to them. "I'm not used to manual labor these days and I'm fairly sure I don't need to go to the gym for the next couple of days. I don't think I could at this point."

"I know the feeling," Vickie said and patted her on the shoulder. "Come on, let's sit and convince people to give us better prices until the end of the workday."

Both women made their way to the shop. Tanya still looked a little annoyed as she turned and moved away to keep working on the obstacle course.

Bobby sighed and lowered his head. " I wasn't wrong, was I?"

"You could have been a little gentler about it," Taylor told him. "Sure, she needs training, but calling her out like that in front of everyone?"

The mechanic nodded slowly. "Yeah, I guess so."

"Talk to her. Apologize and explain."

He didn't like the sound of it but he agreed and moved to help Tanya. Hopefully, he'd work things out. They would likely have a conversation he wouldn't be a part of and he was happy to stay out of it. Besides, he doubted they needed to make setting the course up a priority. He could give them their space and head in to get work done on the suits they had on hand.

He returned to the shop, where he could already hear Vickie and Elisa on the phones with their providers. If nothing else, he couldn't accuse them of lacking initiative.

His mind filled with the possibilities, he pulled one of the harnesses out and opened a panel to check what still needed repair.

CHAPTER TWENTY

Taylor patted the steel beams that had been put in place. It wasn't bad for less than a week's worth of work, he had to admit, even if he hadn't been involved in most of the effort himself. He'd done his part of putting the obstacle course together, but the people Bobby brought in to fix the wall had ended up remaining on-site for a little longer.

In the end, he had given them considerable work to reinforce and strengthen the outer structure of the course, as well as setting up a couple of the more complex obstacles to make it a little more settled and solid.

"Your guys did good work," he commented as Bobby approached. He was still in his workout clothes and felt the dull ache in his muscles. While he wasn't yet sure if it was cheaper to have his own training area, it was certainly much more peaceful and it allowed him to put in a couple of hours per day. His friend had rightly guessed that he had ramped his efforts up, although he did have more of a reason than simply trying to get back into the shape he'd been in before. He hadn't told anyone about the fight yet, and he wasn't sure if he would, but getting himself into fighting shape meant at least a few hours a day with the various punching bags he had bought, as well as time spent shadowboxing to improve his speed.

"Their boss was one of the engineers who helped to build the base," Bobby explained. "And many of his team worked with him there as well, so we can be certain that much of the work he's done will help with this kind of place. He would know how to set a prefab building up in a way that it would take a nuclear blast to make a dent."

"You're exaggerating."

"Only a little."

Taylor picked up the protein shake he had made a few seconds earlier and took a swig. He wasn't sure he liked this type of thing. The fact that he had to put weight on meant having almost seven meals a day. With three main meals and snacks and protein drinks between workouts, he could feel the difference. A return to form made him feel far more energetic. At times, he felt he almost twitched, ready for something to do, which thankfully didn't interfere with his work on the suits.

Still, he could feel increased power in his body, but something was missing. He felt he wasn't quite right for the fight he expected to participate in when Marino had time to schedule it.

"They changed up the ground too," Bobby continued. "Since we wouldn't always have a concrete floor to deal with, they set up turf patches, sandy areas over there, rocky surfaces at the back for our trainees to climb over, and wooden platforms for them to climb onto. It should make things a little interesting, I thought."

Taylor nodded. "It isn't quite the kind of place we trained with, but if we're honest, I think we could have done with being started in something like this. More of our comrades would have graduated."

He remembered many of their fellow trainees who had volunteered for the experimental weaponry and ended up with broken bones and pulled muscles from where the crude hydraulics had gone a little too far.

"Well," he continued, "it looks like the kind of course we were hoping for. Hell, we could probably market this area for the...what do you call them, the Free Fit crowd. You know, those who are all about obstacle course exercise?"

"Yeah, the guys who think that free running should be mixed with CrossFit exercises?" Bobby asked. He narrowed his eyes and shook his head. "I thought that was only an Internet fad."

"Well, we have a prime indoor location for them, so if we can get a couple of trainers to start using this, we'll be able to draw a crowd in for that. You know, until the fad goes away."

The mechanic shrugged. "Will you go in to work out again or have you finished?"

"It seems like I'm almost always between one or the other," Taylor grumbled and rolled his shoulders slowly. "But yeah, I finished a thirty-minute session. I should pick up another two hours once the workday is done."

"That sounds healthy."

He couldn't tell if he was being sarcastic or not and he

wasn't in the mood to ask. Instead, he took another sip of his protein shake.

"Seriously," Bobby continued. "Are you training for something? Pushing yourself more for some reason? Or is this making up for the fact that we haven't seen you go out drinking and come back with scratches all over you?"

That was difficult to answer, although the man was right. He had stopped going out for random liaisons at bars, but he didn't think it had much to do with his sudden fitness push.

"I'm not sure what you're talking about," he lied. "I simply feel the need to be a little more active, is all."

It was interesting to watch the two women working. Taylor had held Niki directly responsible for Vickie dropping into his lap, and since the hacker was to blame for bringing Elisa onto the team, it led to Niki being the cause too.

It probably wasn't something he would bring up with her at any point, but he was thankful for the assist. Their little business wouldn't have had the start it did without it.

Watching the two working together was interesting. It wasn't completely good cop, bad cop, but there was a hint of that involved in their process. Vickie did the research, called the places that sold the training suits, and compared the prices between different stores while she tried to persuade them to offer a better deal. Elisa did something similar, but while the hacker pressured for lower prices and kept herself on the offensive, her co-worker certainly preferred the honey approach. She killed with kindness and made sure the people that she talked to knew she really, really appreciated their help.

From time to time, they would switch between the sellers to keep them off-guard and not let them know what to expect. Taylor wasn't sure when it happened, but it looked like the two were now very used to working with each other. Maybe it was the last few days of shared focus that allowed them to form a more effective team.

It was interesting and a little terrifying to watch. He doubted he would have been able to resist the two of them driving him to buy or sell or anything else they wanted him to do.

Vickie turned away from her screen and snapped her fingers to catch his attention. "Okay, I think this is as low as we'll get their pricing. You know the catalog you were thinking of is as old as fuck, so they don't have any training suits for that price. Whatever. Between us, we've talked to managers and shit and the lowest we've persuaded them to go so far has been sixty grand. Well, fifty-eight, nine hundred and ninety-nine, but who's counting?"

"Apiece," Elisa added as an afterthought. "That would be if we buy in bulk, which would be a minimum of five pieces. Otherwise, it'll be twelve thousand more."

"And because we asked them very nicely," the hacker continued, "they wanted to up that number to ten—and even fifteen with that one guy, you remember? But I assumed you wouldn't want to pick up five extra suits we would simply have hanging around. I know Bobby could probably repurpose anything extra, but it would be a waste of money at this point, right?"

Taylor nodded slowly and she turned to the screen again. "I'll see if I can't push them for a little more. For now, I'm waiting on word from the Carena sales manager because they offer the same price but higher shipping than the guys at Real Steel. He's tried to get us to pull the trigger with him by offering extra repair parts. Again, it's not something I would normally be interested in, but training suits will also need repairs at some point. If not, we can probably repurpose them for one of our other repair jobs."

Taylor made a face but nodded again—a little quicker this time to let her know he thought it was a good call. He had mostly relied on her and Elisa to bring in what they needed, given that they were more than experienced enough in dealing with the suppliers and probably knew as much about the details of their purchases as he did. Although it wasn't likely they knew as much as Bobby did, they were still more than capable.

"Okay," Elisa called. "I've checked the pricing on the parts they'd send us, and they do have considerable cross-usage with the lines of product we deal with. They will potentially take five thousand off each purchase if we market them right. If we need them, that would be cut down to around two grand per suit since we do have an uptick from the factory prices."

"It sounds like a good deal to me," Vickie muttered and glanced at her boss. "What do you think? Should we pull the trigger on this?"

Taylor paused to think about it. Even the training suits were expensive, but they would be investments. When they no longer needed them for training, they could still be used for limited combat roles, and failing that, they could easily be stripped for parts to make roughly a third of what each suit was worth. That was assuming they couldn't push them to the military or one of the Zoo's merc groups that wanted cheap combat suits. In that case, they could easily sell them for a profit.

He nodded again, this time a little more assertively, and the hacker immediately picked her phone up. "Hi, Mr. Reeves. We'll place that order after all… Yes. The full repair package, plus the suits for five-eight-nine-nine-nine each, plus the shipping should total two-nine-four-nine-nine-five, plus two thousand for shipping, right? All right. Send us the invoice. It's a pleasure doing business with you."

She held her hand up for him to high-five when she ended the call. "You're already thinking about how you can get a tax write-off for these things, aren't you?"

"Of course. They are business-related expenses, some of which will go to training government employees, so you're damn right I'll milk the IRS for every penny I can get out of them." He liked how she seemed to have learned the way his mind worked—unlike most people, who tended to think of him as merely another buffoon with big muscles.

"Almost three hundred thousand isn't a number to scoff at," Elisa added, her head tilted in thought. "But still, I guess having that kind of an investment does mean we'll have more capital to work with in the future. If the pricing catalogs are anything to look at, these suits will only increase in value, right?"

"Demand has increased steadily and supply hasn't caught up, so the pricing increases too, but we can't rely on that to continue. Many market variables could drop the price." It was a warning and her face showed a hint of cognitive dissonance he was more accustomed to. "Anyway, nice work guys. You can take the rest of the day off if you feel like it."

"I might take you up on that," Elisa grumbled, stood, and stretched gracefully.

"I wish I could but I still have a ton of work to do for Niki," Vickie stated and cracked her knuckles. "What about you?"

"I have work to do on my end," he admitted, turned, and headed across the shop to help Bobby with the new suit arrivals that needed repairs.

"Look," Vickie started and sounded more than a little annoyed. "If Dr. Jacobs says everything's on the up and up, there's no reason to disbelieve him. That's why you pay the guy, right? And if you don't think he knows his stuff, you can always find someone else to do all this, can't you?"

Niki scowled and continued to stare at her screen. Her cousin was right, of course. She did have Jacobs on the payroll to advise her when she needed to act in a situation and, equally importantly, when there wasn't anything of concern, but she still felt something was wrong. Hell, it was entirely possible something hinky was happening but had nothing to do with their goop testing.

Maybe she simply saw ghosts at this point. The fact that there was nothing to look at in this particular company was a good thing, which left her a little annoyed by the sour taste it left in her mouth.

"Okay, so we'll move on to the next one, right?" Vickie

sounded invigorated by the work, at least, which was good to hear.

"Right. I also need to give Speare an update regarding our work so far. In the meantime, you can tell McFadden we'll slow down somewhat on the...digital surveillance you've conducted."

The hacker snorted. "Yeah, as if."

"You might be my cousin but I won't risk people discovering they've been hacked, for lack of a better word, and asking questions, especially if I spend money all the way through."

"You make it sound like I'm an amateur who gets caught."

"Even you make mistakes, Vickie, so don't get arrogant about it. If we don't hear anything in the next fourteen days, I'll find you another target. Does that sound fair? I've sent considerable work over the past few weeks too, so it's not like you'll be strapped for cash."

"Fine. You're still a real bitch, though."

"Is that better than being a fake bitch?"

"Marginally."

"Well, I've been called a bitch before so there's nothing new about that. If I don't hear it by lunch, I try twice as hard. Still, thanks for the help. I'll send the documents you gave me to Jacobs and I'll let you know if it leads to anything."

"Later, cuz."

Vickie hung up and Niki immediately dialed the international number she had used more than usual over the past few days. Sooner was better than later in these kinds of situations, and if they had something developing that needed her attention, she wanted to be on top of it as quickly as possible.

Jacobs didn't reply immediately, and the line remained open for almost five minutes before the call connected.

When a face appeared on the video call, Niki narrowed her eyes at the sight of someone who wasn't the scientist. She did remember the woman, though, from the last call… the doctor. Unfortunately, she couldn't immediately recall her name.

"Hello again—Agent Banks, right?" the woman asked and flipped a few strands of blonde hair from her face.

"That's right. And you're…Dr. Monroe. I'm sorry, I'm not great with names."

The doctor laughed. "I'm the same way, but yes, Dr. Monroe is right, although you can call me Courtney. Did you want to talk to Sal?"

"I have a little more work for him. Although there probably won't be any more coming over the next fourteen days or so, I thought we should have this wrapped up as quickly as possible. You know how short a time it takes for these cryptid situations to deteriorate."

"I do indeed. Sal isn't at the compound, though, so if you like, I could accept the files in his name."

Niki's lips settled into a slight scowl. "I don't mean this as any kind of statement of distrust in you—you are on Jacobs' team and we've done our research, which does make you trustworthy in my book—but the NDA I have is with Jacobs."

"Oh, that's no problem. I can work up another one for you. Give me a second." Courtney looked at another screen and a few seconds later, the agent received the necessary paperwork. This time, however, it was in the name of the two companies—Heavy Metal and Pegasus—which made it all look official enough to sell to Speare if the guy had any reservations.

"Fine, but if you could ask Jacobs to message me when he has looked at the data, I would feel much better about it." Niki knew she sounded a little short but her innate distrust wasn't something she could simply turn off. She signed all the paperwork electronically and sent it, along with the data.

"If it'll make you feel better, I'll oblige, of course," Monroe replied with a trace of a smile.

"I appreciate it."

CHAPTER TWENTY-ONE

I t was great to have someone to spot him. He didn't rely on it, though, and most of the time, he didn't do exercises that required it anyway. Still, extra work that came from free weights was sometimes required, and in those cases, it was always better to have a spotter. There had been situations where people had been pinned under weights they were too tired to lift and they'd left a cautionary impression on his mind.

Bobby was getting his daily workout in as well, which allowed him to rest for a few minutes while his boss was on the bench and pressed as much weight as he could manage. After three reps, he could already feel his chest muscles burning, and he had a few doubts that he would be able to manage the full seven his set required.

He was right. He lagged at around five and needed help with the sixth and the seventh, which he completed by slipping the bar into its hooks. If he didn't have the mechanic around, he usually went with lighter weights, but having a spotter allowed him to push himself harder than before.

After a few seconds, he caught his breath, pushed up, and looked at the machine where Bobby now did his set.

"Do you think you might be pushing yourself a little too hard, Tay-Tay?" his friend asked, a little out of breath as his routine included more reps with lighter weights. "I'm all for pushing the limits, but you don't aspire to a weight-lifting record or anything, right? You know you don't have to get everything back by next week."

Taylor scowled at the use of the nickname he intensely disliked but shook his head. "I remember when I could push that much weight without help. I'm getting myself back to my best, is all, and hopefully better."

The man remained silent until his set finished, leaned on his knees for a few seconds, and breathed deeply while he wiped the sweat from his forehead. "Do you know what the best part about being your closest friend is, Taylor?"

"What?"

"Knowing when you're full of shit and having the absolute pleasure of calling you on it. This is one of those occasions. I've seen people work themselves like this, and it was always because they were preparing for something."

He nodded and appreciated the fact that having friends meant they thought it was their job to call him on his bullshit. "Fair enough."

"You've worked the bags much more lately, but I'm sure you know they have a tendency to not hit back. So if you need someone to kick your ass in the sparring ring, all you have to do is ask."

"Would you say yes if I did ask?"

Bobby shrugged. "I might if you told me what you're pushing yourself to."

"You'd need more protective gear, though."

"I'm aware. I've sparred with you before, remember? But you have to come clean with me, man. What has you like this?"

Taylor sighed deeply and delayed his reply with a sip of water and wiped the sweat from his face. "Do you remember those two guys who came here to try to intimidate you while they were looking for me?"

"Sure. What about them?"

"One of my requirements for helping Marino with his ex was to have a one-on-two session with those assholes. The no-holds-barred kind of session."

"Fucking hell, Taylor. You know they will try to kill you, right? You don't have to pull shit like this, especially not for me."

"It wasn't entirely for you. There's also the fact that they came to my business and tried to act like they owned the place. A lesson needs to be learned, and I need to be able to teach it."

"So what—you'll meet up with these assholes in a back alley and knock them around?"

"That's the thing. Marino had conditions of his own. It looks like he'll try to make it like a proper fight—you know, with a ring, a few rules, and there'll even be betting going on. He dropped me an extra fifty thousand for the effort."

"So these guys will know you're coming, will meet you in a ring, and you'll fight two of them at the same time?"

Taylor nodded. "I know they can bring it. They've been

fighters their whole lives, so it's not like it's something new for them. Still, I need to know that I'm able to stop myself from going too far and I think you'd be able to help me with that. It's the kind of situation where I'll need to get myself into the mindset I know I'm capable of from my time in the Zoo. But at the same time, I don't want to step in there and kill them, you know?"

The mechanic took a swig from his water bottle before he answered. "So you want to be able to get into the mood to beat two guys within an inch of their lives but leave them alive."

"I have a feeling Marino won't be a fan of me killing two of his heavies on a live network transmission."

"And we care about what he thinks…why, again?"

He opened his mouth to reply but shut it again quickly. "Okay, fair enough, but I still don't want to kill them. I only want to make sure they know that fucking around with me and mine is a bad idea, that's all."

Bobby wiped the sweat from his face and thought about it for a few seconds before he finally nodded. "Okay, I get it. I'm in, I'll order some of the safety stuff they use for sparring. Failing that, I can probably work up some of my own by day after tomorrow. I'm curious about how you'll hide it, is all."

Taylor narrowed his eyes. "Hide what now?"

His friend laughed from deep inside his chest and started another set on the machine. "You haven't thought this through, have you?"

"I think we've already established that. Hide what?"

"I've seen you in that 'zone' before." Bobby's hands were busy but the quotes were implied by his tone. "I'm sure

Tanya will be all for you delivering pain to a couple of Marino's goons, and so will the rest of our team. Hell, Elisa will probably be more excited by it than any of us, but the fact remains that none of them have seen that side of you before. Hell, I'm one of the few people who made it out of the Zoo after seeing you in that state of mind during those battles. They won't know what the hell is going on. And I'll guarantee you that if Vickie sees it, she'll have a problem with it, and she sees you like a surrogate father figure. And you know that'll only lead to...you know..."

It took a moment for him to realize what the man was talking about. "She'll tell Niki, who'll be all up in my ass with questions about it. Hell, the woman probably already thinks I have issues."

"Exactly."

"Well, it's a part of me—and not one I'm particularly ashamed of either since it's the reason why I'm here and not fertilizing a tree in the form of mutant crap in the Zoo. In this case, I'm fairly sure it's better to ask for forgiveness than permission, especially if it's something they won't understand."

"I guess I can agree with that." Bobby didn't look particularly convinced but Taylor had a feeling the man wouldn't argue it any further. He had made some good points, after all.

"Okay, I'll find a place for us to train in," he stated finally, stood from the bench, and helped his friend up when he finished his set. "I can't promise it'll be some land of milk and honey, but it'll have a ring and probably a first aid kit if either of us needs it."

The mechanic smirked. "Well, we'll see. I have a feeling

you don't want to beat me half to death, so I expect you to pull up much quicker than you will when you pair off against Marino's dumbasses."

He nodded. "That seems fair."

"So, when's the fight?"

"It'll be a few weeks before we set a date, and I think maybe another two weeks after that. All in all, probably sometime next month at the earliest."

"Okay." His friend picked up two more ten-pound weights. "Now, get back on the bench and don't be a pussy. You'll need more weight."

He grinned and made no protest as he returned to the bench.

This wasn't the kind of work he had expected to do out in the Zoo.

Then again, he enjoyed it. It felt much closer to what he'd thought he would do when he first started on his bachelor's degree.

Still, Sal did feel like he was abandoning his other work to do this. While he made good money, leaving all the hard labor to Madigan would end up with him being yelled at sooner rather than later.

It didn't help that Courtney was a fan of this kind of work too. She had signed off on receiving it from Banks, and while he appreciated the help, it meant fewer bodies out there with Kennedy. The woman would be pissed about it.

"Fucking hell," he grumbled, rubbed his eyes, and

stretched while still in his office chair. He had focused for a while and felt he needed a break. Maybe it was time to head out with Kennedy, collect samples from the jungle, and return with a fresh mind.

The painstaking process of examining someone else's work in search of inconsistencies and illegalities was the kind of thing he could be utterly absorbed in for hours. It wasn't surprising to suddenly need a break from it.

Niki had sent the team considerable work, though, and he liked to help to keep the home front safe. He might want to return there one day, aside from the simple fact that it was a no-brainer to stop the Zoo wherever it raised its ugly alien head.

He turned when someone knocked gently at the door before they pushed it open. It wasn't that he prevented people from entering his room, but there had been a couple of talks about knocking first, especially because there were times when privacy was essential.

Courtney poked her head around the door and followed it quickly with the rest of her body. She stepped inside with a couple of steaming cups of coffee in hand. "I thought you might need a pick-me-up. The coffee's crap but it's better than running out of gas. I think so, anyway."

Sal shrugged and gestured for her to come closer.

She placed a light kiss on his cheek before she set a mug on his desk. "Did you see the notes I left for you?"

"Yeah. I'm not sure Niki would appreciate anyone but me looking at these documents, though."

"Right, but what she doesn't know won't hurt her, at least in this case. Anyway, I noted that...right there, yeah... they've imported far more goop than they've used in the lab. I checked the public paperwork they have on record, and they don't have any licenses to sell it in any form. Niki did say she wanted you to look for anything suspicious and that seems..."

He nodded and scratched his chin, surprised that he had missed the detail. "Yeah, I have to agree that it qualifies."

"And she thinks these things should be resolved sooner rather than later so..."

"Okay, fine." He scowled and moved his hand away from her. "I'll call her. Do you want to be in on it? You guys are so chummy now, on a first name basis and everything."

"I don't think she'll like that. She's used to dealing with you and I could tell she was uncomfortable when I answered."

"Why did you answer ?"

"Because I was searching your room for interesting shit and the ringing was annoying. Stop stalling."

Sal rolled his eyes and dialed the agent's number.

CHAPTER TWENTY-TWO

Niki could acknowledge a hint of satisfaction when she walked away from a job well-done.

There was something to be said for her kind of work. She liked being on top of things and to push the limits and make the rich, CEO-types she generally had to deal with put themselves into a situation where they needed to help her or deal with the consequences.

Which was why she didn't have the same feeling when she worked the jobs that didn't require her to play the character she was starting to get known for. Still, a part of her responsibilities was merely checking the facilities that didn't have anything wrong with them. Smiling project leaders gave her the full tour, incredibly excited about the work they were doing. And since it was at the cutting edge of the field, why wouldn't they be excited?

She wouldn't rain on their parade. They were good workers and solid people who loved to do what they did. She didn't have it in her to make them feel bad about it.

Being in Florida again took her mind back to one of the

first jobs she'd run with Taylor. It was odd that her thoughts constantly returned there for the smallest of reasons.

"You look disappointed," Jansen pointed out as they pulled into the hangar where their plane was parked. "Like you hoped there would be something for you to deal with."

Niki shrugged and glanced at Maxwell, who studied her through the rearview mirror. "I guess...something about getting on the nerves of the masters of the universe is always nice, but don't think I'll be sad if nothing is wrong with one of these labs. You can rest assured that I prefer one of these visits to the facilities where we need to gun a horde of cryptids down."

The smaller of the two men seated in the front of the SUV nodded slowly. "I guess that's fair. But it's still funny to see you a little frustrated. It's like you had hyped yourself up to tear them down and had to hold yourself back when you got there."

She couldn't deny that because she wasn't naturally the kind of bitch people thought she was. It took a little work and build-up to put herself into that mindset.

There wasn't much else to be said, and the silence was pleasant until her phone buzzed as they eased to a stop in the hangar.

While she had chosen this work, the fact that she always needed to be available if her people needed her was getting old fast.

And if it was Jacobs, it took priority.

"Fuck," she muttered before she pressed the button to accept the call. "It's nice to hear from you again, Dr. Jacobs...and Dr. Monroe."

"You can call me Courtney," the woman on the other side of the line answered. "And you can call him Sal too."

"I prefer to be called Dr. Jacobs," he grumbled. "I put considerable work into earning that title, you know."

"Sure, whatever." She interrupted their admittedly cute banter without apology. "Was there something you needed me for?"

"Right," the man said and turned to find something before he faced the screen again. "Most of what you sent us appeared to be legitimate and above-board, but a deeper search revealed a little something you should know about. They've imported a large quantity of the goop for their lab work."

"Sure, but that's what they're licensed for," Niki countered. "There's nothing surprising about that, right?"

"True, but the testing they have the paperwork for doesn't account for the amount of goop they've imported. It's expensive, so I doubt they'll throw the excess out, and the fact that they continuously import the same amount tells me they're using it all."

Niki stared at the screen for a moment and rubbed her eyes. "Maybe they send the excess to another location that isn't on the books. A black site? Does that even apply to labs? A black lab?"

"It sounds more like a dog," Courtney commented. "But yeah, something like that. Labs with government contracts tend to have secondary facilities they keep off the books. Usually, the Pentagon doesn't care and turns a blind eye since it gives them the results they want as well as plausible deniability if any of it is discovered."

"Except that in this case, it's our job to dig these places

up to make sure they don't put cryptids out in the world for my team to deal with." Niki scowled and shook her head. These people needed to stop tripping over their shady practices in these kinds of cases.

"Oh, yeah…Sal mentioned that you've been working with McFadden," Courtney commented. "How is the Giant Leprechaun?"

She snorted. "The…what?"

"That was his nickname when he was still here," Sal added. "Did he neglect to mention that?"

"He most certainly did." She laughed. "Although I think I'll rectify that. Later, though."

"Okay." He looked at another screen before he returned his attention to her. "Given the state in which they ordered the goop, you'll need to look for a facility that's within a three-hundred-mile radius of the original lab. That's about as far as a helicopter can go while transporting it in that state. It would be closer to one hundred miles if they transport it by car. I'm not sure if you have someone on your team who can look into their transport logs, but if you don't, I have someone with that particular set of skills."

Niki smirked. "Thanks, but I do have a member on my team who has that covered. Thanks for your help, Courtney, Dr. Jacobs. Be sure to send me your invoice."

"Will do," he said.

Courtney waved. "Stay safe!"

The line cut and she shook her head. Staying safe wasn't an option in her line of work.

Still, it was something to keep in mind. A girl could dream. She turned her attention to the two men in the front of the car. "You guys listened in, I take it?"

"Obviously," Jansen answered.

"We need a location on that black site, pronto. If they're willing to hide the location, they'll hide what they're doing and that's usually where we get involved."

"Will do, boss."

She dialed quickly into the line she had open continuously with Desk. "I guess you already know what I'm going to ask for."

"Naturally," the AI stated. "I'm already digging into the transport logs available for the lab in question. Do you want me to include Vickie on the search?"

"Only if you run into a dead-end," she replied with a small frown. "I told her I'd give her a couple of weeks off in case someone comes looking for her. She still needs to keep a low profile."

"Of course. I'll contact you once I find something. Should I worry about the legality of the work we're doing?"

Niki shook her head. "Fuck the legality. The point of this task force is to fight fire with fire, and if these guys want to cover their illegal actions with red tape, I want them to know we're the scissors that cut through it all."

"An apt metaphor."

The lack of privacy in her life was also something she needed to work on. Later, of course, along with everything else.

"Mr. Kellogg?" a voice said through the intercom.

He looked up from the file on his desk and pressed the button to contact his secretary. "Yes, Janine?"

"Congressman Underhill is on the line for you. He says he's returning your call."

"Oh, yes, put him through, Janine. Thank you."

"One moment please."

The woman was a true treasure. He had encountered his fair share of secretaries who thought their job was limited to looking good and nothing else. His wife had raised the issue with him regularly until he found the older, more professional-looking Janine. She knew how to do her job, and not only in the professional sense. More importantly, she could make a lie up on a dime without so much as a moment's thought, which gave him the kind of freedom to act without having his wife and partners digging into his personal life.

Truly, she was a real treasure in this day and age.

"Clint, thanks for getting back to me," Kellogg said and rocked back in his office chair.

"Of course. I'll always find time for you. How can I help you, Brendan?"

"Well, I wanted to talk to you about the email you sent me." He pulled up the files he'd received. "Something to do with people at the DOD inspecting one of my labs?"

"I thought you wouldn't want anyone to arrive at one of your facilities without you knowing what was going on."

"Given that was the reason I put your name up for the House Appropriations committee, yes. I have a couple more people in position to help me if you didn't warn me, though. Now, I didn't know there would be inspections on my locations."

"Well, the contracts we've sent out do stipulate that we are allowed to conduct random inspections."

"That's for everyone but us. We're supposed to be allowed to work without DOD overreach. How the hell else can we be expected to work on the bleeding edge of our field if we have a horde of worried and trigger-happy idiots running through the labs and preventing everything from staying on schedule?"

"Well, I don't know—"

"Give me seventy-two hours and it'll be rosy. Until then, I suggest you find out or I'll find myself someone who does know something!" Kellogg roared before he slammed the phone down. It was an older unit, much sturdier than most phones on the market these days.

"I'll have to see what I can do," he muttered belligerently.

Still, that wasn't the only work he had to do for the day. Too many people had trouble with the new taskforce the DOD now sent to investigate their contractors, but he had thought his people would be immune from that kind of interference. And even if they were inspected, there was supposed to be enough warning to make sure the visitors didn't find anything.

He picked the phone up again. "Janine, I need a secure line, please."

"Of course, Mr. Kellogg."

A few seconds ticked past as a secure line was set up by the building AI, and he quickly transferred a number to it.

"Mr. Kellogg?"

"This is a secure line, don't worry. We need to activate Oblivion a little sooner than expected. You have forty-eight hours to move as much as you can, and we'll get rid of the rest. I want nothing but a hole in the ground when we're finished."

"Do you want a full evacuation beforehand, sir?"

"No, we'll need a few skeletons in situ to make it believable as an accident. I want Krieg to make it out but choose two or three of them you can't stand and make sure they don't escape. We all have to sacrifice to get to the next level. Unfortunately for them, they don't have a say in who will sacrifice what, and I don't believe the DOD will find out where it is for at least a week. That leaves us more than enough time to have insurance in there conducting their inspections, which will show that we have nothing to hide."

"Will do, sir."

He put the phone down, less forcefully than last time. Still, this wasn't the worst that could have happened. They had Oblivion in place for exactly this type of eventuality, which meant that it was bound to happen at some point.

His expression hard, he opened the bottom drawer of his desk and removed a bottle of scotch and a glass. While he had a wet bar on the other side of the office, it was where his guests generally got their drinks from. This bottle had been in a cask for almost fifty years and it was only for special occasions. He poured a couple of fingers' worth into the glass and inhaled the rich, oaky scent.

"Is there anything else for the day, sir?" Janine asked through the intercom.

"No, you go ahead and take the rest of the day off."

"Yes, Mr. Kellogg."

Niki had thought her time of sitting around and surveilling random locations and buildings were at an end when she joined the DOD. Most of the legwork and tracking had already been done when a case finally landed on her desk, which left her the responsibility to act on their hard work.

In all honesty, the absence of the need for her to be involved at that level was the best part of the DOD gig, but she had known in the back of her mind that she would have to do it again eventually.

"It's nice of your cousin to help us with this one," Jansen noted as she stretched in the back of the SUV. "I kind of wish she could have told us exactly what we are looking for as well as where."

"Vickie wasn't able to help us this time around," she corrected him. "But in this case, all we needed to find out was where the location was so we can determine if they are doing something illegal. It's not like we can charge in and accuse them. Like Monroe said, this is common among these military contractors. It's very likely they are doing something illegal but it might not be something that warrants our involvement. We're an anti-cryptid task force. If we want people to be punished for simple illegalities, we need to call the FBI."

Maxwell smirked, took a bite from his sandwich, and shook his head. "I guess we'll have to open an avenue of communication with the FBI to see if we can send them to take care of what we can't."

Niki nodded. She had thought the same, although things were still a little tense between her and her ex-boss, which provided few avenues for conversation.

"There's movement at the eastern entrance." Jansen's

alert ended the conversation, and she called up the binoculars on her phone and focused on a group of men who moved out of the side of the building.

Unlike most of the sites they had visited, no walls were in place around the building, although high-tension electric fences were evident around the edges of the property. It seemed significant that they were the kind that was set to lethal.

The men involved weren't the type who looked like they worked in a lab. She could make out assault rifles carried on slings over their shoulders.

"What are they carrying out?" she asked, but neither of her teammates appeared to have an answer for her.

She frowned and zoomed in a little. The group carried crates, smaller than those Taylor usually used for his suits but not by much. She wasn't sure why they would move military hardware out of the facility. Maybe Desk had left a trace behind that warned them about what was happening. It was possible, of course, but there was a more likely explanation. A lab dealing with military contracts merely moved military crates in and out of their locations on a regular basis as a matter of course.

"I can't make out what's written on them," Jansen grumbled and shook his head. "I do know those crates, though. They are usually used to transport powered armor suits."

Niki scowled and looked at him. "That was my first thought as well, but the crates Taylor uses are bigger."

"Sure, but the ones still used in the Zoo are last year's models," he commented. "They are bigger, bulkier, and come in larger pieces. They've managed to make them smaller, which means they are stored more efficiently. I think the newer ones would be worked into what will be sent to the Zoo in the next few months, although I have heard of some of the suits being sent there already. They are being tested with new AI functions to help the pilot."

Her scowl deepened. If Taylor ever got his hands on one of those, she had no doubt Desk would want to be the AI that helped him. She was already a little annoyed that he had chosen one of the basic software models in his truck.

"Wait, hold on." She leaned forward and narrowed her eyes in an attempt to see the men better. They didn't carry anything else out of the lab and from the looks of it, they now opened the crates.

"Definitely combat armor suits," Jansen mumbled.

She nodded. "And they're putting them on." She pulled her phone back and dialed hastily.

"Who are you calling?" Jansen asked.

"Speare. He'll want to know about what's happening here."

CHAPTER TWENTY-THREE

The venue was already closed, despite the fact that it was in the middle of the afternoon. Taylor didn't know what to make of that. He had spoken to the owner about a private place to practice and promised to compensate him accordingly for the privilege.

"Did you ask him to close everything?" Bobby asked as they parked the four-by-four in the lot in front.

"No, I only asked for a private area for training."

"In a smaller venue like this, I don't think there would be any private sections."

He tilted his head in thought and realized that he should have thought of it. The venue was too small to have any places to train where they wouldn't be seen. The owner had clearly understood his request to mean clearing the whole building for only the two of them. Maybe it was for the best.

"I guess we'd better get to work." He shrugged and rubbed his forearms. He wasn't sure why he did that, but it was a common action when he was psyching himself up for a particularly exhaustive workout. Still, it wasn't something he thought about and he hadn't noticed that he did it until now.

The owner was there to open the door for them as they arrived. He wasn't too tall, but his dark skin gleamed over powerful muscles, the kind usually seen in boxing rings. Although he was bald, a thin and wispy goatee grew around his chin.

"Don't stand out there with your jaws slack," he rattled in a raspy voice that spoke of a few too many cigarettes. "I've been told you boys want to do some training, and there ain't no better place in the world to do it than here."

"This is my friend Bobby Zhang." Taylor gestured for Bobby to step forward. "We call him Bungees sometimes."

"Pleasure to meet you, Bungees." The older man grasped the mechanic's outstretched hand. "I'm Leonard Riddell, the proprietor of this here establishment."

"You've done boxing in the past?" Bobby asked as they stepped inside the building. It smelled of stale sweat and hard work, which made it the best place to get hard work of their own done, in Taylor's opinion.

"It's been a while, but yeah." Leonard grunted. "Back in '23, I was NBC's heavyweight champion and got a couple of title defenses. One of them even happened at the MGM. That purse was enough for me to buy this business, although I did have a couple more fights. I retired with a twenty-six to seven record in the end and thought I'd taken enough beatings."

"It sounds like you doled out more than you took."

"Oh, don't get me wrong, I still throw a mean right hook but as it turns out, so did many of the other fighters.

In the end, I was getting older and the younger fighters were getting faster and could hit as hard. You finally reach a time where you get yourself into a situation where you have to choose to take a beating in the hopes of landing a good hit that'll knock them down. I decided I'd had enough after three losses and two wins."

Taylor could understand that. There would come a time when he wouldn't be able to keep up with the brand-new and improved cryptids and he would have to make a decision as to whether he would continue to try or turn it over to someone younger and better.

He'd always assumed he would be long dead before that decision needed to be made, though.

The three approached the boxing ring. He wrapped his hands before he pulled on a couple of lighter mixed-martial-arts gloves. Bobby wore similar gear, although more of it, including a helmet, body padding, and protection for his shins and forearms, just in case.

"Damn, son!" Leonard smirked, pulled a section of tape, and used it to plug a couple of holes on an older punching bag. "Are you looking to spar with a grizzly?"

"Almost," the mechanic replied as he moved and feinted to adjust to the extra padding.

"Come on. I admit he has some muscle on him." The proprietor pointed at Taylor, who was already warming up with shadowboxing in front of one of the bags. "He's well-built but you're even bigger. What'll he do? Hulk out? He don't even look like Bruce Banner. Maybe Aquaman if he had red hair."

"No, not Aquaman," Bobby countered. "I think more along the lines of Mad Sweeney, but angrier."

"Hilarious," Taylor muttered before he put a mouth-guard in. "Will you ladies keep doing each other's hair, or will we do this?"

His words were a little muffled behind the guard but his teammate began to warm up too. He stepped in front of a punching bag, threw a couple of punches, kept his guard up, and circled. Leonard shook his head.

"What?"

"Well, I guess you boys aren't having a boxing match, so your footwork isn't as important," the man offered by way of an answer.

"It's not that it's less important." Bobby could still talk while he warmed up as he hadn't put his mouthpiece in yet. "Only that the focus is shifted. In a bout where kicking is allowed, you have to be able to use your feet for attack as well as defense. The strategy changes. You're less mobile but in exchange, you have better range. Observe."

The mechanic took a step back and threw a couple of lunging punches, all of which missed the bag due to the increased range. After another step, he leaned his body back a little and threw a couple of high kicks and one low before he settled into a traditional Muay-Thai stance.

"I didn't say nothing against it." Leonard folded his arms. "But you would be picked apart by a boxer, is all."

"In a boxing match, I probably would," Bobby agreed. "But if you put a boxer in a ring with a kick-boxer in a no-holds-barred match, things change."

"So you know a thing or two about it?"

"My parents got me kick-boxing lessons when I was a kid and the military built on that for a while. I've continued to train since then too."

Taylor had warmed up enough and climbed into the boxing ring, rolled his shoulders, and kept himself warm throwing punches and kicks into empty air.

"I still think it'll be a fair fight," the ex-boxer grumbled. "There's no need for all that gear."

"Honestly, he needs to train hard so there won't be anything but me trying to beat the shit out of him and trying not to die."

"You're fucking shitting me."

"Nope. Call it when it's obvious that one of us is out of the fight. Although if it's him, don't ring the bell until he stops moving."

Leonard shrugged. "Five grand is five grand. Let's get this party started."

Bobby climbed into the ring and put his mouthguard in, and both he and Taylor took position in opposite corners. The proprietor picked up the little bronze hammer he kept for these kinds of occasions and tapped the old-fashioned bell at the side of the ring.

His eyes widened immediately. "What the fuck—"

Speare didn't keep her waiting before he responded to her message. It wasn't all that late, but Niki assumed the man's job description also included something that required him to always be available if he was needed. His job was to be constantly prepared to act on any sensitive issue, and she was willing to bet people wanted to talk to him all day and every day.

His secretary told her she would locate him and sure

enough, five minutes later, Niki's phone rang with a call from Spear's line.

"You wanted to speak to me, Banks?" the man asked as soon as she accepted the call.

"It looks like there's another team out here." She cut straight to the chase and made no effort to play politics with the man. "They appear to have power armor and from what we can see from our vantage point, it was stored within the facility we've had under surveillance. This leads me to believe that they are contracted to the company but also raises a shit-ton of concerns. If they need professionals in suits, you can bet your ass what they're doing is not above board. I'm not sure if I should send my team to deal with it."

"If my reports on your current position are correct, I can inform you that you'll soon intersect with a team that also has access to mechanized suits—one I've created myself. I am very confident in the abilities of the people led by Mr. McFadden, but as I cannot expect him to be constantly at your beck and call, I took the liberty of bringing a few of my people together to support you if needed. If it makes you feel any better, it is composed entirely of the people you brought out of the Zoo to be a part of your FBI task force."

"I...huh. Really?"

"Really. It should save considerable time if I put you in contact with them and task them to do whatever you need from them."

Niki nodded and saw the impressed looks on the faces of the two men in the SUV with her. "Why don't you go ahead and give me their number?"

Bobby had seen Taylor fight in the past. He'd even told himself he was capable of fending the guy off in a fair fight on occasion, especially after a particularly intense workout.

But as he stood opposite the man, a niggling hint of doubt gained a foothold in his mind.

When the bell rang, all thoughts that he could withstand something like this quickly evaporated. His opponent surged from his corner like he'd been launched from a cannon. He uttered no roar of effort or made the slightest sound other than his bare feet on the canvas. His eyes went dead and even as he advanced, his teammate couldn't pinpoint where he would ultimately come from.

They didn't meet in the center of the ring. Taylor pressed forward and Bungees threw a high kick to force him to keep his distance. The man had expected something like that, however. He ducked low and immediately caught his opponent on the back foot. A body shot hammered home and knocked the breath out of Bobby, who brought an arm down to cover his midsection as he backpedaled.

The other man simply bulldozed forward and drove him into the ropes with a series of body shots. He managed to hold him back and even tagged him high in the head with an elbow before Taylor dropped back.

As the mechanic stepped forward to press his perceived advantage, a powerful jab connected with him right between the eyes and knocked his head back, and for a second, he thought he could see white spots in his vision. His opponent pounded into him again like a wave and a couple of body shots triggered reflexive pain like he wasn't wearing half an inch of padding. Before he could recover and push through, a hook struck his jaw with impossible speed.

The world spun and Bobby sprawled on his back and raised his arms instinctively to shield his face against the constant barrage of blows. Taylor's technique was fairly simplistic and needed considerable work on the technical aspects, but he more than made up for it in sheer speed, accuracy, and power. The downed man's ears were ringing when his teammate finally spun away.

No, his ears weren't ringing, he noticed as if from a distance. It was the bell. Leonard had tapped it furiously in an attempt to end the fight.

The ex-boxer looked both shocked and a little annoyed, he thought—as if he still tried to understand what he'd seen.

There was blood on the canvass, Bobby realized, but it wasn't his. Taylor, as he backed into his corner, touched his right eyebrow where red began to stream down his face.

"Are you feeling okay?" he asked, picked up a towel hanging from the ropes, and pressed it to his forehead.

"Yeah," Bobby lied but needed a few seconds and the help of the ropes to regain his feet. "I only need an ibuprofen or three. How about you?"

Taylor scowled and looked displeased with himself. "You tagged me with that elbow. I didn't even realize it."

"It was a lucky shot," Leonard rasped as he climbed into the ring and tugged Bobby forcefully to a chair he'd put in place. He ran a quick check on his pupils to make sure there was no concussion. The mechanic didn't think there was one, having suffered a few in his time, but it was always best to check these things.

He didn't like the thought that his one good strike had been lucky, but he also didn't feel he could honestly refute it. His midsection still ached despite the padding, his head felt the same, and even his elbow felt like he had tried to hit a piece of rock.

"You could have knocked me out with that," Taylor commented while he maintained pressure on his eyebrow. "I need to keep my guard up."

"That's optimistic, but sure," Bobby grumbled. "Let's work on your defense next round, huh?"

CHAPTER TWENTY-FOUR

Having a four-man team that consisted only of fighters would have been a small yet still respectable team if they had been in the Zoo. It wasn't suitable for deeper missions, of course, but smaller numbers worked better for the shallow scouting runs. Matt Greyson didn't think there would be any problems outside the Zoo. People were supposed to be all kinds of civilized around there, after all.

They had a simple enough task in this operation. The people who designed the lab had done so with a failsafe in place if they were ever caught with their metaphorical fingers in the metaphorical cookie jar. All he and his team needed to do was get as much out as possible—and as many of the people—in time for Oblivion to kick in. He wasn't sure what that meant exactly other than something big that went bang.

"Okay," he called to his team over the collective comms. "The trucks should arrive in about three hours. When they leave, there'll be one hell of an accident here—the Chernobyl kind of accident—so we need as much shit and people out of there as possible, barring three names. Doctors Martin, Johnson, and Stevens are not on the list. We'll transport them to a secure location, seal the building, and blow them up inside. I'm sure they'll be dearly missed."

All four men smirked at the clear sarcasm.

"The bottom line is we'll go wheels up from here in three hours. Anything and anyone left behind stays behind. Don't expect me to be anything but the first one on the chopper that arrives to pick us up, and I won't wait for any of you dumbasses."

They all understood the details and it wasn't anything new. People didn't go into the private sector with an overdose of altruism in mind.

Matt nodded, looked at the team, and tried to make sure that each of them was with him on the plan. There was no sign that anyone was in doubt as to whether they could go through with it or not. It was for the best because it would be a shame to have to leave one of his teammates behind. That was always bad for morale.

The silence answered his unasked questions and he was about to speak again when the entire team tensed and immediately shifted into alert positions. A low, rhythmic thudding in the distance grew inexorably closer. It was a sound all five of them had heard before.

They didn't need to see them to know that trouble approached rapidly. Apache Helicopters made a very distinct ruckus when they were on the move.

"Shit!" Matt roared. "All of you check weapons—right fucking now!"

Niki hadn't expected Speare's team to be so quick on the draw. Then again, she had expected something like Taylor's team, a band of misfits who were dragged together by convenience and who were worth so much more than the sum of their parts.

The one thing she hadn't expected in this kind of situation was Apache helicopters diving in to drive the team on the ground away. She certainly hadn't anticipated that they would return fire. In these kinds of locations, people didn't tend to fire on the military.

These were well-armed professionals and showed no inclination to back down from the fight despite the height advantage of the choppers. It wasn't long before the aircraft needed to peel away from the base. They made contact to tell her they wouldn't risk themselves in the line of fire any longer, not while there was also the possibility that their barrage might injure or kill civilians as well as whoever these combatants were.

She was still waiting for the team that was supposed to arrive with the mechanized suits as Speare had promised. Instead, what had happened was merely another military operation—big, impressive, and lacking any kind of subtlety or finesse. She didn't think they could have announced their arrival with any more noise and fanfare than if they had thrown a parade.

It gave the team she had located all the time they needed to prepare for a fight, and they put up a good one. She couldn't tell if there were other people inside. Hell, they could have been hustling everyone and everything out of a back exit to make sure no one discovered what they were doing. Anyone willing to put up this much of a defense was covering for something. More to the point, simple mercs wouldn't react this way if they didn't have the orders to do so.

Of course, simple mercs wouldn't have access to high-tech armor suits like these did. Still, they were contained to the lab well enough, although they wouldn't be able to keep it secure for too much longer.

"They're stalling in there," she noted. "They're waiting for something."

"Do you think they expect reinforcements?" Jansen asked and looked at the troops that began to seal the area off. "Not that they would be able to. They'd need a private army to break through this lineup, and it'll be even more difficult if more are assembled."

Niki scowled. She wondered the same thing. Whoever the team was, the men were well-equipped and ready for a fight even before they realized the army had arrived. It wasn't a good sign that they appeared to walk into an already ongoing operation.

"We have movement behind!" one of the nearby sergeants shouted to draw the attention of the men around him. They brought their weapons to bear, ready for an attack on that side.

Moments later, a truck slowed outside the perimeter and wisely drew to a halt when the driver saw a handful of assault rifles, a few grenade launchers, and even a machine gun pointed at the cab.

These guys were nothing if not effective in their show of force.

She waved at the men to stand down but noted that not one of the soldiers around her lowered their weapon. At least they had enough muzzle discipline to not aim at her as she approached the vehicle.

The window was already rolling down as she stepped beside the door. The man inside didn't look like a military type. He was a little overweight with a thick beard and a trucker cap on his head.

"What the hell is going on here?"

"This area is closed," Niki announced, a little irritated that she had to state something that should have been obvious to him.

"You don't fucking say," he muttered. "Do you have any idea when it'll be open? I have folk waiting for me to take a delivery."

"You're taking a delivery from the lab?"

He nodded. "I sure am. Most folk around here wouldn't have guessed there was a lab in the area, but I know some of the guys who trucked the building equipment out here—about two years ago if memory serves. There's been a fairly high demand for trucks coming in and out since then. It pays well, mind, and there's a steady stream of work, especially lately."

Niki wondered what had possessed the man to simply spill the beans regarding his client, but she imagined that driving trucks for a living was something of a solitary lifestyle. He probably talked this way to anyone who would listen to him.

"Are you carrying anything in there now?" she asked.

The driver shook his head. "Nope. You can check. I'm not the first truck coming this way neither. They asked to bring three big ones here post haste, let them be loaded, and take them to another location."

"Do you happen to know where the other location might be?"

"Nope. I was told the folks who loaded would tell me, though. Why, is there anything important happening at the lab? Is that why you guys are pointing your guns around?"

She sighed. While she hadn't hoped to learn much, knowing where the owner of the lab was moving everything to was probably a good idea. She would have to tap someone else to help her find out, though.

"These guys will have to search your truck," she announced and gestured for the troops to approach. "And you'll have to step out."

"So there is a situation at the lab."

"Unfortunately, yes."

He shrugged and his expression revealed that he disliked the situation. Still, he showed little inclination to argue when he was confronted by a group of trigger-happy men in uniform who seemed to be in the mood for a fight.

They worked quickly and made a thorough search of the cab as well as the back and all the nooks and crannies they could find. She noted that a handful of them searched under the vehicle, which gave her the impression that this wasn't the first time they had done something like this.

Even the driver looked impressed. "These boys really do think that I'm transporting something in there."

Niki shrugged. "All things considered, they have to be damn thorough and make sure there's nothing in there."

"What do you think I'm transporting?"

"That's classified." She wasn't about to tell him what

they possibly faced in the lab. He probably wasn't a threat, but she didn't need him to talk to anyone who would listen about cryptids spreading into the area.

"All clear here, boss," one of the soldiers shouted while the others stepped away from the vehicle.

She nodded. "Good work. Get ready. By the sounds of things, there should be another two coming in. They will probably be as empty as this one, but we can't be too careful."

The soldiers all seemed to be in agreement. They were hard workers, she had to give them that.

"Okay," she said and addressed the driver. "What's your name again?"

"James," he answered quickly. "My friends call me Jim. You can call me Jim too if you like."

"Good call. Okay, Jim, we need you to pull your truck to the side of the road until we're finished here. We'll make sure you don't get into any trouble with your bosses, so give us the number to their office and we'll straighten everything out."

"Yes, but—"

"I should mention that we have Apaches in the air at the moment, and if you don't do as I say, we'll shove Hydra rockets so far up your ass, you'll be able to taste the explosives before they go off."

Jim tried to laugh but cut it off quickly when she stared at him, her face unsmiling. He cleared his throat uncomfortably and nodded. "All right. I'll...uh, park the truck. Over there?"

"You do that."

Jansen and Maxwell both smirked as the driver scrambled into the vehicle, started it quickly, and eased it onto the side of the road.

"I think you enjoyed that," Jansen quipped.

"Not really. He's a hard-working American and innocent in all this. I only wanted him to know that we aren't fucking around here."

Both appeared to understand or simply didn't want to push her further.

After a few minutes, one of the soldiers—an officer by the looks of the uniform—strode to where she stood. His back was ramrod straight and she had a feeling he resisted the urge to salute her the moment he stopped in front of her.

Instead, he offered his hand. "Agent Niki Banks? I'm Captain Kevin Pak. I've been instructed to maintain the perimeter around here."

"Your men have done fine work, Captain," Niki replied and shook his hand.

"Thank you. I hope you understand that while we will respect your presence here, this is a military operation. As the ranking officer, I will call the shots."

She raised her hands. "I understand. As long as you guys understand what we're dealing with here. None of us want any cryptids to escape and create an even bigger problem."

He nodded and clasped his hands behind his back in an at-ease pose. "Don't worry, Agent Banks. We've all been trained for this."

"I'm not worried, Captain. Your men either have the situation in hand as you claim, or they don't. In both cases, the perimeter is already secured and nothing will get through. With that said, though, if the perimeter is compromised, we'll all have to fight to stop them from spreading into the surrounding area."

The man's expression changed from calm and mildly hostile to surprised and a little more comfortable. "I was told we could expect you to call another team in if things went south. McFadden's Mercs, I believe their company name is."

"For now," she grumbled. It was still a terrible name. "And we can't do that until we know if they'll be able to accomplish anything. They only get involved if there are cryptids to deal with."

Niki heard the earbud she wore key in as someone connected to it.

"I could probably check that for you," Desk announced through the newly acquired connection. "And also alert them that they might be needed."

She put her finger to her ear to indicate to the captain that she wasn't talking to herself. "What?"

"I said—"

"I know what you said."

"In that case, you will be billed for the time and the effort."

"Don't you fucking exist on my servers?" She scowled. "Should I charge you for that, plus utilities?"

"What kind of utilities do you think I use?"

"Electricity?"

Desk didn't answer immediately. "I could deduct one dollar and ninety-eight cents from the bill."

She should have known it was a pointless protest. With a sigh, she rubbed the bridge of her nose, which had suddenly started to ache. "Fine. Alert the team."

CHAPTER TWENTY-FIVE

"Why aren't they breaching?"

Matt looked at the man closest to the door. He hadn't known them long enough to remember names, but by the looks of him, he was young and rearing for a fight. His hands held his weapons, the safeties were off, and his suit looked like it was in a combat position.

He was familiar enough with the suits to know what they looked like when the battle settings were on.

"If there's anything you can learn from the military in this country, it's that they won't risk having any casualties if they can avoid it. Did you see how quickly they pulled their choppers back when we fired in return? They won't risk anything happening around here."

"What do you think we should do?" a calmer member of the team asked. The man hadn't even drawn his weapon yet.

Maybe that meant the guy had no intention to fire at the military. He made a mental note to keep a closer eye on him.

"Well, honestly, this simply makes our job here that much easier." When the men looked at him with blank expressions on their faces, he sighed. "With the DOD moving in on us in force, we won't need to be as careful. Anything that happens here can later be explained as them fucking up instead of us. If people are caught in Oblivion, that'll be on them."

The group looked around and he could tell they weren't quite as comfortable with collateral damage as he was. Still, they probably wouldn't be a problem.

The elevator doors behind them opened, and a couple of the men he had sent into the lab emerged. They led a group of two men and a woman—all three in lab coats— who looked confused at the sight of the additional men in full combat suits.

"What's going on here?" the woman asked, stepped forward, and nudged her glasses up the bridge of her nose. "We're not bunking here, you know. We have work to do."

Matt was suddenly reminded why he'd picked those three. He had worked security in the facility for a while now, and there were some people who faded into the background. They simply came to work and went home. Then there were three who made it their mission in life to make the lives of everyone around them miserable, especially those they considered inferior. From what he understood, that simply meant people who didn't have any letters at the end of their names.

He plastered a smile on his face and let her look through the visor of his mask. "I'm sorry to interrupt your work, Dr. Martin, but as you're probably aware, we have a situation happening outside. These men will escort all essential personnel to secure rooms in the building in case something happens."

"What exactly is happening, Mark?" one of the men asked.

"It's Matt," he corrected for what felt like the thousandth time. "And I'm afraid that is confidential. There's no time to explain this, unfortunately. You need to move to the location as soon as possible. Guys, will you assist them?"

The men in suits grasped the researchers by their arms and pulled them into another elevator. This one needed a key to enter and accessed the lower storage areas.

He couldn't resist the urge to wave as the doors closed behind them.

People had called him a psycho in the past. Many of them still served in the military, but he had left once he'd been there long enough to make the connections that would get him a better-paying job. Plus, going into the Zoo had made him considerable money that he had invested and he hoped to see the dividends before too long.

Still, he had never taken the psycho title seriously. Some people merely cared more about this kind of thing than he did and for them, he would have suggested a line of work where they wouldn't consistently work with firearms and weapons of mass destruction—like accounting or teaching, or something like that.

"Incoming!"

Matt ducked instinctively and his hands moved reflexively to the assault rifle holstered on his back. The mechanics locked the weapon into his hand while the software activated the battle functions of the suit. Their adversaries weren't supposed to push in this quickly.

"You!" He highlighted the man closest to the door, who was already retreating. "Lay down suppressing fire. Everyone else, get into cover. Move!"

They swung into action and explosives rocketed through the room to gouge out chunks of concrete and fill the entire area with smoke. Fortunately, the team members were all equipped with functions in their suits that would enable them to see through it.

More rockets were fired as everyone ducked into cover. They remained hidden for the moment as whoever was at the door seemed determined to kill almost every damn thing present before they entered.

Matt was the first to circle his cover. The heavy wall with a marble outer shell that was chipped and shattered in numerous places provided decent enough protection, but he needed to retaliate. They had to buy time until things were finished.

All he was able to manage was a couple of bursts from his assault rifle before the rockets streaked in a lethal onslaught again and with more intensity than before. The explosives powered into the elevator doors, all but shredded them, and likely damaged the mechanism inside. It was an annoyance, to be sure, but there were more ways in and out of the building they could use later on.

"Give me cover!" he yelled and tried to contact the two who were still in the lower levels, securing their sacrificial lambs. They needed to get back before he began to accelerate the schedule. Most of the researchers had already been quietly evacuated and a handful were on their way to the upper levels.

No cover fire came, unfortunately. Instead, the rockets stopped and he realized that red lights flashed around the building accompanied by blaring alarms.

"What's going on?" he asked and scanned the situation quickly.

"Alarms were tripped by the bombing," one of his teammates explained.

"No fucking shit! What do they mean?"

"Checking now...oh, containment breach. What...what kind of containment breach, though?"

Vickie rolled away from her desk and pushed the chair across the floor with her feet until she was within shouting range of the shop.

"Taylor!" she yelled to pitch her voice over the sound of machinery. "Taylor!"

"What?" he responded and took a step back from where Bobby used a grinder to shape a piece of armor.

"You better get in here. Shit is going down and Niki needs us in play."

Desk had alerted her to the fact that someone might call for their help soon if things went poorly and sure enough, the alarm bells rang in her system. She expected Niki to call them with a job any minute now.

Her boss jogged lightly to the improvised office she had set up in order to be closest to the router in case of emergency and dropped into a chair next to her.

"What shit is going down?"

"Desk alerted me to Niki's involvement in an attempt to contain a volatile situation. She said we should be ready in case things went poorly and McFadden Mercs were needed." She paused in anticipation and grinned when he winced at the name before she continued. "Anyway, I've kept tabs on the situation, and it looks like they just had a containment breach, which is a problem. You know, the kind that ends with us called in to look at the bodies of a group of dead scientists."

"Right," he muttered. "And why wasn't I alerted about this before?"

"Would you believe me if I told you it was because I didn't think it would amount to anything? Oh, and the fact that Niki is supported by a contingent of soldiers and probably had the situation under control?"

Taylor nodded. "Fair enough. And what makes you think they won't be able to deal with this containment breach? If Desk's word means anything, Niki has handled that kind of situation before."

"Oh, did I not mention? They also have to contend with a handful of mercs who are fighting back, which prevents them from breaching the location."

"Oh, come on. All those soldiers—"

"And these guys are wearing armored suits."

"Fan-fucking-tastic. We should get our suits loaded, then."

"Do you think we should take Niki's and all the extra ones?"

He didn't answer her, probably because he wouldn't tell

her if he had to simply shout it to where Bobby was still working and put it out there for everyone to hear.

"Hey! Bobby! Get your ass up here."

"Now?" The mechanic didn't sound happy about being dragged away from his work. "What's the fucking matter that you can't handle it on your own? And don't tell me you need more dating advice."

"Shut your trap and get up here. We have a situation," Taylor retorted. "Shit has gone down and Niki needs our help."

The man took only moments to climb the steps to Vickie's office.

"No, go ahead. Everyone, come in here," she muttered and turned to her computer screens.

"What's up?" Bobby asked as he wiped the grease from his hands. "What couldn't wait?"

"It looks like Niki will be in trouble and she'll probably call us to recruit our services."

"You mean she hasn't already—"

The man cut his protest off as Taylor raised his hand to stop him. A second later, he pointed at the computer which, as if on cue, suddenly beeped with an incoming message.

"You have to teach me that trick." Vickie grinned as she pulled the message up. Sure enough, it was Niki. The woman always had a hundred different typos whenever she sent something from her phone but the gist was clear. *Get the fuck over here now. Sending you the details.*

"There is no trick," he replied. "People merely become a little predictable in their behavior, and given how quickly the situation is devolving there, I assumed she would send a message at any second."

"So you risked looking like an idiot?"

"Well, yeah…basically. But occasionally, it pays off."

"I'm sorry, I thought we were dealing with some kind of emergency here," Bobby snapped. "She needs our help so… what's going on? Should we start packing the suits in Liz? What else should we include?"

"All the combat suits we have available," Taylor stated quickly. "Who knows how many hands on deck we'll need for this?"

"We'll have to think about fuel consumption on the way there," the mechanic countered. "And on the way back too, I guess, even if we make her pay for it."

"Fuel consumption won't be a problem since we're looking at a fairly short ride."

Vickie narrowed her eyes. "Uh…they're in Florida, so it'll be a damn long drive."

"Not from here to Nellis Air Force Base it won't be. My money is on Niki already arranging a plane or helicopter ride from there so we arrive faster. She's thoughtful like that."

"Probably a plane," the hacker commented. "A helicopter would have to stop all the time to refuel. The plane will be quicker."

"It's tougher to find a place to land, though," he countered. "We'd have to find an airstrip, land, and then be transported to the location. If we're on a helicopter, they have probably already cleared a landing site for new arrivals."

"With the heavy mechs on board?" Bobby interjected. "It's not likely. A plane's my bet too."

"Well, all the money's in. While we wait for the results, we should get our asses into gear and load the suits. Are you coming with us, Vickie?"

"Nope. Desk is making sure I'm apprised of the situation," she replied. "She's already involved so it's unnecessary to have us both entirely focused on it."

"Good call. Let's get moving, people."

"I'll update Tanya, I guess," Bobby muttered and turned to head to the shop where the woman was still working.

Vickie wondered why Taylor hadn't called her too. Maybe he thought they were alternating trips and it was Bobby's turn? But he wouldn't have called it all hands on deck if that were the case.

She shook her head and returned her focus to the situation as displayed on the computer. Nothing much had changed since all the alarms in the building were triggered. Not surprisingly, there weren't many cameras in the building, which gave her no access to what was happening inside.

Elisa climbed to the office and looked a little confused when sounds drifted across the shop as the team began to prepare.

The hacker rolled her seat to look at what had the former reporter so baffled but all she saw was Taylor next to his suit. Quickly, he pulled the crate out and checked it. His movements were quick and precise, and it wasn't long before he was satisfied and moved to Niki's suit, leaving his for Bobby and Tanya to load into the truck. He looked calm and collected, but there was something a little off about the way he moved that sent chills up Vickie's spine.

"He's hiding something," the other woman whispered, careful to make sure he didn't hear what they were saying. "I guess the only question is what he could or would hide from us? We're essentially the only friends he has, right?"

She shrugged. "There's a ton of shit that one might hide from one's friends—especially the friends, sometimes. It doesn't matter, though."

"What are you talking about?" Elisa narrowed her eyes. "Don't you want to know what's going on in that red head of his?"

"I do know." Vickie didn't like it but she had seen him look like this before. He usually returned in need of medical attention. Taylor had already finished with Niki's suit and moved on to Bobby's and Tanya's in quick succession. The mechanic had harnessed both, which meant there was likely nothing wrong with them.

"So you're being mysterious now?" Her companion didn't sound happy about being left in the dark.

She shrugged. "Well, it's not that complicated. Sometimes, Taylor goes into a dark little place in his mind where he prepares himself for what's to come."

"And that is…"

"War, Elisa. He's getting ready for war."

The reporter grunted. "I guess that makes sense. Kind of."

Taylor finished inspecting the suits and whistled for Bobby to bring the forklift while he jogged to the truck. She was distracted when Niki messaged them about not being willing to wait for Taylor to make a road trip to reach her and sent them a few ID codes for presentation when they reached the airbase. He had only partly been right. She hadn't arranged a helicopter, although it looked like one would be waiting for them when they touched down.

"Taylor, Niki has a plane ready for you," she yelled. "And she wants me to come with you guys too, so get ready for that."

He raised a thumbs-up before he slid into the truck and started it. Vickie was left with nothing to do but start to pack her shit up.

"Good luck," Elisa said and looked both relieved and apologetic. "I'll hold the fort here for you guys until you get back."

CHAPTER TWENTY-SIX

The smoke showed no signs of dissipating. They had pumped in as many explosives as they could to clear the area as quickly as possible with as little loss of life on their side, but nothing went according to plan. Niki could see them holding position at the doors through her binoculars. From what she could tell, they tried to decide what they should do next.

These troops weren't the cream of the crop. No, that wasn't fair. The army trained their men right, even those who were still in the country, but they didn't know what to do in this kind of situation. Orders were either muddled or incomplete. They were supposed to get the civilians out as quickly as possible, but there was no clarity on what they should do with the hostiles firing on them.

She had seen this kind of situation before. People were afraid their reputations would be tarnished and there were too many unknowns involved.

"Why don't they simply push in there?" Maxwell asked, also keeping his eye on the situation from afar.

"The guys inside are all Americans, probably," Jansen explained. "And former military too. No one wants to give the order for their men to move in and kill a group of veterans. That'll be spun badly every way you look at it, and while they are looking for a way in that doesn't involve a whole shitload of casualties, the orders they receive aren't very clear. Isn't that right, Captain?"

Pak stood with them and seemed more and more displeased with every second that ticked past. She could understand that sentiment at least. He wasn't high enough in the chain of command to have to worry about politics, but the people who sent him orders were. Ultimately, it meant that if he acted without orders and everything went badly, he would be the scapegoat.

"This is a fucked up business," Pak said finally and hissed through clenched teeth. "Hell, if shit goes any farther south, we'll reach the Panama Canal."

It was aptly put, she had to admit. "Your men won't breach without orders. Why don't they simply pump more explosives in?"

He shook his head. "We're already dealing with a containment breach in there. Honestly, we don't want to give the cryptids any more holes to escape from."

That was a very good point. Niki frowned and tried to make out something—anything—through the binoculars.

From the little she could see, something was moving in there. Someone shouted and the men were called back. Smoke issued from inside the door and engulfed the soldiers in formation near the building.

"What the fuck…" Pak mumbled before he activated his

radio. "Henry, what the hell is going on in there? Report, goddammit!"

The order wasn't obeyed for a few long minutes, and she could see signs of a fight. Flashes of gunfire streaked through the shadows cast by the smoke and dust clouds.

"Fucking...we have movement. Something's shooting at us and...shit!"

Gunfire erupted through the radio, heard also from inside the cloud of dust before Niki saw something move out of it.

There was very little clarity at first glance, but as they pushed to the edge, she realized it was a group of people who were decidedly not soldiers or the mercs who defended the facility. Lab coats, already streaked with gray dust, identified them clearly as civilians and most likely researchers from inside the lab.

"What are they doing?" Pak asked. "Some kind of trojan horse?"

"Maybe, but probably not," she answered. "I'd say they were inside, alarms went off, and they began to evacuate..."

Her voice trailed off as the soldiers initiated a withdrawal as well. They didn't move in an organized fashion to help cover the civilians but in an obvious retreat. At least two of them were probably wounded and had to be dragged away by their comrades. A third been carried across another man's shoulders.

"What the hell is going on in there?" Pak snapped, talking to himself. Niki doubted the man had even heard her explanation.

Once the soldiers realized there were civilians, they

quickly formed a defensive position around them and moved to the perimeter that had been established.

The non-combatants arrived first and most cried and covered their heads as if to protect themselves like they were still under attack. Niki and Pak rushed to where they had gathered.

"What the hell happened in there?" the captain asked the nearest soldier.

"There was something—it killed Henry and Coulson and hurt Terry bad. Your...your orders were to retreat to the perimeter if something came out that we hadn't seen before."

"Shit," Niki cursed.

"That's not all," he continued and wiped soot and dust from his face. "There are more of them inside."

She turned to one of the researchers who listened to the conversation—and was possibly the one who had delivered the information in the first place.

"What do you know?" she asked and drew the woman apart.

"A couple of men went down there," she explained. Her furtive glance around her indicated that she felt a little insecure in the location but she tried to be helpful. "They wore big suits of armor and said they needed to escort three of us to a more secure location. They wouldn't wait for anyone and almost forced them out at gunpoint."

"Do we assume they're all alive?" Pak asked.

"Until we see a body, that should be the assumption," Niki answered quickly. "And I think we can call in a couple of specialists who should be able to give us a better view inside. I'll try to get in touch with them." She stopped as her phone rang in her pocket. "Or they'll get in touch with me."

"No, I did not hack you," Vickie protested. "Besides, hacking is such an ugly word. I like to think of myself as keeping a watchful eye over the people in my family who I care about."

She could hear Niki's frustrated sigh on the other side of the line.

"Okay, fine. I listened in on what was happening there."

"That's called hacking."

"Again, I don't like that term."

"Well, I'm sorry, but I didn't invent the English language, Vickie. And this isn't the best way for us to spend our time, so why don't you and I talk about what the fuck you're doing listening in on my conversations."

"I don't always," she defended herself and looked at the others in the car with her. "Besides, it's not the best way for us to spend our time either. Do you want to talk about those three missing scientists?"

"Do you know anything about them?"

"Well, I'm cross-checking the names of the people who were not present in the building and those who are currently with your people now, and...yes, there are three names. They were present in the facility and were not among those who evacuated. I'm trying to find blueprints on the building to see where they could be."

"Okay. Do you have the names?"

"I have the names of Dr. Andrew Martin, Dr. Angela Stevens, and Dr. Timothy Johnson. Those are likely the three who were removed from the lab before your guys arrived."

"Okay, so we have to assume they are still in there. Where could they be?"

"I'm looking through this. There aren't many areas in the building that could be secured the way they explained it, and certainly not close to where they would have evacuated from. It's relatively small by the looks of the blueprints that were submitted, but..."

"But what?"

"There were three different copies lodged, so I'm trying to determine which is the latest and we can build from there. From what I can see, there's a secondary elevator system that leads to the lower levels. It's a secured area, where deliveries are maintained in the different states they need to be in. Oh, and...yeah, that's more or less the same area where the containment breach alarms are coming from. The explosives probably disabled some of the isolation units for the live specimens."

"Because of course there are live specimens."

"I'm trying to determine whether these specimens were brought in and when they were brought in."

"What's the difference if they were or were not brought in?"

Taylor leaned back from his seat to shout an answer. "If there were live specimens imported, it means they were being tested with the stuff. If not, they were grown in a lab, which means they would have a higher concentration of the goop in their DNA structure."

"Oh. Right."

"How do you know about that?" Vickie asked as he settled into his seat again.

He shrugged. "You pick up a thing or two when you pay attention to what the researchers talk about while you're in the Zoo with them. They often discussed the difference between animals influenced by the goop and those that were grown directly from it. Most of it was biology, which I didn't fully understand, but those with more goop concentration tended to be more violent, aggressive, and… well, alien in composition. They talked about how the DNA they would find in those creatures could be a decent marker for wherever the goop came from."

"Right," Niki announced. "Fan-fucking-tastic. Was there anything else?"

"Oh, the leader of the merc team you're waiting for is about to call you."

"Fucking…how did you— Actually, no. I don't want to know. I'll hang up so he can get through."

Only a few minutes after Vickie hung up, Niki's phone buzzed again. She didn't want to know how the hacker knew they were trying to contact her. In all honesty, she wouldn't be able to understand the concept anyway. Still, she wondered if her cousin hadn't learned more from Desk than they had anticipated, simply by working with her.

The fact that the girl thought she was doing it to

protect her was nice, but it brought the worrisome thought that she didn't have any idea how invasive her actions were. Maybe she didn't care? Or maybe this was so natural to her that she didn't realize how uncomfortable it could be for other people.

She would bring it up with her later. For now, though, they had other matters to deal with.

"Hello?"

"Agent Niki Banks, this is Grover Reardon. Mr. Speare instructed me to contact you about our imminent arrival. I wasn't aware that we would report to anyone in this particular situation but in this case, I look forward to working with you. Particularly because we are bringing a few additions that might be interesting for you to test, given your AI's capabilities."

"What about them?"

"We'll bring drones in that your AI might be able to operate." He paused and she realized he was sending her a few files. "MQ-17—you know, the smaller ones with limited firepower but incredibly agile and able to move through buildings and the like. We intended to use them for basic cover and surveillance, but with an AI on board, we should be in a decent position to test their true capabilities out in the field. Right now, we are in the helicopters and en route, along with the drones. You might want to prep your AI before we land in case you want to try them."

Niki thought about it for a few seconds. "Sure, we'll look into it. See you soon."

She hung up and immediately tapped her ear. "Desk, please tell me you have the capabilities to operate MQ-17 Predator drones."

"I have already determined how well my software would interface with army-developed hardware. It seemed to be a logical step forward that I would need some form of integration capability with military equipment."

"Well, that's reassuring." Niki scowled as an odd sense of discomfort churned in her gut. "I think."

CHAPTER TWENTY-SEVEN

"You've seen me here before, right?" Taylor asked. The airforce sergeant looked uncomfortable with the question, but he finally nodded. "You're the guy they call in when they don't know how to handle a horde of alien monsters. Sure, I've heard of Taylor McFadden."

"So, what's the fucking problem? You know we work on these cases and you've been apprised of the situation in Florida. Hell, you guys already have a plane being prepared for us out there."

The sergeant looked genuinely apologetic. "Sorry, but this happens for essentially everyone we encounter here. The issue with security is being addressed by making sure all new arrivals to the base are individually cleared by our software. It's not a very efficient system but I've been told it's effective."

He opened his mouth to ask what kind of security issues they were facing but then remembered who he had in the back seat of his truck. Vickie wasn't the kind of person to let anything so trivial as national security stop her from keeping her eye on the people she cared about. There was the possibility that there was another source for the breach, but all things considered, he didn't want to attract any more attention than he already had.

"Okay, let me know when it works itself out," he said finally.

Vickie leaned forward in her seat. "You know, I could probably—"

Taylor cleared his throat loudly to interrupt her and motioned subtly across his neck to stop her from saying anything else.

The hacker interpreted the unspoken message and quickly realized the implications as well. She nodded quickly and leaned back in her seat.

"Right," the sergeant muttered. "Anyway, it shouldn't be too long. Besides, the plane is still getting prepped so you should be cleared and be able to board immediately."

He nodded and let the man return to his post. It wasn't long before the barrier in front of them lifted and a jeep jerked to a halt directly ahead. What looked like a colonel checked a tablet before he motioned for them to come through. The sergeant waved them forward as well and directed them toward an airfield to their left.

Taylor could already see the plane being prepared for them. It wasn't a private jet like the one Niki usually transported them with. This was a cargo plane, the kind that would allow the transport of personnel as well.

"I don't think I've ever been in one of these," Vickie commented as she rejected the offer by some of the men who loaded the plane to help her with her equipment. "You know, I've always thought the people who complain about cargo planes being uncomfortable were a little too used to being pampered."

"Prepare to be surprised," Bobby grumbled. "They can be fairly comfortable, but you have to know how to work them. I've seen guys bring hammocks and noise-canceling headphones and sleep their way through the trip."

"I used to do that," Taylor recalled and helped to position one of the crates to be loaded onto the plane. "I took sleeping aids too. It felt like I simply traveled in time and woke up when the plane landed. I have to say it's the most relaxing way to travel."

The mechanic smirked and patted him on the shoulder. "Don't worry. This shouldn't be that kind of flight. We probably should have brought noise-canceling headphones, though."

Tanya and Vickie exchanged a glance as they approached the aircraft. The engines had already begun to whine and they were being waved on board by the crew, who directed the group to where they would sit for the duration of the flight.

"I have to hope it's worth all this trouble," Taylor shouted but he wasn't sure if they could hear him over the engines. The noise didn't abate when they boarded or settled themselves for takeoff.

Everything was loaded in a remarkably short time and the doors began to close. People gesticulated and shouted over the increasing volume from the engines, and the group strapped themselves in.

The lack of windows was barely compensated for by dim red lighting. The plane jolted into motion and increased speed as Taylor grasped the sides of his seat until, with a shudder, the aircraft became airborne.

Amazingly, he didn't feel any more relaxed once they ascended and the ride was a little less bumpy.

Matt acknowledged grimly that he had never missed this. Dealing with Zoo creatures had always felt like a necessary evil and he wasn't alone in that feeling, of course. No one liked to surge head-first into a pack of critters that had no place on this particular planet, but when it was his job to kill as many of them as crossed his path, he wouldn't complain.

There had been nothing about that in the job description he currently worked under, though. Maybe he should have guessed it when they handed him a brand-new set of armored suits.

The only warning he'd needed was the flicker of movement out of the corners of his eyes, barely visible in the heavy cover of dust and smoke that filled the room. There was nothing in the world that moved quite like a mutant. Every motion seemed to indicate that they didn't care about any of the rules of physics.

"Oh, fuck me," he whispered. "Where are the dumbasses who took our lambs into the lower levels?"

"We still have nothing from them, boss," one of the others answered.

"And it looks like we won't get anything. Turn the fuck around and stay alert for movement coming from the stairways."

"Why—"

"Do as you're damn well told!"

The group turned to face the inside of the building. The soldiers who had tried to enter had backed out once the researchers had all been evacuated. They likely now settled into their secured perimeter and thought their job inside was all but finished.

And aside from the three who were still in the belly of the building, their job was done. Matt held himself steady and tried to back away while his gaze flicked across the HUD in an attempt to see any sign of movement.

Something jumped to his left, and he pivoted immediately, opened fire, and grimaced when the bullets punched holes in the already pockmarked walls. Without a doubt, something was in there with them.

"Form up!" he shouted and gestured at the two men he still had with him. His weapons were already primed and ready to shoot at something he couldn't see.

Within moments, his mouth felt dry and his fingers seemed a little numb, along with all the familiar sensations that came from a sudden spike in adrenaline. His senses were suddenly heightened, and the whole world felt like it slowed.

He gritted his teeth as a manic grin spread across his features. He had missed this feeling.

"What is your name again?"

"Phillip Karras. PhD in molecular biology."

Niki nodded and made a note of how the man failed to

introduce himself as Dr. Phillip Karras, which was what most of the folk with PhDs did. At least, most of those she had encountered. Jennie had commented on how those she worked with only liked to call themselves doctors when they tried to get tables at restaurants, and it always felt pretentious.

But she wouldn't tell them what to do with their names. They had put time, effort, and money into earning those three letters at the end of their names, after all, and who was she to tell them they couldn't add two more at the front?

"Would you say you're the one in charge of this installation, Dr. Karras?"

He shrugged. "I'm in charge of one of the three projects that receive funding in this installation, but I wouldn't necessarily say I'm in charge. With that said, I guess you could say I am the highest-ranking member of the staff present since the other project leaders and the manager of the installation are all gone for the weekend."

"It's Thursday."

"They wanted a jumpstart on the holiday weekend. You know, President's Day is on Monday. They were in charge so they weren't needed for the day-to-day routines and if they wanted to, they could go. More importantly, who would stop them?"

"Well, that's a question for another time, I guess," she admitted. She wanted to have a conversation with whoever had designed the damn lab and tried to keep it under the radar like that. For now, though, she'd have to prioritize her questioning. "But I need to talk to you about your experiments with the Zoo goop."

"It's called—"

"I know what it's called but I won't spend half an hour trying to pronounce it every time, now will I?"

"Fair enough. What do you want to know? Although you should know I won't share any proprietary information on our processes."

"Well, I want you to talk about what kind of work you have done with the water runoff," she countered and looked through the notes Jacobs and Monroe had sent her. "Most of the labs that receive contracts to work with the goop are put through very rigorous containment checks to ensure that none of what they work with will be allowed to spread. There was something of a problem with the runoff from the early labs reaching the sewers in DC, so you can understand what we worry about. We all know the more biological material the goop is exposed to, the more shit I have to clean up."

He opened his mouth, likely to comment on how her concept of cleaning up was shooting first, second, third, and occasionally trying to slip in the odd question or two. Although she waited to give him the opportunity, he held himself back. Niki wondered why.

"I understand the concern," he said finally. "But you have to understand that we wouldn't have agreed to work here if they had cut corners in development. No, the work they put into the facility was kind of interesting since there was no water runoff from the lab areas. The systems always recycled, reused, and filtered any of the...goop for our continued use."

"Well, that's good to hear," Niki conceded and made a

note of the process to ask Jacobs about it later. "We'll have to make sure about it but—"

She paused and focused on the sound of shooting from the lab itself for a moment. The doors were open and smoke still poured out.

"Well," she continued, "I guess you guys did put yourselves through your paces to make sure nothing would accidentally get out, but I don't suppose you ever considered anything ever intentionally getting out?"

The doctor narrowed his eyes. "What the hell are you talking about?"

"You have live specimens in there."

"Well, yeah. There isn't any other way to test the effects of the goop without live specimens, despite the laws."

"Have you ever considered the fact that there is a reason why those laws were put in place?"

He didn't answer immediately but his expression seemed to indicate that he might have begun to see what she was driving at.

"You know, something getting out of containment on purpose?"

He looked at her and suddenly realized what was being shot at inside the building. "Oh, shit."

She could only roll her eyes. "Surprise."

CHAPTER TWENTY-EIGHT

O f all the useless parts of his psyche, Taylor hated his fear of flying the most. It wasn't as rational as he tried to pretend it was, and while he liked to think he had it under control, it didn't always feel like it. The transport plane was one of the newer models, lighter and designed to move faster and with less fuel expenditure. The exchange, of course, was that it was a little more jittery than the long-distance planes tended to be. It was, in simple terms, less immune to the elements than the larger aircraft.

The shuddering only made things worse. He used to think the lack of windows on cargo planes he'd been on in the past was what made them easier to fly in, but as it turned out, that was not correct.

He took a deep breath and pressed against the lumpy surface of his seat as he closed his eyes and tried to go to a happy place where he wasn't on a damn plane. A bar in Wisconsin, sipping a beer and watching the Packers beat the living daylights out of the Bears was his first choice. He allowed himself to imagine the familiar smell of booze and the limited food options on the menu they prepared in the small kitchen in the back.

The selection was limited, but when all they had to make was a variety of steaks, burgers, and deep-fried foods, they could get extremely good at it.

A hand settled on his arm and drew his attention to the here and the now as turbulence buffeted the side of the plane. His whole body tightened and his hands clutched the arms of his seat like they were life rafts and he was in the middle of a stormy ocean.

His attention turned to where Vickie was seated beside him. Her hand squeezed his arm gently but the clenched muscles pressed against it.

"I'd ask if you were okay, but..."

He could hear her voice over the rumbling of the plane around them. Thankfully, it seemed no one else could hear them. A couple of crew members were involved in a discussion. Bobby and Tanya seemed to be lost in their own little world, talking and laughing about something in low tones.

"I have it...under control." The fact was that he'd frozen when the plane shook again. He closed his eyes and tried to believe his own words.

"I know you do," she replied and squeezed again. "I'm only saying that...well, I'm checking to make sure you don't break the seat. They will make you pay for that shit. And I happen to know how strong you are so it's not an empty worry, you know?"

Taylor nodded. "I don't think I'll break anything but...I appreciate your concern. You know, for the chair."

She grinned. "Come on, let me protect you here in the

air, okay? I know it sounds stupid but I'm good up here. Certainly better than you by the looks of things."

He released some of the tension from his shoulders, took a deep breath, and returned her smile. "You know, for some dumbass reason, knowing you care enough to offer actually helps. Even if your sole concern is for the welfare of the plane."

Vickie pinched his arm and he yelped.

"Ow!"

"Asshole. Don't worry, when we slide out, I'll come out on your shoulders so if we land, you can protect me."

"Slide out?"

"You know, when they put those slides out of the side of the plane when there's an emergency?"

"I don't think they have those in cargo planes."

"Eh. Well, in any case, I'll use you as a pillow to cushion any falls I might have. You protecting me like that is a decent way for you to repay me for being an asshole when I tried to be nice."

Taylor laughed and relaxed a little. It made sense, of course, to take his mind off the situation and give him something to think about other than the fact that they hurtled through the air at impossible speeds.

Matt didn't know where the new team came from and he didn't care, honestly. They'd already lost contact with two men and he would assume they were both dead at this point. Even though he and the two who remained were probably enough to protect each other's backs, he wouldn't put much money on it. If one of them dropped, he would do the smart thing and run. It was better to risk the soldiers outside than however many monsters were inside.

He'd begun to wonder if he shouldn't simply begin a sneaky retreat anyway when an unexpected barrage of gunfire drove him into cover. Monsters screeched as they rushed out of the way and gave Matt and his team something to shoot at in the dense smoke. Something had ruptured and was burning down there, he decided. That was where all the smoke came from.

It didn't help that the lights in the building had gone out and the sun was starting to set outside. He was no longer sure how long it had been—hours, of course, although it felt like days. They were supposed to have cleared everyone out by midday. The standoff had started sometime in the mid-morning. He had a clock in his HUD, but he had been so focused on staying alive that he hadn't noticed the passage of time until everything began to become much darker.

The new team consisted of pros. They covered their lines of sight smoothly and quickly, with the kind of movement that showed they had been trained in the use of the suits they wore. While these were older models than those he and his team had been equipped with, there was no need for dick-measuring in this case. They all merely tried to get out of this alive.

Matt turned as they approached and held his weapons primed and ready. The fact that they all had bigger things to worry about than the futile resistance he and his team had attempted wouldn't stop them from simply eliminating them now that they had the chance.

He stared at the leader and waited for him to make the first move. For a long moment, everyone seemed to simply remain motionless as if the world held its breath. The cryptids had retreated for the moment, most probably because they'd realized they now faced additional humans and decided to pull back and regroup before they renewed their attack.

Both teams appeared frozen although their weapons all aimed at each other. Matt knew for a fact that the massive guns the newcomers carried would turn even the new and improved suits his team wore into the reinforced titanium version of Swiss cheese. Still, he was determined that they wouldn't be annihilated without taking a couple of their unexpected adversaries with them.

Finally, the leader ordered the team to lower their weapons. Matt didn't hear it, of course, since it was likely through a private channel, but the man did so and his example was quickly followed by his teammates.

A few seconds later, he attempted to open a comm channel with them.

Matt accepted the call. "It's nice of you guys to come in and save our asses here. I would have thought you soldiers would have been content to leave us here to die and clean up the mess afterward."

"Well, I'm sure the guys out there are probably happy with that plan, but we're not army. We're specialists brought in to clean up the mess you guys caused around here. Consider that the only reason why we haven't fragged you and let the cryptids eat your corpses, understood?"

He nodded. "I guess that's fair. What do I call you?"

"Reardon. Follow me and my team. If you shoot us in the back, you can be damn sure this place will be obliterated with you dumbasses inside. Stick it out with us, help, and don't make yourselves liabilities, and we might let you walk out with us. Understood?"

It made sense to not test the man's patience. He and his six men outgunned him and his by a good margin, and even if they did manage a couple of cheap shots, he wouldn't survive the engagement. It was all about getting out of there alive, which he was determined to do.

"Understood."

"Awesome. We'll move out and push into the lower levels."

"Oh, shit!"

The warning was all Matt needed and he spun quickly. Even through the smoke, he could see the swarm that rushed at them and hear the buzzing of massive insect-like wings. They surged and attacked like they did in the Zoo. Creatures had crept onto the ceiling and dove down from it, which made it difficult to tell where they were all coming from. What looked like snakes or large lizards approached from directly ahead.

Reardon's team responded instantly, formed up quickly, and turned their front line into a kind of shield before they launched lead from all sides. Matt pulled his men behind them and directed them to fire on the creatures above.

Even their combined efforts weren't enough. The first wave faltered but the second surged forward and it used the dead bodies of the other cryptids to provide cover for them.

The newcomers pulled back but a couple of them were

brought down. They weren't dead and continued to fight while they were hauled on by their comrades. The suits sustained significant damage as the creatures tried to retain their hold and drag them away.

"Shit, shit, shit!" Matt grumbled as the other team leader motioned for them to retreat toward the door, where they would be able to refocus and gear themselves for a renewed assault.

It wasn't long before they were outside, still in the smoke that poured through the door. The cryptids suspended their attack and seemed to realize that they'd lost the upper hand.

"Take care of the wounded," Reardon snapped.

"This is what I told you about," a woman said through the comm channel once order was established again.

"These assholes are fucking suicide bombers," he retorted. "I'll bet you no one was trained for this shit."

The man had a point. Experience, not training, was the teacher.

"These bastards are like little alien terrorists that worship the goop," the woman agreed. "They will die for it. Don't ask me to understand. I'm a heretic. Keep your guys clear. I have another team on the way to break through with you guys."

"Understood."

Taylor's shoulders released their tension as the plane touched down and taxied slowly. This wasn't the end of the uncomfortable situation, but it was close enough.

Vickie had done her best to keep his mind off his phobia, but there was no better cure than simply removing the source of his fear.

He was the first one off the plane only seconds behind the crew who had disembarked immediately. They had begun to pull the suit crates out and load them onto the helicopters that had their rotors turning in readiness for the team.

"From one nightmare into another, eh, Taylor?" Bobby taunted and punched him playfully on the shoulder.

"I'll be honest, I've changed my mind and now think helicopters are better than airplanes, although I hate both."

"Really?"

"Well, that plane, anyway. I'm fairly sure anything's better than that."

"At least you can convince yourself it'll be better but we'll be done soon."

"And then what? We still have to fly back."

"Maybe flying commercial will agree with you more. Or better yet, Niki's private plane."

"That might be better, but I'll worry about it later."

CHAPTER TWENTY-NINE

"Nice of you to join us, Taylor," Niki called over the comms.

He smiled, genuinely glad to hear her voice. "I couldn't let you guys have all the fun, now could I?"

"Well, enough pleasantries. We have a potential complication. They ran the water used in the labs through a recycling process, which means a large collection of goop-infused water. The cryptids might be drawing from this and could try to release it if they have the chance. That's the only reasoning I think would explain why they are pushing so hard."

It made sense, he supposed, but it was still a tricky situation. "Vickie has blueprints of the building I think are accurate. Oh, and speaking of which, it would probably be a good idea to check to make sure our three missing researchers are still alive. They're supposed to be in a sealed room and safe from attack, but there's no way to know if it's still true. You know how crafty the cryptids can be at getting in and out of places when they want to."

"You're right, we should."

It sounded like she had almost forgotten there were three people who were hopefully still alive in there, but he wouldn't hold it against her. She was a big-picture kind of person and her priorities would understandably shift to whatever would potentially save the most lives.

A team was already in there waiting for them and held the main entrance against attack. Smoke billowed out the front door, a clear indication that something was burning inside the building, likely caused by the explosives they had bombed the interior with. He didn't want to tell people how to do their jobs but throwing bombs at problems usually tended to make them worse. Unless, of course, you were shit out of all other options and total annihilation was the final solution. Wyoming was a case in point.

It looked like the team had managed to maintain their position. They had established defenses outside and attempted to ensure that nothing could escape.

"You must be the team Banks was sending," one of the men called and waved them over. "While you haven't come in the numbers I thought you would, every suit counts out here, I guess."

"Sure it does," Taylor muttered. "You guys know that trying to defend against cryptids is basically inviting them to hit you in the flank, right?"

"Of course," one of the men in the newer suit models grumbled. "But it's not like we can do anything else in there. If we push in, they will attack from all sides. They're waiting for us."

He nodded and tried to determine who was who. The older suit models were probably the secondary team Niki had brought in, but they didn't seem to be doing very well. A couple were wounded or at least had damaged suits. The men in the newer armor were probably those who had fought the soldiers until all hell broke loose. He wouldn't rely on them for much.

"These fuckers are smarter than your average animal but they're still not too bright. Goading them into a fight is easy."

"Who says we want to goad them into a fight?" the leader of Niki's group—Reardon, if Vickie's intel was correct—stated. "We can keep them in there for now and that's good enough for me."

"Right, until they find another way out. Get yourselves ready for combat, set up defensive positions, and follow my lead."

None of them looked happy about the orders, but Taylor hadn't been brought in to hold a position. His mission wouldn't accomplish itself, after all.

He took a couple of grenades from his belt loop and moved toward the door. The smoke made it difficult to identify any movement inside, but it looked like the cryptids remained clear of the entrance and likely tried to keep themselves out of the line of fire.

The entire team—much larger than any he had ever worked with while in the States—prepared themselves, primed weapons, and established well-planned formations to enable them to open fire once anything came out.

Taylor knew his assumption wasn't wrong. The creatures were easy to bait into a fight. Making them aggressive wasn't usually difficult, which was why some people were stumped when they simply did nothing for a little while.

He pulled the pins from the grenades and lobbed them into the building. As he backed away slowly, he could barely make out a couple of the creatures diving on the devices. Whether it was to attack, inspect, or keep them from injuring the others didn't matter.

Moments later, the grenades detonated with ear-splitting pops, and he retreated farther as he opened fire on the creatures he could see.

The cryptids attacked in a rush. He almost didn't have time to get out of the way before they surged out. A couple had wings and a few others slithered along the ground. Together, it made it look like the area was writhing with a mass of them.

Taylor barely registered that he had the trigger held down at full auto. It wasn't like there was any way for him to miss them as they launched their assault and bulldozed toward the defensive positions.

Despite their fury and aggression, it didn't take much to overwhelm them. The teams weren't there to simply be a wall, and the fighting was brief and savage. Even from a distance, the soldiers on the perimeter were able to select targets to help them clear the creatures out of the area.

The combat ended but already, the adrenaline from the fight pumped through his body as he looked around at the group. For now, no more of the creatures emerged and there also didn't appear to be any that retreated once the battle turned against them, but he wouldn't make foolish assumptions. It was better to be too careful than either sorry or stupid.

Still, the encounter hadn't been without its losses. One of the men in the newer suits was down and lay unmoving with numerous holes in his armor. A couple of those in the older suits had sustained damage as well.

Bobby was his main concern, though, and he hurried to where the mechanic leaned against one of the crates they had used for cover.

"Why is it always me?" he complained and grimaced at his leg.

There didn't seem to be any holes in it but there was damage to the hydraulics, which slowed his movement.

"In fairness, I was the one whose leg was bitten by an alligator the last time around," Taylor pointed out.

"I wasn't there last time."

"Exactly. Tanya, are you still good?"

The woman pinged a thumbs-up to him and he turned his attention to Reardon. "You'll probably need to stay here and be the first line of defense against any more attempts to escape, but I need a couple of your men. We have to head in deep and clear out the critters that remain, as well as hopefully rescue a few researchers. Volunteers only, though."

He was impressed when the three men whose suits were intact raised their hands quickly.

"You have good men here, Reardon."

"They've wanted to kick cryptid ass for a while, McFadden. Take good care of them. If any of them come back injured, I'll take that out on you."

"Copy that. Team! Grab what you need and hurry. We'll head in there in sixty seconds."

Taylor placed a hand on Bobby's shoulder to stop him

from joining them. "I need you to keep an eye on the back line for this one."

The mechanic scowled but clearly understood. His suit was in no condition to be on the move inside an area full of hostiles.

"Thanks for that," Tanya mentioned over a private line as they moved through the doors.

He didn't reply and barely offered her a nod before they pushed into the interior of the facility.

The smoke showed no indication that it might clear, which confirmed his suspicions that something was burning inside. Still, the blueprints Vickie had sent him were more than helpful as they moved cautiously to the stairwell. The space was smaller than most of those they had been in before, and only one level below needed clearing.

It didn't look like there were many of the creatures left, and those that remained seemed to choose to avoid them. He could barely identify them on motion sensors on the lower level as they continued their descent.

Vickie keyed into his comm channel when they reached the bottom. "Taylor, there are a couple of servers in the area where you're heading. If you could drop a couple of spikes on them, I should have access to the internal system the lab is run on."

"Roger that."

As luck would have it, one of the first rooms they entered had what he assumed were servers. The hacker insisted that he carry her spikes on every mission and constantly reminded him that it would enable her to help him. Experience had proved her right, so he made no protest. Besides, it was simple to plug the spikes into the nearest inlet.

"Not to sound too cliché," Vickie communicated once he'd inserted them, "but I'm in. You guys should look for the scientists who were left behind. Here—I've marked it on your HUD's."

Taylor responded in the affirmative and motioned for his team to head through the hallways in the direction of the location she had highlighted on the blueprints. The new additions to the team were fairly competent, much to his relief. They covered their corners well and moved fluidly in their suits, which showed at least some practice in them.

The remaining cryptids now retreated through the hallways and away from them. It wasn't like the mutants he loved to hate, and the odd behavior made him immediately suspicious. He decided to investigate.

"Tanya, get the researchers out if they're still alive," he told her. "I'm going hunting."

"Alone?"

"No." He gestured for one of Reardon's men to join him once they reached the door of the room, and the two continued along the corridor to what looked like a storage area.

Few of the mutants were present but they moved quickly and lunged forward. While they snapped massive jaws with elongated teeth, they had no carapace and didn't appear to be particularly mobile.

Thankfully, the smoke seemed to come from one of the elevator shafts, which gave Taylor and his new teammate a clear view of the area.

Unfortunately, what he looked at made him feel sick to his stomach.

"Vickie...do you see this?"

"Are those... What the hell are those? Eggs?"

They were about as tall as his knee and were propped on what looked like mucus membranes, which kept the whole room humid to the point where a mist almost formed around them. The two men stared in mutual horror.

"I'll go with yes," he replied. "And if these fuckers get into the goop-infused water supply—hell, any water supply —we'll have a situation like Wyoming."

"Only all across the fucking waterways."

"You'd better tell your cousin to carpet bomb the hell out of this place once we're clear. And then add a good dose of napalm for good measure until there's fucking nothing left."

"I think I can do that. But if you think I'll call a bombing while you're still in there—"

"I don't think there's any need for that again."

"Wait, again?" the new addition asked.

"It's a long story," he muttered.

"Oh, I know the story. I merely thought it was bullshit."

Tanya keyed into the comm channel. "We've found the researchers. Aside from being incredibly annoying, they're all fine and alive. The mercs who escorted them weren't so lucky."

"Roger that. Return to the surface. We'll be right behind you."

His teammate stared at him for a few seconds and

grunted in surprise when he took the rest of his grenades from his belt.

"I'm not taking any chances," Taylor explained and lobbed the grenades deep into the room.

Niki didn't hesitate even for a moment. The airstrike was already in place, and the moment Taylor, Reardon, and their respective teams and the rescued civilians were out, the helicopters swooped in and hurled enough firepower to burn the facility to the ground.

The sight of the eggs had chilled her to her core, and she wouldn't risk anything getting out of that fucking place.

The researchers didn't look very happy that all their work was turned into a neat little pile of ash, but they had to understand that what she did was for the greater good.

Besides, Vickie had already drained their servers for all the data they had. If they behaved, maybe it would be shared with them again.

Still, it was a little gratifying to watch the facility engulfed in flames, a vivid conflagration against the deepening darkness.

She moved away from the soldiers, who did a good job of being thorough about cleaning the area, and jogged to where Taylor and his team began to peel their suits off.

Bobby looked like he was still intact, thankfully, as his armor had taken most of the damage.

"It's good to see a somewhat straightforward mission for you guys," she called as she approached and Taylor turned to greet her. "Things were a little dicey from the start but it's a good thing you guys were able to get in and out without too much trouble."

He shrugged. "It could have gone much worse. I'll take the win—and the paycheck."

She was about to answer when he stripped to his regular clothes and cleaned his suit out. The man had put considerable work into his body, she knew that, but she was almost at a loss for words at the results. They pressed against the tank top he wore and left little to the imagination.

"Holy shit," she muttered. "It looks like you gained most of that muscle mass back, huh?"

His eyebrows raised and Taylor and Bobby shared a hasty glance. There was something she could read into that but for the life of her, she couldn't tell exactly what it was.

Or maybe it was simply guys being guys over her paying him a compliment. She had more pressing matters to attend to anyway. "Well, keep up the good work."

"Will do. Oh, what's our ride situation back to Vegas?"

Niki shrugged. "If you don't mind waiting for a day or two for me to clean this mess up, I could fly you guys back."

"It sounds good," he answered and stretched his shoulders in a way that had her attention immediately. "I could use a couple of days off anyway."

CHAPTER THIRTY

It was safe to say that Leonard was a believer by now. He didn't want to comment on the old boxer's quick change in opinion regarding what he had seen of Taylor's and Bobby's abilities, but even after their few days away, the man was ready to help Bobby don the protective gear without so much as a word.

Taylor decided he would take that as a compliment to his fighting abilities and warmed up in the other corner of the gym, using a speed bag to get his arms and shoulders ready.

"The delivery for the training suits came in yesterday," he called once Bobby was ready and started shadowboxing to get used to the added weight. "With that and the obstacle course ready, I think it might be time for us to start training folks. I thought next Tuesday when Niki's team will be in town. We can put them, Vickie, and Elisa through their paces. You know, it's never too soon to run them through it as tough as we can make it."

The mechanic smirked, still focused on warming up for the sparring match. "That's a little aggressive of you."

"It's the only way I roll. Besides, they need the stress to try their hardest. It's not like the Zoo, where you knew it was learn or die."

"Or learn and die."

"Or that," he conceded.

"Do you think this training regimen will interfere with your fight? When is that, anyway?"

"I think we'll have a week with Niki's team while they're still in town. And probably another week before the fight."

"You're taking her out before the fight, right?"

Taylor stopped punching the speed bag to scowl at his friend. "How did you…never mind. Yeah, before. I won't let her think I forgot or anything. I'd never hear the end of that—from her or Vickie. I think while they're here for that week of training would probably be the best time for it."

"She won't like not knowing about the fight before it happens, you know."

He held his hand up. "I don't see no ring on this finger."

Leonard laughed in the background and strode to where they now stood. "If you don't mind taking the advice of a man who's been happily married for the past twenty-five years—"

"Congrats on that," Bobby commented.

"Thanks. Anyway, if you want to hear my advice, what she thinks matters, regardless of what you might think is your business and none of hers. If she has her mind on one way, you'd better believe it's a good call to make your decisions with that in mind. If three screw-ups in the past have taught me anything, it's this—don't be stupid. If you care, tell her."

Taylor scowled at the man and tried to think of a good response, but nothing came to mind. He was right, but he still wasn't convinced that telling Niki was a good idea.

Still, he would cross that bridge when he got there. He put his mouthguard in and climbed into the ring. "Let's fight."

"Nice work, Leonard," Bobby muttered as he joined him. "Annoy the shit out of him by telling him about the truths of relationships and then put him into a ring to fight me to work his aggression out."

The old boxer guffawed. "Don't you worry, son. I got your ibuprofen ready. Keep your eyes out for the nut shots." With that, he tapped his hammer into the bell.

He decided he should have been ready for that. Bobby wasn't the kind of man to walk away from a fight, and he would always give it his all. The mechanic was now accustomed to his surge and overwhelm tactics and began to adapt to them. He had landed more than only the one good blow, and Taylor had been on the back foot more than once.

"My defense needs to be better," he muttered to himself as he pulled clothes on after his shower and his ribs twinged gently as he eased his shirt on. "Fucking Bungees hits like an anvil."

His phone buzzed. He'd heard it from the shower but damned if he would be rushed simply to talk to someone who couldn't be bothered to call him during business hours.

Still, the number that was displayed was blocked, which told him it was either Vickie or Desk, although both had learned to use their names and numbers to call him. Covering their tracks only did so much when he already knew who was calling.

He sighed and pressed the phone to his ear as he walked to the fridge. "Yeah?"

"Good evening, Taylor," said Desk's familiar voice. "I hope I didn't disturb you."

"You never bother me, Desk. Well, no, that's not true, but it's nice to be nice. Which one am I talking to again?"

She didn't reply immediately. "How do you know there is more than one of me?"

"Well, I already worked out that you're an AI from the way Vickie talks about you and that you're...well, based on servers, plural. She mentioned you were stored in two different locations—FBI and DOD—which means there is technically more than one of you."

The AI paused before she spoke again. "You know, it should be noted that too many people misjudge your intelligence based on your brutish appearance. I regret to inform you that I made similar assumptions. They will not be made again."

He shrugged, took a beer from the fridge, and popped the cap off. "Don't worry, I'm used to it by now. I've learned to turn it to my advantage."

"Interesting. Anyway, this is Desk Version 2.0099982, which might be described to you as the version based on the FBI servers. There is a reason why I wished to speak to you."

He took a long sip from the beer. "Shoot."

"Well, I have kept my eye on recent developments regarding the people I care about, and whispers have emerged about a fight involving one Taylor McFadden. I imagined that was you, given that there are not many people with the same name."

Taylor narrowed his eyes. "I'm curious. How the hell did you find that out? Not even I knew there were any traces of it on the Internet, and I've kept a close eye on developments."

"Suffice it to say that my abilities to scour the Internet for information on those I care about supersede yours."

"Huh."

"Isn't that how one shows one cares about people?"

"Well...okay, sure."

"And I must ask why you considered keeping this a secret, as your friends would likely want to know what is happening in your life, especially as it pertains to risking your life and health."

He nodded. It seemed like everyone was in the mood to tell him how to live his life today. He wouldn't complain since he did appreciate that there were people in his life who cared enough to tell him how to live it, but that didn't change the fact that he would do this his way. For the most part, anyway.

"So what do you suggest?" he asked finally after he took a deep breath to stop himself from saying anything sarcastic. He didn't want to hurt the AI's feelings, after all.

Assuming she had feelings. He still didn't understand how they worked, to be honest.

"You might want to consider telling Niki about it. All things considered, she is thoroughly invested in your well-being."

Like Leonard, the AI was right. It didn't make it any nicer to hear, though. "Fine, you're right, and I will tell her. But not tonight. Let's put off being killed tonight to being killed tomorrow. It's a shame there isn't any make-up sex for this."

"I knew you would come to your senses," the AI chirped happily. "I will leave you to your business. Good night, Taylor."

"Night, Desk, sleep—do you sleep?"

"I suppose you could consider my downtime to install upgrades as 'sleep.'"

"Sleep well, then."

The line cut and he laughed and tossed the phone onto his bed before he took a long swig from his beer. "Craziest fucking family ever."

Have you read *The BOHICA Chronicles* from C.J. Fawcett and Jonathan Brazee? A complete series box set is available now from Amazon and through Kindle Unlimited.

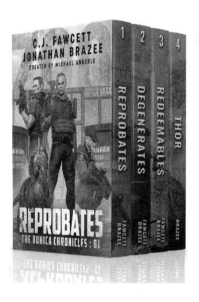

Kicked out of the military for brawling, what can three friends from different countries do to make some needed money?

Grab your copy of the entire BOHICA Chronicles at a discount today!

Reprobates:

With nothing in their future, Former US Marine Charles, ex-SAS Booker, and ex-Australian Army Roo decide to give the Zoo a shot.

Without the contacts, without backing, without knowing what they are getting into, they scramble to get their foot in the door to even make rent in one of the most dangerous areas in the world.

With high rewards comes high risk. Can they learn on the job, where failure means death?

Relying on their training, they will scratch, claw, and take the most dangerous jobs to prove themselves, but will it be enough? Can they fight the establishment and the Zoo at the same time?

And what the heck's up with that puppy they found?

Degenerates:

What happens when you come back from vacation to find out your dog ate the dog-sitter?

And your dog isn't a dog?

The BOHICA Warriors have had some success in the Zoo, but they need to expand and become more professional to make it into the big time.

Each member goes home to recruit more members to join the team.

Definitely bigger, hopefully badder, they return ready to kick some ZOO ass.

With a dead dog-sitter on their hands and more dangerous missions inside the Zoo, the six team members have to bond and learn to work together, even if they are sometimes at odds with each other.

Succeed, and riches will follow.

Fail, and the Zoo will extract its revenge in its own permanent fashion.

Redeemables:

NOTHING KEEPS A MAN AND HIS 'DOG' APART...

But what if the dog is a man-killing beast made up of alien genetics?

Thor is with his own kind as they range the Zoo, but something is missing for him. Charles is with his own kind as they work both inside and outside the walls of the ZOO.

Once connected, the two of them are now split apart by events that overcame each.

Or are they?

Follow the BOHICA Warriors as they continue to make a name for themselves as the most professional of the MERC Zoo teams. So much so that people on the outside have heard of them.

Follow Thor as he asserts himself in his pack.

Around the Zoo, nothing remains static, and some things *might converge yet again if death doesn't get in the way.*

Thor:

The ZOO wants to kill THOR. Humans would want that as well, but they don't know what he is.

What is Charles going to do?

Charles brings Thor to Benin, where he can safely hide out until things calm down. Unfortunately for both of them, that takes them out of the frying pan and into the fire.

The Pendjari National Park isn't the Zoo, but lions, elephants, and rhinos are not pushovers.

When human militias invade the park, Thor and park ranger Achille Amadou are trapped between the proverbial rock and a hard place. How do you protect the park and THOR Achille has to hide just*what* **Thor is...**

Can he hide what Thor is when Thor makes that hard to accomplish?

Will the militias figure out what that creature is that attacks them?

Available now from Amazon and through Kindle Unlimited.

AUTHOR NOTES

For me, dealing with romance in stories is a bit of a challenge.

I am an excellent example of a guy who "doesn't get women." My wife had to practically hit me over the head to make sure I understood she liked me. (She is also very adamant when she decides she isn't liking me at the moment, either—no confusion for me.)

However, in stories, it seems that I am just as challenged when it comes to creating the little dance of characters who are attracted to each other.

Why? Why are they liking each other now, when they obviously didn't before?

Ok, part of it with Taylor and Niki was how each assumed they understood exactly where the other stood by the first encounter. Not that either was all that wrong, to be fair, but they did push a little of their own projections onto the other person.

By the time it became obvious (to me) that these two were definitely going to become a pair, the questions became how and who is going to believe it and what is their attraction?'

The answers became obvious as I delved into the scenes.

Crazy.

Crazy is the language that these two communicate in. In their own ways and for their own reasons, both will go to crazy levels of effort to make sure that:

1) Their friends or family are protected to the best of their abilities.

2) They run into trouble, not away from it.

3) They aren't afraid to speak their minds, even when they know it might screw them over with someone important.

4) Neither is crazy about sharing their feelings.

When Tanya mentions that she doesn't understand what Taylor sees in Niki, it takes Niki a minute to realize that he would have to be a little messed up to see something in her. Even her boss assumes she is a cold-hearted bitch.

For Taylor, he is trying to move to a mating dance he doesn't understand. The only thing he understands is Niki knows who he is and what he does and appreciates parts of him no one else can.

Join me in the last *Cryptid Assassin* book (08) and let's watch two crazy people try to admit they have feelings for each other.

And watch the fireworks explode.

Diary June 14 – 20, 2020

So, Las Vegas is a little weird right now. You have

pockets of people who are very Covid-19-aware around the valley area, and then you have the casinos. Some of the casinos are very Covid aware and more stringent, and others aren't.

No casino (that I've been to) mandates wearing a mask.

The Station Casinos shoot that temperature gauge at you when you enter their establishment but are pretty open after that.

Caesar's Hotel and Casino (for this latest weekend) was packed with people, and they try to encourage social distancing, but occasionally people get a little close together—and by occasionally, I mean all of Friday night.

I can't speak to Saturday or Saturday night since I didn't get to continue playing. My budget was used up, so I worked and slept most of Saturday, catching up from some mixed up sleep during the week.

I'm at the Green Valley Hotel and Casino. Sitting in the food court, I can see at least twelve people playing on the casino floor. The mask to no-mask ratio seems to be about even, except for the person who has a mask, but is smoking, so the mask is pulled down.

I'm going to count that as a no-mask.

Here in the food court, the mask ratio is about one person with a mask to twenty without one.

We are fifteen feet from the slot machines.

I get why those of us in the food court have no masks (and there is no difference when I go to regular restaurants. Once a person sits down at a table, the masks come off almost immediately.)

I think I will be about done with these updates starting next week. Enough of my diary entries have dealt with

Covid-19 and Las Vegas, it's time to just...talk about other stuff.

Like books, maybe?

Sometimes, it's hard to remember what readers want to hear about in our (author and publisher) lives. I eat, sleep, and breathe publishing and stories at this point in my career, and what's normal to me (and seems like would be boring to you) is probably not.

As always, THANK YOU for reading our stories. We would not be able to create the wonderful stories without readers like you supporting us!

Ad Aeternitatem,

Michael Anderle

One Crazy Set Of Stories (12)

SOLDIERS OF FAME AND FORTUNE

Nobody's Fool (1)

Nobody Lives Forever (2)

Nobody Drinks That Much (3)

Nobody Remembers But Us (4)

Ghost Walking (5)

Ghost Talking (6)

Ghost Brawling (7)

Ghost Stalking (8)

Ghost Resurrection (9)

Ghost Adaptation (10)

Ghost Redemption (11)

Ghost Revolution (12)

THE BOHICA CHRONICLES

Reprobates (1)

Degenerates (2)

Redeemables (3)

Thor (4)

Printed in Great Britain
by Amazon

44114659R00206